DARKNESS & Grace

By Kathryn Schleich

PUBLISH HER™

DARKNESS AND GRACE © Copyright 2021, 2022 by Kathryn Schleich

All rights reserved. No portion of this book may be reproduced, stored in a retrieval system, or transmitted in any form or by any means—electronic, mechanical, photocopy, recording, scanning or other—except for brief quotations in critical reviews or articles, without the prior written permission of the publisher.

Company and/or product names may be logos, trade names, trademarks and/or registered trademarks and are the property of their respective owners.

This is a work of fiction. Names, characters, places and incidents are products of the author's imagination or are used fictitiously. Any resemblance to actual persons, living or dead, is entirely coincidental.

ISBN: 979-8-9865220-3-6 (Softcover)
ISBN: 979-8-9865220-4-3 (Ebook)
Printed in the United States of America
Second Printing: 2022

Published by Publish Her, LLC
2909 South Wayzata Boulevard
Minneapolis, MN 55405

Cover design by Kayla Franz

For Stephen

a note from the author

"Darkness and Grace" was inspired by real-life events involving people I know in the early 1990s. Each time I would discuss the true occurrences, people would comment, "This is a great story. You need to write a book." After initial trepidation, I recognized this was not only a story worth telling, but it was one that comes to an author only once in a lifetime.

Originally published in 2007 under a pseudonym with the title "Shades of Darkness, Shades of Grace," this book is a work of fiction. To write the narrative, I employed aspects of historical fiction, using authentic news accounts, world events, settings and descriptions involving entirely fictional characters. "Darkness and Grace" is of the domestic thriller genre in which close relationships can prove to be far more dangerous than the world at large.

Kathryn Schleich

character list

Kay Pierson-Scott .... Oldest of the Piersons' three children
Tim Scott.. Kay's husband
Paul Pierson ....Kay's middle brother
Rachel Pierson .... Paul's late first wife
Pamela Schaeffer Pierson...Paul's second wife
Jack Pierson .... Kay's youngest brother
Michelle Pierson ....Jack's wife
Ruthie Pierson...................................... Jack and Michelle's daughter
Sam Pierson .... Jack and Michelle's son
Beverly (Bev) Pierson........................... Kay, Paul and Jack's mother
William (Bill) Pierson............................... Kay, Paul and Jack's father
Jeanne Daly....................... Michelle's mother and city councilwoman
Michael Daly..Michelle's father
Annette and Donovan Schaeffer .... Pamela's parents
Ron Baker ....Pierson family friend and homebuilder
Sandy Baker............................ Ron's wife and Pamela's close friend
Linda Petersen...Paul's secretary
Doug Castleton...Pamela's first husband
Kaitlin Pierson ....Paul and Pamela's baby daughter
Tom Dixon .... Pierson family attorney
Heather Carlson .... Kaitlin's nanny
Lula Faye Simmons ....Pamela's friend
Juanita Chavez .... Pamela's co-worker
Walter Rixmann .... Pamela's boss
Malcolm McBride.................. Pierson Properties insurance executive
Margot Paliulionis.......................... Minneapolis Star Tribune reporter

prologue

FEB. 12, 2001

Minneapolis Star Tribune
Dog returns home with severed leg
By Margot Paliulionis, Staff Writer

The owner of a German shepherd near Chisago City made a grisly discovery when the dog came home Tuesday with part of a woman's leg. The dog's find prompted an intensive search in the heavily wooded area north of Chisago City near the Wisconsin border, employing dozens of law enforcement officials from surrounding counties.

Although police are not certain they are dealing with a homicide, authorities are hoping a tattoo on the woman's leg may offer clues to her identity. The tattoo, found on the ankle, includes the drawing of a red rose with the inscription "Foxy Lady."

Pathologists are still examining the leg as state police and other law enforcement agencies continue to review missing person reports from Chisago, Hennepin, Ramsey and neighboring counties. Little additional information is available until pathology tests are completed, which are expected to take several days.

PART ONE

chapter one

JUNE 1996

It was not a typical wedding ceremony—the uniting of two people in matrimony, professing their love in the presence of family, friends and God. It was a resurrection from the dead of sorts, the shedding of grief and melancholy and accepting the chance for grace and new life.

I could feel the swirl of excitement and anticipation of beginning a journey, free at last of the sorrow that had claimed Paul's heart. For a year after his wife's death from ovarian cancer, my middle brother seemed like little more than an empty husk, hollow-eyed and distant, barely functioning. We all mourned Rachel's loss, a vibrant life cut short, but Paul, who'd always been the most sensitive person in our family, had become the walking dead, and no one knew how to save him.

Losing one family member was devastating; losing two was unacceptable. Our family made a commitment to pull Paul back out into the world, inch by inch if necessary. He could be stubborn, bringing us to the point of exasperation more than once, but our diligence paid off. An encounter with friends reminded Paul that life was not static but fluid, and that he could choose to exist trapped within the dark abyss of mourning or liberate himself and rejoin the living.

Pamela Schaeffer had been willing to take the risk of challenging Paul to recall the person he had once been. Her effervescent presence served as a reminder that even as a widower of 31, rediscovering happiness and living life to the fullest was a possibility for Paul. We'd confronted and forgiven an earlier error in judgment on Pamela's part. Now the joy and promise of this day had banished any fleeting misgivings we might have had about the union.

At a few minutes past 7 p.m., the air came alive with the melodic strains of Pachelbel's "Canon in D Major," and the wedding procession began. From my place at the middle of the wedding party, I could see my husband, the Reverend Tim Scott; Paul; our youngest brother, Jack; and two groomsmen take their places at the altar. The groomsmen each wore a black tuxedo, accented in burgundy.

Paul was handsome in black tails and ivory accents. Appreciation and love crossed his face as our parents started down the aisle.

Regal in a chiffon sheath of pale lilac, her silver hair elegantly coiffed, Mother clasped Dad's arm as they walked together to the first pew. In their early 60s, they made a distinguished and striking couple.

The music built to a crescendo as my sister-in-law Michelle, my brother Jack's wife, commenced her walk wearing a slim A-line gown in dusty rose silk. Each bridesmaid wore an identical dress, but Michelle was particularly lovely, her lithe figure gracefully floating along the aisle, auburn hair setting off her pale skin and green eyes.

Walking down the aisle behind her, I recognized the smiling faces of co-workers from our family's real estate business. Every person here had weathered the tragedy of Rachel's death and Paul's heartbreak, and I was touched that so many had wanted to celebrate this occasion with us.

Sandy Baker, Pamela's maid of honor, followed, and as she approached, I felt a surge of gratitude. It was Sandy and her husband, Ron—business associates and family friends—who had introduced Paul and Pamela. Sandy had met Pamela at the hospital where they both worked as lab technicians. She saw in Pamela a vivacious person living every pulsating beat of life, exactly what Paul needed.

We faced the congregation as Jack and Michelle's two young

children made their way down the aisle as flower girl and ring bearer. At age 6, Ruthie was whip-smart and as rambunctious as could be. Getting Ruthie into the rose silk dress was akin to roping a small wild animal, but with blonde curls framing her face, she was nothing short of angelic.

Walking in perfect step was her 3-year-old brother, Sam, a miniature of his father, down to the impish twinkle in his blue eyes. The children were supposed to stand next to Sandy until Pamela reached the altar. Once they turned around and saw the throngs of people, they made a beeline for the safety of Michelle.

As the majestic "Trumpet Voluntary" began, the congregation rose and turned to await the bride. On the arm of her father, Pamela was radiant in an ivory silk beaded gown, lustrous blonde hair falling to her shoulders. A jubilant Paul walked the few steps to meet her.

Tim welcomed everyone to this celebration. Jack stepped to the podium, reciting scripture from the first letter of Paul to the Corinthians. "Love is patient. Love is kind. It is not jealous. Love is not pompous, it is not inflated, it is not rude. It does not seek its own interests. It is not quick-tempered; it does not brood over injury. It does not rejoice over wrongdoing but rejoices with the truth. It bears all things, believes all things, hopes all things, endures all things. Love never fails."

Jack returned to his spot, and a soloist sang an operatic rendering of the "Wedding Hymn." As the music soared, Michelle leaned in close to whisper, "You were absolutely right to insist I give Pamela a second chance."

I knew what she was referring to, and I thought the incident had been dealt with to everyone's satisfaction. I smiled in silent acknowledgment.

Tim and I had been married 10 years, but I never lost that sense of pride in watching him do what he loved. "In the scripture reading from Corinthians, we see the many ways in which we are called to love one another. Paul and Pamela, what you are doing here today is proclaiming that love publicly. As we heard in the reading, love isn't always easy. It takes work. So, I would say to the both of you to put yourself in that place—Paul is always patient and kind; Pamela is never boastful or conceited. Paul is never rude or selfish; Pamela does not brood over injury.

"Would Paul and Pamela and the wedding party please come forward for the exchange of vows?"

Paul clasped Pamela's hand as they met Tim before the altar, the wedding party standing on either side. Tim invited the couple to face one another and join their right hands. Paul repeated his vows in a strong and clear voice: "I, Paul, take you, Pamela, to be my wife. I promise to be true to you in good times and in bad, in sickness and in health. I will love and honor you all the days of my life."

I am not sure how many of us thought we would ever see such a glorious day, but the ceremony seemed to pass in a blink.

chapter two

The Lafayette Club overlooked Lake Minnetonka, the largest lake in the Twin Cities metropolitan area in Minnesota. Our family had been longtime members, and I had been to the club often enough to know it was an elegant setting, but tonight guests were transported to another world. White netting arced across the ceiling and tiny lights shimmered over the Crystal Ballroom, which had been transformed into a lush flower garden. Candle and flower centerpieces accented each table, giving the feeling that we were dining outdoors under a canopy of twinkling stars. The oblong windows behind the bridal table overlooked Crystal Bay, and against the backdrop of a cotton candy-streaked sunset, a few boats were silhouetted against the evening sky.

An army of servers in black attire circulated with silver trays brimming with finger foods as the bridal party formed a reception line in the center of the ballroom. As Paul and Pamela greeted guests, I chatted with co-workers, family and old friends, and we shared the universal lament that the only time we all got together was to marry or to bury someone. We were, at last, doing the former.

Dinner was announced, and we took our places at the head table, looking out across the full ballroom. I had attended more wedding dinners than I could possibly count, but they did not often include filet mignon and lobster tail, which was Pamela's choice. Throughout the sumptuous meal, there were frequent interruptions of silver tinkling on crystal, a sign for the bride and groom to kiss, and they happily obliged.

After a dessert of chocolate mousse wedding cake was served, all the single women gathered as Pamela threw a pink rose bouquet, which Ruthie promptly caught. As tradition dictated, Paul removed Pamela's lace garter and threw it into a crowd of single men; this time the lucky recipient was one of Paul's last single friends, which prompted hoots and hollers from the crowd.

This had been an exceptionally long day for the children, and my sister-in-law Michelle's parents, Jeanne and Michael Daly, would be taking them for the night. As little Sam fought to stay awake, they determined it was time to go. On their way out, they stopped by the bridal table to say good night, Sam peacefully asleep on Grandma Jeanne's shoulder. Ruthie was excitedly showing off her bridal bouquet. "See my flowers, Mommy! It means I'll be the next one to get married," she said, waving the flowers in front of her parents.

"Well, let's hope not for a while," Michelle said with a laugh.

"Like not until you're 35," my brother Jack deadpanned. "Hey, thanks for coming, Jeanne and Michael. We appreciate your taking the kids for the night."

"Our pleasure," Michael replied.

"Bye, Mommy. Bye, Daddy," Ruthie said, still waving the treasured bouquet.

Shortly after, the wedding dance commenced. As Paul and Pamela took the floor for their first dance to Nat King Cole's romantic ballad "Unforgettable," Michelle sat next to me, her voice soft and tinged with regret.

"You know, I still feel guilty about what happened and how I reacted. But that night, all I saw was a drunk gold digger who was not in love with Paul but in love with his money. I'm grateful you were so persistent that I hear Pamela's side, but even then, it wasn't easy to forget."

The incident had been an agonizing experience that had caught everyone off guard. Paul and Pamela had announced their engagement on New Year's Day, and soon after that, Jack and Michelle, along with Tim and I, took them out for a celebratory dinner. We chose the Lake Elmo Inn. It had been the setting of many Pierson family special occasions, from Easter brunch to anniversaries, and was our first choice for such happy circumstances. The inn was tucked along the main street of Lake Elmo, a small Minnesota town that retained a rural charm while surrounded by sprawling cities and burgeoning suburbs. Only a few miles from the Wisconsin border, it meant driving from one side of the Twin Cities to the other. Even so, the food, service and memories made it well worth the trip. We would toast Paul and Pamela's happiness and hear their plans for the wedding.

The evening had started out well, the couple asking each of us to participate in the ceremony. Paul and Pamela had both been through major life traumas, and as their gift, Mother and Dad had offered to pay for the wedding. Pamela started drinking the moment we were seated, ordering a double shot of Jack Daniels. Within 30 minutes, her manner transformed from charming to surly; her voice grew louder and more obnoxious with each drink.

As Pamela was in the middle of describing her designer gown, the custom bridesmaid dresses, the invitations and the flowers, our waiter appeared, carrying a tray of lemon sorbet. "What the hell is this?" she demanded.

"It's a sorbet, ma'am, to cleanse your palate before the main course."

"I don't want this! Just get me another drink!" She swatted at the waiter as if he were an annoying fly.

"Pamela, please keep your voice down," Paul said, his tone colored by embarrassment.

"Don't tell me what to do!" she snapped. "I just need to relax, and you're being an asshole." We were acutely aware of the other patrons staring at our table, but Pamela was indifferent. "Has Paul told you about our honeymoon? Three weeks in Paris, London and Rome, staying at the best five-star hotels."

"Wow. That sounds expensive," Jack commented.

"It's not like your parents can't afford it, Jack," Pamela sneered.

"Mom and Dad are paying for the honeymoon, too?" I asked.

Pamela was undeterred. "Of course they're paying for it," she shot back. "They said we could have the wedding and honeymoon that we wanted, and this is what I want."

"What about what Paul wants?" Michelle asked.

Our waiter had returned, preparing to serve dinner. Pamela demanded her drink. "Where the hell's my drink?"

"Ma'am, if I could just serve the main course—"

"I want another drink and I want it now!" she shouted. A second waiter intervened, saying he would bring her cocktail right away, the five of us watching in silence, appalled by this side of Pamela we hadn't seen.

Under the influence of large amounts of alcohol, Pamela was oblivious to her surroundings. She continued talking, blithely describing the trip she and Paul had made to Dayton's department store to choose their bridal registry items. The list seemed excessive: Waterford crystal in the Lismore pattern, Irish linens, a sterling silver coffee service. The china and sterling flatware were special-order. Even the ordinary items needed to start a home—cookware, appliances, sheets, towels—were top of the line. Pamela relished describing the list, chattering on about our family's wealthy friends and whom she expected to "pony up" expensive gifts.

As the celebratory dinner continued to deteriorate, I excused myself to use the ladies' room. I rose from the table, and Michelle was suddenly at my elbow. "I'll go with you," she said, and we made our way across the crowded main dining room, conscious of the stares. It was the bridal registry that had sent Michelle into a tailspin. As we entered the ladies' room, she threw her evening bag across the white-and-green-tiled lounge in a rage, the contents spilling across the floor.

"This is not the girl we want Paul to marry!" she shouted. Michelle's outburst caught me off guard and left me gasping for a response. She slammed her fist against the vanity, continuing her angry rant. "We've all been duped! Pamela Schaeffer is a world-class gold digger!"

I couldn't deny that Pamela's behavior was inexcusable, but as a recovering alcoholic myself, I knew firsthand about the stinging consequences of being drunk in public, talking too loudly, stumbling across a room and making an all-around fool of myself. I also knew it could have been an isolated incident fueled by stress. It didn't necessarily point to deeper problems. Even as the older sibling who'd always been protective of both of my brothers—but especially Paul—I thought we owed Pamela a bit of grace.

We replaced the contents of Michelle's purse, and I suggested we give Pamela a second chance. We returned from the restroom just as the evening was ending abruptly. Jack was asking for the check, though desserts were only partially eaten. I hoped we could depart without Pamela making any more of a scene than she already had, but a discreet exit was not to be. We'd been seated in the center of the room, which meant we had to navigate a maze of diners. Pamela stumbled and lurched hard into the nearest table, clinking china and spilling wine as she slammed into it.

"Look what you've done!" one of the diners said angrily.

"Fuck you!" she retorted, and the dining room grew eerily still.

"I am so sorry," I said, mortified. "We will make this right." From the corner of my eye, I saw Jack motion to a waiter, handing him a credit card. He whispered something, no doubt giving instructions to purchase a new bottle of wine for the upset patrons.

Tim and Paul each grabbed Pamela by an elbow and guided her out of the restaurant as gracefully as they could. She was spewing venom at everyone. "Let go of me! You are such fucking assholes!"

Every pair of eyes followed us. In the throes of embarrassment, I felt as if I were burning up. Outside, despite the January cold, I tore off my wool coat.

"What are you doing?" Michelle asked in alarm.

"I'm so hot," I panted, the cold air sharp against my lungs. "This whole evening has been a horrifying mess."

"And you think we should give her a second chance?" Michelle seethed.

In her wobbly condition, Pamela slipped on the icy black street. Tim and Jack caught her before she fell, but she flailed wildly. The men supported Pamela until they could get her into the back seats of the SUV, where she passed out almost immediately.

We reached Paul and Pamela's colonial-style home in Edina—an affluent suburb of Minneapolis—45 minutes later. It took both Jack and Tim to carry Pamela's dead weight into the house, Paul guiding them to the bedroom. Paul was visibly shaken, confessing he had never seen Pamela exhibit this kind of behavior. I did my best to comfort him. On the drive home, Michelle remained insistent that the wedding must be called off.

The next day, Pamela paid a heavy price for her overindulgence. She suffered a head-pounding hangover and couldn't recall much of the evening, particularly the end, and it caused her great shame. I hoped she did not have a drinking problem, but I knew all too well that blacking out was a sign of trouble ahead. Pamela apologized to each of us, contrite in her quest for forgiveness. She said she had let the stress of her job and planning the wedding get to her and recognized her behavior had been abominable. As I thought about how happy she made Paul, and the transformation that had occurred since they met, I was willing to forgive her. She seemed genuinely sorry. Jack and Tim also accepted her apology, believing this was an unfortunate instance of poor judgment.

Michelle, however, would not be so easily convinced. Her response to the apology was chilly, an attitude Pamela sensed immediately. I implored Michelle to give her an opportunity to redeem herself, reminding her of how far Paul had evolved due to her.

To regain Michelle's trust, Pamela began by asking for her input. Michelle and Jack had held their wedding reception at the Lafayette Club, and Pamela consulted her for ideas on the menu, seating, music and decorations. She asked if they would allow Ruthie and Sam to participate as the flower girl and ring bearer. Michelle felt Sam might be too young, but Pamela explained it was important to her to have the children included in what she viewed as a family affair. Michelle began to waver, realizing she was not being fair in holding one unpleasant evening as a benchmark for ending the relationship that had brought Paul so far.

Watching Paul and Pamela's wedding dance cheek to cheek across the polished hardwood floor, Michelle patted my arm and smiled. "I was wrong to be so judgmental. Paul is happier than I ever thought possible, and Pamela is the reason."

"Don't be hard on yourself," I said. "It was a difficult situation for everyone, but Pamela made amends. That's what counts."

Her smile was slightly self-conscious. "I guess that also means I shouldn't be so concerned about how much our dresses cost."

Michelle had been outraged when we discovered the bridesmaid dresses cost $600 apiece. "Think of it this way," I said. "They're lovely and definitely dresses we can wear again."

"True," she responded. "And I'll be wearing it a lot because it's the most expensive piece of clothing I own."

"For me, too," I laughed as Jack joined us.

"What are you two up to?"

"We were just talking about that awful dinner at the Lake Elmo Inn and how wrong I was," Michelle answered.

A ghost of melancholy shaded Jack's face briefly. "Fortunately for us, things worked out for the best."

"That they did," I said.

The next dance was dedicated to the bride and groom dancing with their parents, but the DJ invited others to join the dancing as well.

"We'd better take this chance while we can," Jack said, offering his hand to Michelle.

Tim and I also enjoyed a moment to ourselves. We danced to the wedding classic, Etta James's "At Last," which we had always favored as our special song.

"You look beautiful," he said quietly. "Rose is a gorgeous color on you. And I love your hair—think you could wear it like that more often?"

"You're a pretty good-looking guy yourself. But as far as the hair," I said, touching my dark auburn updo, "the salon appointment was an hour and a half, so I'm thinking probably not." We kissed, and I smiled at my husband. "You know, I hear this song and I think 'at last' is right. We are so lucky, Tim. I really didn't think Paul would ever recover after losing Rachel."

Tim nodded. "It was a tough time for everybody, and I won't deny I had my doubts. Nobody goes looking for pain and suffering, but it's made us stronger and more appreciative of what we have."

Well after 1 a.m. when Friday had crept into Saturday, the newlyweds retired to the bridal suite at the nearby Lafayette Hotel. The rest of us headed to the gifts. The piles had grown so large that the four designated tables were buried. We ferried the stacks of wedding presents to our cars and SUVs, where they would be held for the night. Later in the day we would gather at our parents' home, which we affectionately referred to as Goldenwoods, on the shores of Lake Minnetonka for a leisurely brunch and to watch the newlyweds open their gifts.

Tim finished packing our car and was closing the trunk. "I think that's about all we can take," he told Jack and Michelle. "See you tomorrow."

"What time did Mom say?" I asked.

"No earlier than noon. We've got to pick the kids up from Jeanne and Michael's place, so we'll be over around 12:30," Jack said.

"I don't know about you, but I can use a good night's sleep," Michelle said.

She was right about that. It was past 2 a.m. when we arrived home. By the time we were ready for bed it was pushing 2:45, well past my bedtime. Just before I slipped off into peaceful slumber, my mind drifted over the past year and Paul's metamorphosis. It reminded me of the biblical story of Lazarus, given up for dead. For all practical purposes, Paul had died with Rachel, but our family became closer than ever in the tragedy. We refused to give up, resolute in our belief that restoring Paul's life was not only possible but imperative. The wedding had been a glorious event, filling us all with great joy to participate in their happiness.

chapter three

Mother and Dad had built Goldenwoods—their dream home overlooking Lake Minnetonka—in the early 1990s. Once my brothers and I left home, our parents didn't think the house we grew up in would comfortably accommodate an expanding family of spouses and grandchildren, and they designed the house they had always wanted.

Another of the considerations for building the new house was Mother's determination to make a major career change. She had worked in the property management portion of our real estate company for more than a decade. She oversaw hundreds of properties and tenants, dealing with never-ending crises, from irate tenants, leaking toilets and loud neighbors to illegal drugs and even the occasional dead occupant. What she was not prepared for was a SWAT team surrounding one of our apartment buildings while attempting to negotiate with an emotionally unstable tenant. The hostage standoff and the bloody climax were carried live by the local news. Traumatized by the tragedy, Mother decided she'd had enough of the property management business.

As a hobby, Mother and Dad collected antique Red Wing pottery, stoneware made in the Minnesota town of the same name. Production of the utilitarian pottery began in 1861, and authentic pieces were marked by a distinctive red-winged logo. After the hostage standoff, Mother determined it was the perfect time to make her pottery-collecting hobby a career. In their new home, she mandated that she'd have an office space and room for displaying her collections.

Goldenwoods was a two-story gray-and-white brick house situated on a vast lot that provided easy accessibility to the lake. Its antique-filled hallway led to an enormous open kitchen, the center of all activity and true heart of the home. Modeled on the farm kitchens of the early 20th century, it had white antiqued cabinets lining the walls, modernized by granite counters.

Off the kitchen was a great room, designed for large gatherings and comfort. Two-story windows highlighted the beauty and changing moods of the lake and golden sunsets. Mother's office had long been converted to a sitting room. Her pottery collection had outgrown the house, and she had opened a storefront in downtown Wayzata, Past Treasures Antiques.

Early Saturday afternoon the day after the wedding, we trickled into the kitchen at Goldenwoods. Mother had arranged the breakfast buffet across an oak-topped island at the kitchen's center. A colander of fresh fruit sat in the low farm sink, and pans were laid casually across her eight-burner stovetop.

"Good afternoon," I said to Mother as she organized the food.

Dressed in an open denim shirt over a shell paired with jeans, Mother was casual, but she always looked chic. "Hello, guys," she said, hugging both Tim and me. "Did you sleep OK?"

"Like a rock," I replied. Arms laden with presents, I nodded my head toward the open space. "Take these into the great room?"

"Yep!" Jack called out.

He and Michelle stopped stacking gifts, taking our load and surveying the rapidly filling room. We'd replaced the formal attire from the previous evening with comfortable jeans and sweaters. A good choice for lots of crawling around on the floor and shuffling large boxes. "Are Paul and Pamela here yet?" I asked.

"They just called," Jack said. "They shouldn't be much longer. Michelle, did you bring the camera?"

My sister-in-law rolled her eyes in mock exasperation. "Yes, dear. It's in the case lying on the couch."

Mounds of wedding gifts covered half the great room floor. The newlyweds entered for a leisurely day of enjoying good food and family before heading to the airport, where they would catch an overnight flight to Europe.

"Are you all packed?" I asked Pamela as we embraced.

"Oh, yes. I anticipated we'd be busy with last-minute wedding details, so we've been packed since Wednesday."

Another of Pamela's stellar qualities—organization. When she and Paul first met, she discovered he had no fewer than seven checking accounts, all in various states of disarray. Once they moved in together, she set about balancing the accounts and consolidating them all into one.

Paul stood in the great room, gauging the piles of gifts. "Wow!" he uttered, overwhelmed, his eyes glistening with gratitude. "We might have to build an addition just to make room for all of this."

Ruthie and Sam bounded up the stairs from the backyard, where they had been flying a kite with Dad, who was a few paces behind.

"We get to help you, Uncle Paul!" Ruthie revealed, full of excitement.

"We're probably gonna need it," Paul said, giving his niece a hug. "Did you have fun yesterday?"

"Yes, except for my dress," Ruthie replied. "It was itchy."

Michelle called from the kitchen, "But you looked so pretty."

"You did," Pamela said, planting a kiss on Ruthie's forehead.

"Thanks," Ruthie said with a shade of bashfulness.

"I wooked pretty, too!" Sam announced loudly.

"How about 'handsome,' bud?" Jack said with a laugh. "You were very handsome."

"We're about ready to eat," Mother proclaimed. "Everybody wash up."

Forming a circle in the kitchen and joining hands, Dad asked Tim to bless the meal and this time together as family. Our hungry brood dug into the buffet with gusto. Crisp fruits and vegetables, delectable pastries, potatoes, eggs, bacon, juices and freshly brewed coffee enticed us to fill our plates and not be shy about seconds.

Afterward, we gathered for the opening of gifts. Armed with pens, notepads and a file folder for keeping the cards, Michelle and I took turns keeping track of who had given what. Ruthie and Sam were charged with bringing Paul and Pamela the smaller gifts and assisting to unwrap.

Soon Waterford crystal pieces were being moved to the dining room table for safekeeping, along with settings of the Noritake china and sterling silver place settings. Sets of plush sheets, towels, delicately embroidered linens and French cookware rounded out the piles.

In late afternoon, the high sun still ablaze, I let out a sigh of relief thinking we were done at last. Carrying a large box from their first-floor bedroom, Dad announced, "One last gift from Mother and me."

He gently set the box down before the couple. "But the wedding was your gift!" Paul said.

"This is an heirloom you can pass to your children," Mother explained, her eyes twinkling. She loved celebrations and giving gifts.

Ruthie and Sam were already tearing into the paper. "I'll feel better with you two over here," Jack said, motioning with his hand to the children.

The box was tightly taped, and once split open there were mounds of tissue paper. Pamela dug through the box, lifting out a pitcher or vase. Paul removed a second piece.

Tissue paper came off in layers, Pamela holding a stunning blue-tinted pitcher with a lily motif. Paul unwrapped the matching basin, a hard-to-come-by set that was a unique example of Red Wing pottery artistry.

"Oh my God, it's beautiful," Pamela said appreciatively.

Paul looked at Mother and Dad, shaking his head. "This is just too much!"

"Well, we noticed you've really taken an interest in the Red Wing pottery, Paul, and we wanted you to have a special piece to add to your collection," Dad said.

"This also fulfills the 'something old, something blue' part of the wedding tradition," Mother added, beaming.

Tim and I had also been recipients of rare Red Wing pottery pieces. I knew how much it meant to Mother and Dad that their children had taken a keen interest in their collections. Made in Red Wing for nearly a century, the pottery was an important part of Minnesota history, one our parents meant to preserve. The newlyweds would start married life in high style.

* * *

Paul and Pamela honeymooned in Europe for three weeks. At every major port, they sent postcards to everyone in the family, filling us in on their travels and adventures. By the time they returned home in mid-July, my refrigerator was covered with postcards depicting European landmarks.

They were incandescent with happiness from their breathtaking journey and joyous beginning to married life. Once their pictures and video were organized, they invited everyone for dinner and a guided tour of Western Europe.

In late July, the family settled back into the steady hum of the busiest season for the real estate business. Every so often, I would stop to think about how fast things can change for the better. In just a year, Paul had rediscovered love, and a beautiful wedding had touched all of us. Now it was back to the ordinary events of everyday life, but the prospects had never looked brighter.

PART TWO

chapter four

AUGUST 1996

Our family had been in the real estate business for 30 years, during which time Pierson Properties grew from a three-person office tucked behind Suki's Beauty Salon in Minnetonka to 10 offices and some 400 sales associates scattered throughout the Twin Cities. The main office where Jack, Paul and I worked had been constructed five years earlier as part of a new Edina office park. The one-story building housed the apartment rental and property management division that Jack headed, our new development business that Paul oversaw, and marketing and communications, which was my domain. Including accounting, computer information services and support staff, the office employed more than 100 people.

The office ended up being the drop-off for many wedding gifts. Even after returning from Europe, gifts continued to arrive at the office or their house, causing Paul to lament, "I'll be writing thank-you notes for the rest of my life!"

By August, the stream of gifts had greatly tapered. One afternoon, when UPS delivered a huge box to the office, Jack shook his head in disbelief. "More wedding presents?" he asked.

"Oh yes, gifts can arrive for up to a year after the wedding," I said.

Jack lifted the box. "Whatever this is, it's heavy. With Paul out of town, I'm not sure we should leave this in his office."

"I'm on my way out for a meeting. If you'll carry it to my car, I'll deliver it to Paul and Pamela's house."

"Maybe I should come along. It'll take two of you to get this into the house."

"Jack, we can manage just fine," I said with mild annoyance, feeling quite confident I could handle the lifting myself.

"Only making an offer."

Jack settled the box onto the back seat. "I've got an appointment to look at some new promotional items after I drop this off. Back in a couple of hours," I said.

"No more pens! Find something sales associates and leasing agents view as useful that's not overly expensive," Jack said, slamming the door.

I nodded in agreement as I climbed into my car. When I arrived at Paul and Pamela's house, Pamela's white Volvo station wagon was parked in the garage. Even with Jack's admonishment not to move the package myself, I tried anyway. My efforts only wedged it against the cloth seats. Under my beige linen jacket, I could feel perspiration and realized it would take both Pamela and me to move the package.

As I walked through the garage, I noticed the Volvo hatch was open. The back was packed to the limit with boxes of all sizes. Looking closer, I recognized several wedding gifts. Colored dots on each of the boxes caught my attention—a label on a crystal pitcher read $50, on a toaster $65 and on a Crock-Pot $30.

The door to the house opened. "Hi, Pamela! I've got a package for you and Paul."

Pamela stood at the threshold balancing more tagged boxes. I could see she was wearing a white halter top and shorts, which showed off her slim, tan legs. Her blonde hair was styled in a casual ponytail. She gave off an air of pristine cool in the stifling heat.

"Kay! I didn't hear you pull up. What are you doing here?"

"I have a wedding gift that was delivered to the office," I replied, beckoning toward my car. "It will take both of us to carry it into the house."

Pamela set her boxes on the hood of the Volvo, contemplating the packages. As she followed from the shade of the garage into the brilliant summer sun, I could've sworn I heard her mumble under her breath, "Ugh. More shit."

"Pardon?"

"Nothing," she said, waving me off as she assessed the large box. "Let's bring this into the garage."

We pushed and shoved until we got the bulky box out of the car, then carried it like two movers grabbing hold of each end, setting it on the garage floor. In the summer heat, even cool Pamela had started to perspire as we caught our breath.

I was curious about the items loaded in the Volvo. "Do you need help with those boxes in your car?" I asked casually.

Pamela brushed a wisp of stray hair aside with her hand. "I'm selling the duplicates at a friend's yard sale; the rest are being put in storage. Want something to drink?"

I followed into the kitchen. "No, I'm fine," I said, trying to process her comments.

My face must have betrayed my surprise. Her eyes narrowed. "Oh, Kay, I'm not giving them away, for chrissake," she said, the sharpness rising in her voice. "We don't have enough room for everything. We need a bigger house, or we can't keep it all. And Paul is in complete agreement with selling the duplicates. We'll give the money to charity."

She seemed to be avoiding eye contact. I kept the conversation cordial. "If space is a problem, we'd be glad to store some presents for you until you and Paul have the room."

Pamela took her time filling a glass of ice with water from the faucet. "If you want to store them, fine. But you might end up having this stuff for quite a while."

"We do have the room, and it's no trouble," I said.

"Let's see what this one is. You'll probably end up storing it too."

She grabbed a knife out of a drawer, slitting open the cardboard box, and together we lifted out the silver wrapped package. Opening the attached card, she read it aloud: "'Eleanor and Frank Parker.' Must be one of the employees." Tossing the card onto the counter, Pamela ripped off the wrapping paper to reveal a large crystal punch bowl with service for 20 in matching plates and cups.

"You can take this too," she said, her manner vigorous.

My gut reaction was to protest, but I kept quiet. She'd been forthright about selling duplicates, but something felt off. I just couldn't put my finger on it.

We loaded the items in my car, and then Pamela said briskly, "I need to get going. See you at family dinner on Sunday." I realized I was 20 minutes late for my own appointment. I gave Pamela a quick hug and sped across town with the discarded treasures.

* * *

By the time Tim arrived home that evening, our Mission-style dining room table was covered with everything from crystal to small appliances to picture frames. "What is all this?" he asked, the stacks forming various geometric shapes across the table's surface.

"Wedding gifts for Paul and Pamela. Most of them I recognize."

Tim examined an exquisitely appliquéd tablecloth. "Why do we have them?"

"I stopped by to deliver a late present. When I arrived, she was loading all of this into her car. Pamela told me she was selling the duplicates and moving the rest into storage, because they lack space. Except, every single item has a price tag. It was strange."

"Well, we did something similar," Tim said.

"But not to this extent." I lifted a crystal clock off the table. "This was a gift from Fran Smith, a longtime sales associate. It seems rude, don't you think? And Pamela was not exactly thrilled to see me."

"But she admitted some items were being sold, didn't she?"

"Yes," I said with a roll of my eyes, sensing defeat.

Tim looked at the crystal clock. "Maybe she just doesn't like it, and this was a polite way of letting someone else who would like the clock get enjoyment from it."

I hated it when Tim played devil's advocate. "OK, so maybe I'm jumping to conclusions," I acknowledged.

"Lord knows we gave all of our duplicate items to charity," Tim continued. "And there were plenty of items that we didn't like or couldn't use that we're still storing in the basement."

Now the presents Pamela had deemed unacceptable would also be in a basement closet, carefully packed but unclaimed.

chapter five

Labor Day brought the official end to summer. Most Minnesotans lament that summer is never long enough, taking advantage of every opportunity warmer days afford. Typically, in the fall and winter seasons the real estate sector of our business slowed. But during the mid-1990s, mortgage rates began declining so the housing market was gathering momentum. Development and home sales remained brisk.

During early fall, Paul and Pamela announced they were building a new home in Woodbury, one of St. Paul's fastest-growing and expensive suburbs. Affluent subdivisions had names like Wedgewood, Interlachen Woods and Eagle Valley.

"Woodbury is a wonderful community, with great schools and businesses," Paul gushed, unrolling blueprints amid the cluttered desk.

Of Mediterranean architecture, with two-story arched windows in the great room, the house would occupy a wooded lot in a new subdivision overlooking the centerpiece, Colby Lake.

"From the blueprints it looks huge," I said.

"What's the square footage?" Jack asked as we examined the drawings.

"Just over 5,000 square feet," Paul said.

"So just a shack," Jack said with a mischievous grin. Just as quickly, he was all seriousness. "Are you sure you can afford this?"

"We're selling our house, of course," Paul said, waving away concern. "Fran Smith is the listing agent, so we're in good hands. There have already been two open houses, with another set for Thursday."

Fran was the sales associate whose wedding gift was now being stored in our basement. Don't bring that up, I thought and listened to Paul talk.

"We've spent almost a year making renovations, so it's appreciated substantially. Edina is a premier location. With the housing market on the upswing, the sale should provide a solid down payment."

Edina, like Woodbury, was an upscale suburb but had been in existence far longer. From the early 1950s when the suburb first began taking shape, it was an address with cachet. It was also a place brimming with childhood memories, as it was where the three of us had spent a happy childhood. That comfortable familiarity was one of the main reasons we built the main location of the business in Edina, plus we all lived nearby in the west metro area.

"What about the drive?" I inquired. "Your commute is going to go from 10 minutes to at least an hour in traffic. You might as well be on the other side of the world."

Paul laughed nervously, adjusting his glasses as he spoke. "Yeah, the drive's terrible, but my schedule can be pretty flexible."

"You couldn't pay me to do it," Jack interjected. "Crossing the bridge on I-494 alone would make me nuts. But it's your house."

Jack's comment was a fact of life. As the Twin Cities grew, navigating traffic became more difficult if one had to cross one of the rivers that wound through or bordered the metro, but particularly the Mississippi, which separated Minneapolis from St. Paul. Mighty and swift, Ol' Man River was a persistent reminder that nature dictated the engineering achievements that melded the two cities.

I returned to the topic of their new home. "When will the house be completed?"

"We're hoping to be in by Christmas. If not, then right after the first of the year."

"Well, it sounds lovely," I said. "I can't wait to see it."

"Don't worry, Sis," Paul said, giving me a squeeze. "We'll have a great big housewarming party, which will give us something to look forward to in the dead of winter, when it's too cold to be outside."

* * *

That fall was glorious, as though an artist's brush had painted leaves stunning shades of burnt orange, mustard yellow and bright red beneath cloudless cerulean skies. 1996 was also an election year. Incumbent President Bill Clinton campaigned for re-election against Senator Bob Dole of Kansas. As native Minnesotans, we'd been raised in a progressive state, informed by the legacies of Hubert Humphrey, Eugene McCarthy, Walter Mondale and others. Our family was politically active; we hosted fundraisers for candidates and canvassed neighborhoods to register voters. Through our parents' activism, we each understood that voting was not a right but a privilege, and I planned to exercise it that afternoon.

Before heading to the polls, I had a meeting to show Jack and Paul the proofs for the new marketing campaign. It was the result of a month long process of researching, designing and revising. A new marketing slogan, "Come Home to Pierson Properties," had been launched earlier that year, but I wanted the final go-ahead for the campaign.

With advertising proofs in hand, I headed toward Jack's office. Suddenly, his angry words from behind the closed door filled the halls. "You cannot afford this house! You're in way over your head!"

"Stop telling me what to do!" Paul shouted back. "I sold my house for a 35 percent profit."

"That's great, but your house payment will be more than $4,000 a month!"

"My wife works too!"

"She'd better, because that doesn't include property taxes."

Paul's secretary, Linda Petersen, and two sales associates anxiously peered around the corner. I knocked, not waiting for a response before entering. "What's going on?" I forcibly shut the door behind me.

"Nothing," Paul fumed.

"Don't be an idiot, Paul! You do not need a 5,000-square-foot house just because your wife wants the status."

"Leave Pamela out of this, Jack!"

In a second I shifted into big-sister mode and physically inserted myself between my two brothers, who stood inches apart. "That is enough!"

"Damn it, Kay. Mind your own business!" Paul said, taking a wobbly step back.

"This is my business and half the office's now too," I said, jabbing a finger toward several employees trying to look as though they weren't paying attention but hanging on to every word. "I don't care if you argue, but you need to do it where the whole company can't hear you."

"Fine!" Paul said, pushing hard past both Jack and me. "If you minded your own damn business there would be no argument. I don't need this shit!" He slammed the door so hard that papers blew off Jack's desk, several floating to the floor.

"Well, that was lovely," I said, exasperated. Stooping to grab loose papers, I glanced out the side glass into the hall, where people nonchalantly stood whispering among themselves. "Wanna tell me what happened?"

"I needed to find some information on the Lake Hills development, and Paul wasn't here. You know what a mess his desk can be, so as I'm sifting through the stacks, I come across the loan papers. I couldn't help but see the amount. This is out of his league."

"And he's mad that you told him so."

"Yes. Nothing wrong with building a bigger house, but the

house they have now was just renovated—and essentially at the company's expense."

I hadn't thought about that. "Well, Dad was OK with it, or he would have insisted Paul and Pamela pay the company back."

"I vehemently opposed the arrangement from the start. There's no way in hell they entertain often enough to justify renovating one house, let alone building an even bigger one."

I wasn't sure what to think. I felt caught in the middle. I was frustrated by my inability to come up with a solution that would satisfy everyone. "The loan was approved, so there's not much we can do."

Jack seated himself, leaning back in the burnished red-leather chair. "I know, but Paul should be smarter than this. He's falling into a lifestyle built on overextended credit that will collapse at the slightest downturn. Sure, things are booming now, but the dead market of 1992 wasn't that long ago."

"What kind of loan is it?" I asked.

"A 30-year fixed," he replied. "I guess I should be grateful it wasn't a five-year ARM, because Paul would really be in trouble."

Jack's concerns were valid. "I could ask Fran how much Paul's house sold for," I said.

The shrill ring of Jack's cellular phone ended our conversation. "No, I'm going to wash my hands of it," he said, answering the phone, "This is Jack."

On a pad of Post-it Notes I scribbled "marketing proofs are ready and don't forget to vote," sliding it toward him. Jack nodded in acknowledgment, and I silently left the office.

The air in the hallway was heavy with tension. In front of Paul's office, Linda sat at her desk, on edge. "Paul's gone," she said anxiously, the lilt of her Southern accent more pronounced than usual. "He's real upset. Didn't tell me where he was going."

I kept my voice steady to reassure her. "I know, but it'll blow over."

Linda's agile fingers clacked against the computer keyboard. "I hate it when y'all fight."

"I do too," I replied wearily. "At least we don't do it often."

* * *

Paul did not speak to Jack or me for several days. Appearing at work each morning he went straight to his office, sequestered behind closed doors. When either of us tried to approach him, Paul insisted he was handling urgent development matters. If he required material about a project, Paul used Linda as the intermediary, shuttling the information back and forth.

"I can't stand being the go-between," Linda fumed, returning the marketing proofs. "Y'all need to sit down and work this out."

I knew she was right. "I understand your frustration."

Her voice was crisp in its anger. "No, you don't! Look around you, Kay. Everybody here is walking on eggshells, afraid they might say the wrong thing. Your problems become our problems, as much as you'd like to think otherwise," she said, making a sweeping gesture with her hands. "It hurts morale when you guys argue."

After Linda's comments, I noticed the inquiring faces of our employees were asking simple questions: "Are you speaking yet? Can we get back to our jobs?" Clearly, action had to be taken to end the divisiveness.

On the Sunday following the altercation, Paul and Pamela stayed away from our weekly family dinner. Aware of the impasse, Mother and Dad maintained neutral ground. "I can see both sides," Dad said as we cleaned up the kitchen after, "but this is something the three of you need to settle yourselves."

They were having better luck at keeping a balanced perspective than Michelle, who ran into Pamela at the grocery store. While clearing the dishes, she whispered, "Pamela was incredibly rude to me. Just a bitch. She said something about how it was 'unfortunate Jack found it necessary to be abusive.'"

Carefully stacking ceramic plates, I murmured, "Abusive? We had an argument and there was some yelling, but no one was what I would call abusive. That's a pretty strong way to describe it."

"Exactly," Michelle responded, beginning to rinse dishes at the sink. "She made it sound like Jack assaulted someone." She turned off the water. "I'm upset about what Pamela said. But this isn't about me. You guys have to make up."

She was right. Our estrangement was harming everyone. If we didn't reconcile soon, Dad would have to get involved. It never came to that, as Paul could only withstand the deadlock for so long—Paul needed to be liked, especially by his family. Jack, on the other hand, could always wait it out—his stubborn self-righteousness was unyielding.

That Monday I was about to call for a truce. Before that happened, Paul apologized to Jack, explaining that he'd felt picked on. Jack said he was only worried Paul was throwing his financial stability to the wind. They ironed out their differences by agreeing that as brothers and business partners they would do their best to stay out of one another's personal business.

Paul made amends with me, reiterating that he did not appreciate his siblings telling him what was best. "But I'm your big sister, I *do* know best," I joked. He didn't smile. "Neither one of us wants to see you get in over your head, that's all."

"I can handle building this house," he said, still defensive. "But you and Jack don't need to constantly be hovering over my life."

"Oh come on, no one is hovering," I replied, taken aback.

"Neither of you think I'm mature enough to handle my own affairs. I can run my life without your interference."

"You're being unfair," I said. "If we did so in the past, it was simply to keep you among the living. Presently, I don't feel that any of us intrudes in one another's lives."

"Pamela feels our whole family meddles too much," Paul said.

"I'm sorry if Jack and I overstepped boundaries about your new house. We are, however, involved in a family-owned business, and that ties us to one another more than other families."

I believed Paul was not seeing the entire picture, but I knew it was fruitless to fight him. A saying our grandfather had told us often when we were kids came to mind: If you get burned, you'll have to deal with the blisters. I genuinely hoped Paul could keep his feet out of the fire.

* * *

I was curious to see the house that was driving a wedge between my brothers. I had asked for a tour, but Pamela said she wanted everyone to wait until it was done. She was working with a decorator at Gabbert's, a local retailer of luxury furniture and interior design. Mother, on the other hand, had already seen the house. I asked her to take a drive with me to the construction site so she could give me a tour.

We visited on a chilly mid-December day when no one was there. While there was work remaining to do on the inside, the curb appeal was impressive. The house was trimmed in ornate stone moldings and window caps that made it look expensive. But I thought it also looked a bit cold. As Mother suspected, the house was locked, but she led the way around to the back.

"This window has a broken latch, and until it's replaced it's pretty easy to open," she said, kneeling next to a basement window that opened after she gave it a good hard shove.

"You've done this before?"

"Sort of," she answered, rising and brushing off her hands and topcoat. "You're the smallest and can fit through the window. Once you're in, come upstairs and let me in."

"Mom!"

"I can't fit through the window, dear."

"Isn't this breaking and entering?"

Mother rolled her eyes. "We can prove we're not burglars. I'll meet you on the porch."

"Don't leave until I'm in! I could get stuck."

After squirming and wiggling, I managed to squeeze my body through the window and dropped into the basement. Mother closed the window, and I found the stairs.

On the first floor, the smell of freshly oiled woodwork and sawdust was pungent. In the entryway I opened the door to a blast of cold air.

"Your father thinks it looks like a bank," Mother said, walking into the vast great room where windows arched two stories to the ceiling.

"Or maybe a medieval castle," I said. "Are those gargoyles over the garage?"

"I suppose."

"They're a little over the top for my taste."

Mother guided me through our tour, noting the many built-ins of desks and bookcases, much like our parents' home. Beautiful. And expensive.

On the second floor, reached by ascending a grand curving staircase, were four bedrooms. In one bedroom a mural depicting Winnie-the-Pooh and friends had been painted. "Is this a nursery?" I asked.

Mother confirmed with a nod. "You know how organized Pamela is. She likes everything planned well in advance. She's not pregnant yet, but they definitely want children."

The rest of the second floor consisted of a large guest room, a study and, as the centerpiece, an expansive master bedroom suite. It featured a sitting area, a massive bedroom, and a bathroom built around a jetted tub, with a dressing room, two walk-in closets and his-and-her vanities.

"I'm beginning to understand why Jack feels the way he does," I said. "This is huge."

"Paul and Pamela certainly won't get in each other's way here," Mother replied.

Back on the first floor, polished granite counters encircled the kitchen with an immense island and stovetop at the center. Mother said all the appliances were special-order commercial versions. "Pamela designed the kitchen for serious gourmet cooking and lots of entertaining."

Despite its beauty, I thought the structure lacked warmth. We left, this time via the garage. "I tend to agree with Dad that it looks like a bank," I said. "The only thing missing is an ATM."

* * *

Winter came and went. It was early summer 1997 before Paul and Pamela held a housewarming party. We arrived on a breezy Saturday afternoon in June, cars lining both sides of the streets for three blocks. Inside the large, open structure was a crush of people, the mass almost suffocating. We were greeted by Ron Baker, whose company constructed the house. Pierson Properties had worked with Ron for years, and he and both of my brothers had become close friends.

"This is an incredible house, if I do say so myself," he enthused. "We're planning to use it as the showpiece in our yearly catalog of homes."

"It is fabulous," Tim agreed.

"Congratulations on a fine job," I said. "Who else is here?"

"Your folks are out back with Sandy, and Paul's giving Jack and Michelle the nickel tour."

"Hey, Sis!" rang out from the top of the oak staircase, Paul leading

Jack and Michelle back downstairs. Jack's gaze briefly met mine. The rigid set of his jaw made it clear that his opinion that our brother had overextended himself lingered.

"Welcome to our abode," Paul continued, heartily shaking Tim's hand. "The bar's out back, and there's food in the kitchen." The bell chimed and Paul opened the massive door to a half-dozen more guests.

Snaking through the crowded house behind Michelle and Jack, I could not fathom why Paul and Pamela would want hundreds of people eating and drinking in their beautiful new home.

Once outside, the scent of fragrant roses collided with the smell of chlorine. The yard was beautifully landscaped, trimmed with manicured hedges and pruned trees. Sunlight shimmered off pristine aqua water that filled a tiled swimming pool and hot tub, two items that had not existed when Mother and I took our self-guided tour in December.

Tim wandered over to the bar to fetch us drinks, and I remained talking with Jack and Michelle. I turned toward Jack. I wondered what was going on behind his pensive eyes, which absorbed every detail. "You're still worried they're in over their heads, aren't you?" I asked.

"Yeah. But we promised to stay out of each other's personal lives, remember?"

Just then, Pamela approached us. "Welcome to our home," she said, slipping into the group, a cocktail in hand. "Have you gotten something to eat?"

"We haven't been here long," Tim answered.

"Pamela," I said, "the house is stunning."

"Oh, thanks. It's our dream home." Pamela waved to another group of guests standing at the bar. "I need to mingle but be sure and eat up. There's plenty, and the caterers will just throw out what doesn't get eaten."

Pamela walked across the lawn, the breeze catching her honey-blonde hair. The flowered sundress hugged her slender figure, showing off every curve. I stepped back from our group, soundlessly watching as she interacted with guests.

"Bill, it's great to see you," she said, throwing her arms around the neck of a man I didn't recognize.

"What a fabulous home. You must be thrilled."

"It's not that big, really, but thank you. Who needs a drink? The bar's right next to the pool. Karla! Stan!" Pamela waved to a couple just arriving, moving through the crowd.

After the rest of the family departed, Tim and I stayed on into the evening, chatting with the numerous guests. Pamela paraded a constant stream of people through the house. She seemed to be everywhere, soaking up the compliments and relishing the attention. In another era, I thought, Pamela could have been a queen mingling among her adoring court.

I couldn't shake the sentiment that something was different about Pamela. There was a subtle yet noticeable shift in her demeanor. A smirk always about to crack the surface. An almost but not quite arrogant tone. And that quick and haughty flipping of her hair.

Paul seemed to be changing too. He had always appreciated high quality, but he had never been enamored by material possessions. Now he owned an enormous house with an equally large mortgage. This house was outfitted with the best technology and workmanship available, from the in-home theater system to the custom-made woodwork, cabinets and appliances. The finest caterer had provided the food, and a popular local band was tuning up instruments poolside.

Twilight had extinguished the sunlight, chirping crickets beginning their song. "That was quite the shindig," Tim said as we made our way along the curving block full of parked vehicles.

"It's not over yet," I said. "I wonder if they'll get any complaints from the neighbors about the music being too loud."

He laughed. "Paul loves a good party. He'll invite them all in."

Growling guitar chords began wafting into the air, the band launching into its first song of the night.

"Here's a question for you," I said when Tim clicked the automatic door locks. "Does it seem like Pamela's becoming more aloof ... or even a bit snooty? Or is it just me?"

"She certainly appreciates the finer things in life," he replied, slipping into the driver's seat.

"You're not the only person who's noticed Pamela has very expensive taste," I said.

I thought back to the argument. Jack's concern that Paul was heading toward a financial chasm did have merit. Even though he claimed not to care, and said this was strictly Paul's business, I knew better. Under Jack's cool exterior lay a soft center, and if Paul were getting into trouble, he would harbor unease, even if never admitting so publicly.

"I'm inclined to agree with Jack that it's Paul and Pamela's call as to how they spend their money," Tim said, starting the engine. "The best we can hope for is that they can afford it."

This was one of the areas in which Tim's and my personalities differed. Some would say we were opposites. He was an eternal optimist maintaining there was goodness in everyone, and he was the first to give someone the benefit of the doubt. As a man of God, Tim understood that evil and inequity could stain human nature. He believed there might be a reasonable explanation for a person's actions, and when there was not, that even those with malicious intent could find their way to redemption.

I, on the other hand, was more suspicious of human behavior. While I'd been an advocate for giving Pamela the benefit of the doubt in the past, the party brought uneasy feelings to the surface. I was becoming apprehensive of her motives. Her outburst at the engagement dinner, her cavalier attitude about discarding wedding gifts, Paul's comment that she thought our family meddled too much. Individually, these things might seem minor. But collectively, the incidents kept creeping back into my psyche, where I would deconstruct and analyze them. Mostly, I was concerned for Paul. Not affording the house was one thing, but he definitely couldn't afford another heartbreak.

As we left the party, I vowed to put my reservations aside and adopt Tim's approach: to be fair and open-minded.

"I imagine you're right," I said as we drove past the house, the pounding beat of the music impossible to ignore. "I do wish them all the best."

chapter six

SUMMER 1997

In late summer, Dad began discussing the idea of selling the company to my brothers and me. He wasn't interested in retiring but wanted to travel and pursue his and Mother's mutual interest in the antique business. In the scenario he proposed, Dad would remain with the company as honorary chairman, continuing to offer input. Paul, Jack and I would each direct a division—much as we did now. As an attorney, Dad's legal advice and expertise were crucial in a competitive industry like real estate. In the new arrangement, Paul, also a law school graduate, would take on most of those responsibilities. The biggest difference was that as owners, we would accept all the risks, as well as potential profits.

We all agreed it was not a decision to be made lightly or hurriedly. Each of us had to determine if we were up to the challenge of running a large business involving hundreds of employees, while accepting the highs and lows of the real estate market. On one hand, there was the enthusiasm of owning the company and moving it from the first to the second generation, but there also was the stark reality that as owners, we would be required to take on the existing debt. We alone would be responsible for our success or failure.

Such risks did not bother me because I had intrinsic confidence in each of us. I believed we were ready to take this step. What concerned me was how this would affect Tim's ministry, as it was a well-known fact that clergy tended to move around. In becoming an owner, I hoped I would not diminish Tim's freedom to change churches when he felt he was becoming stale or desired a new opportunity.

His response was nothing but supportive. "I wouldn't feel tied down," he explained. "Many pastors stay 15 or 20 years in one place. Owning the business is not only a terrific prospect for you, but it also keeps the company in the family, something I know your dad desires."

"You're sure? What happens when you're ready to change churches?"

"Half of Minnesota's residents are Lutheran, so I'm not worried about finding another parish. I might have to commute longer, or we might move to another part of the city, but I'm not uncomfortable with that."

"The risks involved don't scare you?"

"No," he replied. "I'm already indirectly tied to the company just being married to you. And there are always going to be risks involved no matter what you do in life. Here's a chance for you to continue doing what you love, but in the role of owner."

As summer waned, the three of us drew closer to making our decision.

* * *

Labor Day brought summer officially to an end and the unmistakable golden tint of autumn in the air. Paul and Pamela invited the family to come for a day of relaxing and recreation at their home. In late afternoon, the men gathered around the big-screen television in the great room to cheer on our beloved Minnesota Twins as they faced off against the Chicago Cubs at Wrigley Field. Mother and I also were devoted followers, but today was for relaxing and engaging in girl talk around the pool.

"Mommy, can I show everybody my dive?" Ruthie asked.

"Is that all right?" Michelle said, directing her question to Pamela.

"Sure. Hey, Ruthie, can you do a dive off the board?" Pamela called.

Ruthie had to think about this for a minute. "OK," she decided, then climbed onto the diving board in her red one-piece suit, carefully walking out to the end. Hanging her toes over the edge, Ruthie raised her arms straight above her head and pushed off from the board in what was more of a belly flop than a dive.

"Oh, ouch," I grimaced. "She needs to arch her body."

"You OK?" Michelle asked Ruthie's blonde head bobbing to the surface.

"Yeah!"

Mother and Pamela clapped from the sidelines, cheering her on. "Good job!" and "Let's see another one!"

I had served as a lifeguard for several summers in college and decided to help my niece perfect her dive. I joined her alongside the pool. "The next time, arch your body into the dive—like you're a rainbow. I'll show you," I said and hopped onto the diving board, Ruthie following my every move from the water. Positioning myself at the edge, I said, "Watch how I push my body into a curve" and took my dive.

As I was in mid-spring, I heard Pamela distinctly say, "Pretty soon I'll be teaching my own kids how to dive." I kicked to the surface and was greeted by a round of applause. "Pamela! Are you pregnant?" I blurted.

"Yes! You heard that?"

"I was pretty sure the applause wasn't for my dive. Congratulations! When's the baby due?" I asked, gliding under the diving board.

"Late March."

"That's great! When did you find out?" Michelle asked.

"Friday, so I was excited to have everybody over."

Ruthie swam alongside me. "We'll have a cousin!"

"Yep! I can't wait," Pamela said.

While I coached Ruthie and she perfected bending her body into a rainbow as she dove, Sam snuck up behind Michelle. He dumped a pail he'd been filling with water from the hot tub.

"Sammy!" Michelle shrieked as her shirt and shorts soaked through. "I knew I should've put on a bathing suit."

Pamela laughed. "C'mon, Michelle, I've got clothes upstairs you can wear."

The two of them left in search of dry clothing. The Twins game ended, bringing the men outside to join us. The summer sun began its unhurried descent into dusk, a vivid sphere of oranges and pinks. Ever the fan, even the distraction of Pamela's happy news didn't keep me from inquiring, "Did we win?"

"The final score was 7 to 6," Jack replied. "The Cubs are tough, but we hung in there."

"Good," I replied. "We haven't been playing great this year, so we can use every win."

Mother turned to Paul, who was pulling additional chairs around the umbrella table. "Pamela shared your news with us, and it's wonderful!"

Obviously ecstatic, Paul beamed. "Thanks. I let it slip and told the guys during the game."

"So much for waiting until dinner," Pamela said with a laugh.

"Obviously we're excited. An ultrasound is scheduled the week after next," Paul continued. "We haven't decided if we'll find out if it's a boy or a girl."

"Your timing is perfect," Mother said. "With the baby born in the spring, you won't have to go through the summer being pregnant, Pamela."

The rest of the holiday was spent basking in the fading light of summer. It was a special time to enjoy one another's company and celebrate Paul and Pamela's happy tidings.

* * *

Later that fall, Paul, Jack and I made the big decision to formally accept our father's offer to buy the company. For Dad, it was a moment of great pride as he passed on the legacy of the business that he had built from the ground up and continued to guide and grow for more than 30 years. There was also a tinge of the bittersweet in knowing his role would never be the same, no matter how involved he remained.

On a crisp October day under a bright azure sky, we met at our attorneys' offices in downtown Minneapolis to sign the papers. We gathered as both family and partners in the conference room, our emotions running the gamut from fear of the unknown to the confidence of being in charge.

Tom Dixon, our family's longtime attorney, got the proceedings underway. "Any questions before we sign?" he asked.

"No, except that I feel like this means I've finally become an adult," Paul relayed with a hint of anxiety.

I exhaled at our common realization. "Me too, but I'm also scared to death."

Fearless as always, Jack smiled impishly. "You can both waive your ownership rights by signing everything over to me."

"No thanks," I said, laughing. "I'll work better with you than for you."

"Me too," Paul said.

A fit man, Tom's sandy hair gave him a youthful appearance. He took us step by step through what each paper we signed meant. After scrawling his signature on the documents, Paul stepped back from the table with a sigh. "Now we're *truly* in this together."

"I know you'll do just fine," Dad said. "If I didn't, I never would have asked the three of you to make such a big commitment."

Tom stacked the documents neatly together on the conference table, turning to face us. "Your dad has great confidence in all of you," he said. "And now that you are owners, let me offer you a little piece of advice: The three of you have become one entity, but it goes beyond the business. *Everything you do, every decision you make, affects all of you, be it success or failure.*"

No one spoke a word, taking a moment to digest the gravity of Tom's comments. Dad broke the silence. "What Tom is saying is important. It was different with my being the sole owner. Difficulties still affected our family, but ultimately, any decision came down to me. The three of you will have to work together, always conscious of what the other two are doing."

"I'm not trying to scare you," Tom said, observing our solemn faces. "Just remember that no matter what happens, you are family first, and it's never worth it to sacrifice that bond because of money or business interests."

"Don't you trust us, Tom?" Jack asked, a twinkle in his eye.

"Yes, I do. Very much. But I've seen tight-knit families just like yours torn apart over money before. The solidarity of kinship is far more powerful than discord."

With a few strokes of a pen, we altered the course of our lives, bringing both our family and our business into a new era.

chapter seven

Soon after my brothers and I took ownership of Pierson Properties, Paul and Pamela had the ultrasound. The baby's development was right on target, and the technician was able to identify the child's sex, which they chose to learn so they could begin the complicated process of selecting a name. Paul and Pamela would be the parents of a baby girl, whose birth would take place in late March.

They launched into finding the perfect name, trying out ideas on us.

"Pamela really likes Alexis or Morgan," Paul offered. "I like the more traditional names."

"I'm with you," I answered. "The others are too trendy, like something from a soap opera. Mom and Dad offer any ideas?"

"They absolutely do not want to get involved," he laughed. "Although it would be nice to name our child something that's been a part of our family."

Pamela's pregnancy proceeded uneventfully. Both she and Paul took her condition seriously, eating well and often. Paul gained weight along with her, and we joked about who would have the tougher time losing it after the baby's arrival.

"Paul is totally involved in preparing for this baby," Mother said one afternoon in early December. I had stopped by Past Treasures Antiques to deliver a Christmas gift she had asked me to pick up.

We sat in a small snack area at the front of the shop, where antique straight-backed maple chairs surrounded matching tables. "He loves the Lamaze classes and reading up on parenting skills."

"You know Paul. Always wanting to experience life to the fullest."

"He'll make a wonderful father," Mother said. "Speaking of which, Sandy wants to give Pamela a shower and has asked for the names of people to invite."

A baby shower sounded like great fun to me. "Since we know the sex, we could have a theme like 'Think Pink.'"

A few days later, we broached the subject with Michelle. To our surprise, she was hesitant. "You've seen the nursery, haven't you?" she said to Mother and me.

"I know she's got the nursery decorated and furnished," Mother said. "But she'll still need all the baby accessories and equipment."

Michelle shook her head. "Remember when Pamela took me upstairs to get dry clothes on Labor Day? She showed me the nursery. Except for clothes, there isn't much that she doesn't already have."

I said, "That's perfect. Sandy was looking for a theme, and there it is: clothing for a little girl."

The idea of focusing the shower around buying clothing for a little girl turned out to be extremely successful. Pamela received enough to outfit the baby for at least the first year.

* * *

In 1997, Minnesota experienced one of the mildest winters in its history, due in part to the influence of El Niño warming in the Pacific. Instead of the typical long, deep cold spell that makes a temperature of zero seem balmy, the average temperature was a toasty 22 degrees. Many years, March arrived with the area still sheathed in ice and snow, causing many to wonder if the ground would ever be seen again. This particular year, though, spring already was breaking through, and warm days brought forth the first robins, tulips and daffodils. Easter would not occur until almost mid-April, and Tim looked forward to celebrating a sunrise church service without the usual threat of inclement weather.

Pamela was nine months pregnant, her expanding girth and added weight now becoming burdensome. When it became difficult for her to maneuver around the hospital lab, she cut her hours to part time and was just days away from starting maternity leave when her water broke.

Tim and I entered the hospital early on Thursday evening, nearly 18 hours after Pamela had been admitted. We ran into Paul with Pamela's parents, Annette and Donovan, in the lobby, in search of some dinner in the cafeteria. Tim decided to join them for a cup of coffee, while I ventured up to the maternity ward to check in on Pamela.

I had forgotten how much drama was in progress at any given time in a hospital. The hallways always seemed noisy with activity, even though everyone was supposed to be quiet. As I walked along, a hospital chaplain gently escorted two distraught people into a private room where I intuitively knew he bore unfortunate news. On the fourth floor where the maternity ward was located, the scenes were of a different emotional level. Excited family members were taking pictures of their newest additions. The life cycle was just beginning here; it was constantly in motion.

I was about to enter Pamela's room when I heard a loud, shrill voice that stopped me in my tracks. "I need an epidural right now! Do your goddamned job and get my doctor in here!" As a furious blonde nurse came charging out the door, I jumped aside to avoid a collision.

"I wouldn't go in there if I were you," she said, catching sight of me. "She's in a particularly foul mood."

I lingered outside for a minute, before deciding to take a chance. "Pamela, you ready for some visitors?"

"Kay! C'mon in. I was just trying to get comfortable." Clad in the standard-issue hospital gown, Pamela had situated herself among numerous pillows, her massive belly straining against the material.

"Any progress?"

"Not enough. My labor starts then stops, so the doctor's not sure what to do."

"Can I get you anything? A magazine or something else to read?"

"No, thanks. My mother brought me enough reading material for the entire free world," Pamela said, flipping through a large stack of magazines on the table next to her bed. "And needlepoint. What she thinks I'll do with that I have no idea."

"Tim's downstairs with Paul and your parents getting something to eat. We ran into them in the lobby. When did they get into town?"

"You know parents," Pamela said, sounding annoyed. "As soon as my water broke, they were on the road."

"It's their first grandchild and you're an only child, so it's only natural," I said.

The blonde nurse entered the room and firmly relayed protocol. "We cannot administer another epidural. Your doctor is finishing with another patient, Mrs. Pierson."

"Oh, that's all right," Pamela responded calmly, flashing the nurse a sweet smile. "I'll be fine."

The nurse exited in silence, looking slightly perplexed.

Within a few minutes, the others had returned from the cafeteria, and we made small talk as we absentmindedly watched the fetal monitor tracking the baby's vital signs. Paul's nerves were beginning to fray, and it was impossible for him to keep from fidgeting with his glasses or pacing the length of the room.

An hour passed before Tim and I decided we were just in the way. We'd return after the baby was born. On the drive home, I kept thinking about Pamela screaming at the nurse and the quick change in her demeanor when I entered the room. It had flipped like a switch. Yes, she was in labor, but what I detected was meanness, not anguish.

I kept the incident to myself, thinking I may have been judging her too harshly.

* * *

The doctor determined an emergency cesarean was necessary as Pamela passed 40 hours of labor. My beautiful niece Kaitlin Beverly Pierson made her vocal entrance into the world on March 28, 1998. Not a small baby, she weighed a healthy 8 pounds 14 ounces. She possessed a full head of soft brown hair. Paul, completely awed by the birth of his daughter, brought her out to meet the family. Yawning and stretching, Kaitlin was unimpressed by all the commotion and picture-taking.

Our group filled the hospital corridor as everyone took turns holding this brand-new family member. Jack and Michelle helped Ruthie and Sam each have a turn holding their cousin. Closely examining Kaitlin's every inch, Sam finally asked, "How are babies made, anyway?"

I laughed as Jack, normally unflappable, nervously smiled at Michelle. "I'll let you handle that one, Mom," he said, almost blushing.

Without missing a beat, Michelle knelt beside her 5-year-old son. "Babies are made with love," she answered, and Sam appeared completely satisfied with her explanation.

Watching Jack's bewilderment, I slipped an arm around his broad shoulders. "Better get used to it, Dad," I said. "That question is only the beginning."

"I know," he laughed. "But I'm not quite ready for the birds-and-bees talk."

We returned to the hospital the following day. New grandparents Annette and Donovan were thrilled to hold and rock their granddaughter. I noticed that Pamela seemed indifferent about Kaitlin, even slightly disinterested. She'd pass her off to someone in the room whenever she could and only held her to feed her. But I imagined she would get plenty of time alone with her baby at home.

Pamela left the hospital with Kaitlin after three days, and Paul took the next two weeks off. Recovering from the C-section would mean slow going, and Paul wanted to be there to help his wife. Pamela's parents resided in the small college town of Northfield, 60 miles south of the Twin Cities. It was an easy drive, and Annette made the trip every day to lend the new parents a hand.

* * *

Shortly after Kaitlin's birth, Paul and Pamela began talking with Tim about having Kaitlin baptized. Amid the Lenten and Easter seasons, Tim's church calendar was full. To accommodate schedules and family, Kaitlin's baptism was scheduled for the Sunday following Mother's Day.

The baptism offered us the opportunity to give Paul and Pamela something special they had not yet received for the baby: a christening gown. Mother, Michelle and I searched children's clothing stores for weeks and finally settled on a white lace and satin gown and matching bonnet.

"I hope Pamela doesn't feel it's too frilly," Mother said, folding the gown and placing it in the gift box.

"She didn't mention any specifics, except that a baptismal gown was a lovely gift," I offered.

Mother patted the lid onto the box. "If they have other children, it can be worn again. Lots of families keep christening gowns as heirlooms, too."

"You worry too much," I said.

"When are you dropping it off?"

"Later today. I've got errands to run on that side of town."

I pulled into Paul and Pamela's four-stall drive late in the afternoon, under the watchful eyes of the gargoyles. Paul answered the chiming doorbell a bit disheveled in jeans and a cotton sweater. "The house is a mess," he forewarned me. "The cleaning lady was sick this week, so Pamela's been trying to keep up."

That was news. "When did you hire a cleaning lady?"

"About a month ago. With the baby, Pamela has no time to clean, and it'll only get worse when she goes back to work. Want some coffee? It's fresh."

"Sure," I said, following him into the kitchen. "Just black."

Paul sat a bright turquoise ceramic mug of steaming coffee on the kitchen table.

"How are mom and baby doing?" I asked, taking a sip.

"Um, fine," he said, hesitating. "She's feeding Kaitlin now; otherwise, she'd say hello."

I took a long drink. "Don't worry. I'm just dropping the christening gown off." I sat the white box on the oak table. "You know Mom; she buys something and then worries if she's gotten the right thing."

Pouring himself a mug, Paul said, "I'll let Pamela open it. We really appreciate it."

"How are *you* doing, dad?" I asked.

"Oh, you know. A little sleep deprived, which is normal for new parents, I guess. I've been getting up with Kaitlin for all of her late-night feedings."

"Welcome to fatherhood. Oh, before I forget," I said, holding the cup in my hands, "are you coming to family dinner on Mother's Day? No big deal, but the guys are doing all the cooking, which I know you love."

"What's on the menu?"

"Roast beef, I think."

"Sounds great. I could bring a turkey breast too. But before I commit, let me make sure Pamela's feeling up to it. I'll be right back."

I remained at the table deep in thought. What wasn't Paul saying about Pamela? A cleaning lady? The house was big, but there were no kids running in and out, only the three of them. I looked around the vast kitchen with its gleaming granite counters, chrome appliances and shining copper cookware hanging over the island. It was immaculate, as was the rest of the house. A cleaning lady was probably the reason the house appeared picture perfect. I realized some part of me was probably just jealous I didn't have the help.

The silence was shattered by Pamela's piercing voice. "I am not spending another boring Sunday with your fucking family! We'll see them next week at Kaitlin's baptism!"

I sat rigid against the chair, hanging on every word. Paul's reply was muffled. Then it was drowned out by Pamela's shouting. "I don't care if it is Mother's Day! I'm sick to death of your family! If it were up to me, we'd never spend another weekend or holiday with them again!" Paul was speaking calmly, but now the baby was crying, and I couldn't make out any specific words.

I decided I should just leave. As I was placing my half-empty mug in the sink, I heard the clomp-clomp of Paul's shoes on the oak staircase. "Listen, I need to get going," I said nonchalantly, meeting him in the dining room. "Pamela probably wants to spend her first Mother's Day at home."

"Yeah, she's still recovering from the C-section," he replied, agitated. Paul kissed my cheek, escorting me to the front door. "I'll put Mom's card in the mail tomorrow."

I gave Paul a sisterly nod, as if I had heard nothing. "Give Pamela my love. I'll see you Monday."

Paul's cheeks were flushed with embarrassment as we parted. I realized he had the same look on his face in the restaurant the night we celebrated their engagement. The sound of Pamela's angry words—*I am not spending another boring Sunday with your fucking family*—reverberated in my head. I drove aimlessly through the sprawling neighborhood etched out of dense forests and yawning valleys. Perfectly manicured lawns and large, elegant homes gave the appearance of prosperity and contentment. Too often, appearances proved an illusion, I thought. And I began to wonder if Pamela was creating a meticulous façade of her own.

chapter eight

Pamela's proud parents and the rest of the family joyously celebrated Kaitlin's baptism. Seemingly unimpressed by the event, the baby slept through much of the ceremony, waking only to give out a good, loud howl when Tim washed the baptismal water across her head. She was an exceptionally sweet baby, only crying when she had reason to.

Annette and Donovan reveled in their new roles as grandparents, and Pamela gave them ample time with their grandchild. "Oh, you can keep her," Pamela would say whenever someone tried to hand her the baby. "I get plenty of time with her during her late-night feedings." Instead, she chatted with the guests invited to the ceremony and party. Pamela did not seem to be a typical mom, fascinated by and sharing the details of every milestone of her first child. But I wondered if I was overanalyzing, as I often did.

In the kitchen as we prepared trays of meat, cheese and fruit, Michelle said in a near-whisper, "Pamela has a different take on motherhood than most."

"What do you mean?" I asked.

Michelle lowered her voice further. "She doesn't seem to have any interest in bonding with Kaitlin. I've said it before, but it seems like having a baby was another project for Pamela—something to check off the to-do list—and now that the baby's here, her part is finished."

"Everyone is different," Mother said, putting final touches

on a salad. "It may just take her a while to get used to the idea of motherhood. Not everyone is a natural at it."

Carrying a tray of fruit and cheese to the dining room, I noticed Paul at the bar in the great room, where he mixed himself a drink. "Pamela," he said over his shoulder, "do you want a drink?"

"Of course!" she said with a flip of her hair. "Jack and 7UP. And make it a double shot."

It was Paul and Pamela's return to drinking I was most concerned about. Pamela's drunken tirade at the restaurant still gnawed at me. Initially after the incident, their alcohol consumption was limited to social occasions. Then it stopped entirely with Pamela's pregnancy. Now, however, the moment they arrived at Mother and Dad's on Sunday afternoons for family dinner, both made a beeline for the liquor cabinet.

I wasn't the only one who noticed it, as Mother too had warily watched Paul and Pamela's indulgences. "They didn't drink while she was pregnant, thankfully—but they seem to be making up for lost time," she relayed in a voice both knowing and sad. "Mixing alcohol with this family is a losing battle."

As I cast a guarded eye in Paul's direction, I knew all too well what she meant. The genetic heritage that fused our family with alcoholism had scarred at least four generations. Our paternal grandmother's father, Harvey, had an illustrious career as the town drunk. In a curious twist of fate, our parents' families crossed paths years before they officially met, as Mother's police officer father was the only Minneapolis cop who could take Harvey to jail without a fight.

Future generations suffered the blight of alcoholism in increasing numbers. Grandma had seven brothers and sisters, all of whom either died from the ravages of alcohol or spent the remainder of their lives recovering. Many of their children, too, were not able to elude the affliction that fractured their own lives and families, raising the toll of upheaval and premature deaths higher.

Both Mother and Dad said that for the first 15 years of their marriage they drank rarely, if at all. With the emergence of a new culture of experimentation and freedom in the 1960s and early '70s, our parents found their own value structure shifting. Mother enjoyed a glass of wine, but for Dad, those long-dormant genetic impulses suddenly sprang to life. Eventually, chronic health issues and ever-larger pieces of lost memory would set him on the path to sobriety and only intensified Mother's warnings to us. "The Pierson side of the family has a terrible history of alcoholism," she would remind us. "You kids have no idea of the odds you're fighting." In our youthful brashness, we laughed her off.

Despite Mother's admonishments, I paid the price, though the cost was much heavier than we could have imagined. I started drinking as a teenager, first falling for alcohol's perceived sophistication and then bourbon's silken taste and sweet smell. Embracing the life of a reporter in my early career working in media, alcohol allowed me to fit in with an intense crowd that drank heartily and often. If I wasn't celebrating a news scoop, I was crying over a quashed story, and alcohol was always my willing companion. Although I drank nonstop for 15 years, I was able to keep up the appearance of a life in control—or so I thought.

My secret, however, spilled out at an important church function. Every year, Tim's parish held a fundraiser to generate awareness for local hunger issues and raise money for area food shelves. I served on the planning committee, which turned out to be more time consuming and stressful than I thought it would be. I began drinking before the event had even begun. As the live auction was getting underway, I was slurring my words. I ended the evening vomiting on myself and passing out in a bathroom stall.

That event brought a glimpse of my harrowing future. I feared Tim might say "too little, too late." Instead he didn't flinch, proving himself the life partner promised in those marriage vows of "for better, for worse." I chose my life and marriage over alcohol's empty future. I underwent eight grueling weeks in a drug-treatment program. By the time of Kaitlin's baptism, I had been sober nine years.

Paul and Jack experimented too, with plenty of dabbling in other drugs less socially acceptable. Jack drank regularly and smoked marijuana into his late teens, but once he reached his 20s, alcohol and pot both lost their allure. Paul, on the other hand, drank from high school on—the happy, feel-good drunk who was more amusing than menacing. The agonizing realization that Paul and I were soul mates united by the same flawed genetic composition would not come until the saving grace of sobriety.

The suspicions that were already percolating just below the surface rose to a new level of urgency after Rachel died. Paul threw himself into his work, never failing to show up at the office or complete a job. There is an old stereotype of the alcoholic who never misses a day of work but whose life is in total chaos. Paul never admitted to excessive drinking, but there were the subtle signs of memory lapses and questionable health. On top of those concerns were forbidding stretches of despondency, hurling him into bleak emotional corners where despair and suicide began to make sense to him.

I talked to Paul privately about my concerns—several times—only to find myself consoling him through another crying jag. We'd never confronted him as a family, as his upward spiral of redemption always seemed to begin before he crashed headfirst to the bottom. Then, when he'd met Pamela, our worst fears were absolved. Now, eyeing Paul across the room as he filled frosty tumblers with Jack Daniels and 7UP, the emerging pattern was a painful reminder.

What would be said and when were questions I could not yet answer. I knew one simple fact: that what I had faced in my own battle was akin to the story of Jonah facing certain death in the depths of the whale's belly, with only his wits for survival. He would endure, only to be tested repeatedly, and I wanted to warn Paul that I saw our family's past repeating itself. Like Jonah, I made it out alive, but I wouldn't wish the experience on my worst enemy, much less my own brother.

chapter nine

AUGUST 1998

Paul, Jack, Dad and I met for lunch twice a month to discuss various company projects. Any major concerns were brought before our managers for discussion, but this kept us abreast of changes in a fast-paced business.

Our meeting place was always the same: Byerly's Restaurant, next to the supermarket bearing the same name. One of the first upscale grocery stores in Minnesota, Byerly's offered food from around the world, covering the exotic to the ordinary. It also had exemplary customer service and, if one so desired, expensive works of art in the gift shop. The restaurant's attraction was its coffee-shop atmosphere and exceptionally good food. Although the chain had stores throughout the Twin Cities, we always met at the Edina location, across France Avenue from the Pierson Properties office. As was the norm, once we completed the business agenda our conversation turned to a more personal realm.

"When is Pamela planning on returning to work?" I asked on a late August afternoon.

Paul finished his bite of sandwich. "I'm glad you brought that up, because we're making some changes." He wiped his mouth with a napkin. "Pamela has accepted a new position with the Mayo Clinic, which she'll start in September."

From across the table, Jack gave Paul a curious look. "But the

Mayo Clinic's in Rochester, an hour and a half away. That'll be some commute."

Paul paused for a moment, taking a sip of his Coke. "Well, she won't be commuting."

There was obviously more that Paul had to say, but Dad was already a step ahead, interrupting the conversation with a question. "Pamela's going to be living in Rochester?"

I could have sworn Paul was gathering the courage to go forward with this conversation, making eye contact with each of us. "Yes, Pamela will be taking an apartment in Rochester and living there during the week." He paused, letting the revelation sink in. "She's been offered an opportunity as a manager in one of Mayo's laboratories, a position that's too good for us to pass up."

"What about the baby? Kaitlin's only 5 months old," I said, trying not to sound overly concerned.

Paul was the focus of our attention, which seemed to be shaking his nerves a bit. While setting down his drink, the glass slipped from his grasp, spilling cold, sticky liquid and ice over the table. As we scrambled to dry the mess, a waitress appeared with a damp cloth. "I'll bring you some towels," she said.

Paul excused himself to the men's room to wash himself off. As soon as he was out of earshot Jack said, "I have a bad feeling about this."

Jack had taken over the cleaning duties from the waitress, and as I handed off dishes to her, I marveled at how upbringing and genetics poke through at the most interesting times. After wiping up the soda, he took the towels from the waitress, scrubbing every inch of the table before buffing it dry to a high shine.

"Jack, I think that's the cleanest this table's ever been," I said, laughing in amusement.

"I think your sister's right." Dad nodded in impressed agreement as he stepped back to review Jack's handiwork.

Jack directed his gaze toward me, an impish look in his eyes. "Kay," he announced with mock solemnity, "we become our parents. Not that there's anything wrong with that," he added, giving Dad a quick wink.

"I do like things clean and orderly," Dad replied. "I think it's our German heritage. But even I wouldn't have gotten this table so clean."

Jack looked over at me, his eyes dancing. "This from the guy who washed off the office plants in the parking lot."

"They were dusty and nobody else was going to do it," Dad protested. "We're all a little obsessive-compulsive," he added as he settled back in the booth. "But right now, I'd like to know more about your misgivings with Paul's proposed situation."

Jack slid into the booth next to me. "It just seems odd that the best job Pamela could find is in Rochester. I thought she would return to her job at the hospital here, so this is a surprise. You can't tell me there aren't plenty of other positions available here, with so many hospitals, clinics and research labs."

Dad said, "Well, the Mayo Clinic has a reputation the world over."

"True," Jack countered, "but what Kay says about Pamela leaving Kaitlin is a valid point."

Paul returned, seating himself, and Dad resumed the conversation where it had left off. "With Pamela working, what are the child care arrangements?" Dad asked calmly, folding his hands on the tabletop.

"Kaitlin will stay with me," Paul said firmly. "About a month ago we hired a nanny."

"A nanny?" Jack interrupted.

"Not really a nanny," Paul said, a bit flustered. "She's a friend of Pamela's from the hospital who's going back to school. Heather Carlson is her name. She'll be available during most days, and when she's in school, Kaitlin will be at day care."

"Why doesn't Pamela just stay with her current job?" I asked.

"This is a much better opportunity financially," Paul said.

Like Jack, my curiosity was now stimulated, so I pressed Paul further. "What will Pamela be doing?"

"A lot of cutting-edge work with viruses as a means of developing new methods of treatment and drug therapies. We know this means a long-distance marriage, but we talked it through, and both of us feel that the advantages outweigh the disadvantages."

Jack stared at Paul, his face betraying no emotion. "You're sure about that?"

Paul lowered his eyes and replied forcefully, "Yes, this is the best option."

Dad twisted around to face Paul sitting next to him. "When does Pamela start at the clinic?"

"Right after Labor Day." His voice was self-conscious. "If everyone's available, we could use help moving and getting her settled into her apartment."

Our waitress delivered the check, and I began divvying up the amount, which was customary. "OK," I said, "everybody toss in—"

Paul interrupted sheepishly. "Can somebody spot me some cash? I don't have any on me."

Jack gave Paul an annoyed look. "The last two times we've had lunch I've bought because you didn't have any money. Pamela got you on an allowance?"

Paul's cheeks flushed; his response was terse. "Money's a little tight right now. I'll pay you back."

"Here," Dad said, placing a credit card on the check. "I'll take care of this. An expense of doing business."

Jack and Paul were clearly irritated by one another's comments and stewed in silence. Dad steered the conversation back to business matters, but the tension remained heavy between my brothers. I hoped this was not the beginning of another spat. Later in the afternoon I slipped into Paul's office, probing for information and hoping to ease any hard feelings.

"Everything OK at home? You were a little uptight with Jack at lunch."

Paul moaned in exasperation. "Motherhood is not exactly what Pamela thought it would be. And we're having some money problems, which doesn't help. With the baby, we have more expenses. So, I borrowed a couple of bucks from Jack. Big deal. He always manages to throw it back in my face."

"I don't think he means to," I said. "Living apart is an unusual step for any marriage."

Dismayed, Paul fidgeted anxiously. "Jack always sticks his nose in my financial affairs when it's none of his business. Yes, we overextended ourselves, but Pamela's salary increase will help solve that. I don't regret any decision we've made."

I believed everything except his last sentiment, but it was not my place to say. "Well, don't worry about the move. Tim and I will help," I replied brightly, bringing the conversation to its end.

* * *

We helped move Pamela to Rochester the Sunday of Labor Day weekend. Into the bright yellow Ryder truck went the suite of furniture from the guest bedroom; the table and chairs from the kitchen; a couch, coffee table and chairs from the living room; and the big-screen television. Pamela took some of the most expensive pieces of Red Wing pottery, including the blue lily-motif pitcher and basin they'd received as a wedding gift from our folks. "The Red Wing pottery will give my apartment a homier feel," she explained, flipping back her blonde hair with a brush of her hand.

The truck was loaded, and everyone but Paul and I started out for Rochester. I went back into the house for him. The vast house echoed, empty of so many furnishings. "We've got an extra dinette set you're welcome to use," I said as he locked the door.

An awkward smile flashed across Paul's face, revealing just how startled he was by how many of their possessions Pamela had taken. "That would be great, Sis. I can't be feeding Kaitlin in the formal dining room."

Another thought struck me. "Oh! We also have all those extra wedding gifts we're storing in our basement. Some of those items will come in handy."

Paul gave me a puzzled look. "What are you talking about?"

"We've been storing some duplicate items you received. You probably don't remember. In any case, you can put them to good use now."

"I don't remember talking with Pamela about duplicate items," Paul said, looking confused, "but I'll definitely welcome anything you've got."

"I'll get them to you this weekend," I said. *Paul seems to have no clue what she has been up to*, I thought forlornly.

In Rochester, the new apartment was a flurry of activity. Kaitlin watched the proceedings from her infant seat on the kitchen counter, while we formed a line to carry in boxes, Pamela directing which rooms items should be placed in.

Zigzagging back and forth between the truck and apartment, Pamela was abrupt to the point of rudeness. "Be careful with that!" she snapped at Jack and Tim when she thought they had not set a box down gently enough. "Those things are expensive."

Jack was annoyed. "Sorry, Pam," he said, the exasperation intensifying. "We didn't set it down that hard."

"It's *Pamela*," she replied with an annoying flip of her hair.

Jack and I ran to pick up a pizza order to feed our hungry crew late in the afternoon. "Pamela can be such a bitch," he said, still nursing his irritation. "It's not like I enjoy spending Labor Day weekend helping her move."

"We are doing her a big favor," I conceded. "And she is treating us like the hired help."

Jack laughed sourly. "Not only that, but she has a mean streak. Remember when Paul wasn't speaking to us last year?"

"Yeah, after the argument about his house, and Michelle ran into Pamela at the grocery store."

"Right. Michelle didn't tell you everything. Pamela wouldn't even acknowledge her at first, but then she followed her into the same checkout line. She got in Michelle's face—and loudly—about how lousy I was treating Paul," he said, the thrust of his jaw tightening. "I don't give a damn what Pamela thinks of me, but at the top of her lungs she asked Michelle how she could possibly stay married to someone who was so abusive."

I had questioned the use of "abusive" myself. My brow creased. "I assume Pamela thought you were 'abusive'—if that's the term she used—because you and Paul weren't speaking. But he wasn't talking to me either."

Jack nodded. "At the time I thought it was a strange way to phrase the fact that we'd had an argument. But the people standing in line didn't know what she was talking about. She humiliated Michelle."

He turned onto the street of Pamela's new residence. "There's something not right about this move and her new job. We've all noticed the heavy drinking, and why shouldn't we? Nobody's really forgotten what happened at the Lake Elmo Inn. Given that and a tight money situation, I think things are worse than they're letting on. Don't go telling Mom this, but we're gonna have to keep an eye on Paul."

I promised Jack I would keep quiet, but I could also sense the pulsating anxiety building within me. On the surface, Paul and Pamela's story had merit, but the bewildered look in my brother's eyes at the sight of his nearly empty house said differently. Marriage is hard work even in the best of times, and whatever difficulties they faced—financial or emotional—I suspected this went deeper. I wanted Jack and me to be wrong, but I felt very much as I did after Rachel died, sensing that the strain on Paul was starting to send his life careening into turmoil.

At Rachel's death he had watched the life he had planned fall apart. We did all we could to keep him focused and, at that point, alive. I did not think he was in the same degree of trouble, but Jack was right that we would need to keep a close watch on Paul.

The day had been long. When twilight began casting a long shadow over Rochester, Pamela's apartment was freshly organized, and we were preparing to drive back. Except for Paul and Kaitlin, who were planning to remain for the night.

"You know, Paul, there's really no reason for you and the baby to stay here tonight," Pamela said unexpectedly. "I'm too tired to put up with her crying all night, so why don't you take her home?"

Paul wore his emotions on his sleeve, and it was impossible for him to conceal his disappointment. "One more day together for some family time would be nice. Are you sure?"

"I'm sure," Pamela said with a wave of her hand. "I'll be home on Friday, in just four days. I could really use the rest right now."

Paul reluctantly agreed, and outside she sent us off. "Mommy will miss you so much," Pamela said with a trace of overenthusiasm as she kissed her infant daughter on the top of the head.

"She's Grandma's girl this week," Mother said, securing Kaitlin into the car seat. "I'll make sure Paul eats well, too." She reached out to hug Pamela, whose cheerfulness seemed frozen across her face. Standing behind the two of them, I watched as Pamela visibly stiffened, her unresponsive arms limp at her sides.

"I'd appreciate that," she said, pulling away.

Dad honked the horn of the Ryder truck and rolled down the window. "I'll meet you back at the rental lot."

Mother signaled "OK" and Tim maneuvered our Ford Taurus from the curb giving a final wave.

Jack settled into the Jeep's front passenger seat, and I climbed in back next to Kaitlin. Paul went to give his wife one last hug and kiss. It was obvious he wanted to spend more time with her, but Pamela returned his affection with a cursory kiss.

Paul's driver's-side window was open, and he said, "Call me on Tuesday after your first day. I'll be thinking of you."

"Good luck with your new job!" I called from the back seat.

"Love you," Paul said quietly.

"Thanks. See you on Friday," Pamela said, a jaunty smile across her lips.

Paul drove away from the curb as Pamela turned her back and headed into the apartment without a wave or even a look back.

chapter 10

The move to Rochester seemed to buoy Pamela's enthusiasm for returning to work. On the weekends when she was in town, she talked nonstop about the new job, noting that the position was a far greater challenge than the lab work she had done previously. As the warm colors of fall faded into the stark landscape of approaching winter, Pamela came home less and less often, insisting that the demands of her work kept her away.

Halloween fell on Saturday, and the weather was not bitterly cold as was often the case that time of year. With temperatures in the mid-40s, we anticipated throngs of trick-or-treaters at our door. Jack brought Ruthie and Sam over for treats and photographs in their costumes. I was surprised to see Paul with them. Michelle always sewed the kids' meticulous costumes, and this year she designed one for Kaitlin as well. Ruthie, in floating pink tulle, dressed as a fairy princess; Sam was a brightly colored Superman; and Kaitlin was a baby jack-o'-lantern.

Between dusk and nightfall, the kids bounded into our house, bursting with delight at their piles of treats, Paul two steps behind carrying his wide-eyed daughter. Kaitlin was adorable in her orange pumpkin suit, chubby legs in black tights and the pumpkin's stem set atop mounds of brown hair. Laughing and cooing, she was most content, oblivious to Ruthie's and Sam's excitement.

"Trick or treat!" Ruthie and Sam chattered in unison.

"I got gum and candy bars!" Sam announced, proudly opening his bag for me to inspect.

"And Mrs. Fink gave us popcorn balls. See, Auntie Kay?" Ruthie added, grinning.

"You gotta give us candy too, Auntie Kay," Sam pronounced.

"And if I don't?"

"We'll have to play a trick on you," Ruthie replied solemnly.

I dutifully plopped two large Hershey bars in each bag.

"What do you say?" Jack prompted.

"Thank you, Auntie Kay! C'mon, Daddy, let's go!"

"I'll catch up at the next house," Paul said as Ruthie and Sam raced out the door.

"I'll try to slow them down," Jack said, jogging to keep up. "I'm getting too old for this."

"Have fun," Tim yelled after them as he greeted another group of trick-or-treaters gathered on our porch.

"She's so cute, Paul," I gushed. Kaitlin giggled. "Hi, sweetheart. Here's some candy for you. But you can't eat it all."

"She only has two teeth so it could be tough."

Placing candy in the bag, I asked, "Pamela handling the kids at your house?"

Paul visibly stiffened. "She stayed in Rochester," he replied somewhat peevishly. "Couldn't get away until next weekend."

"Well, I'm sure she'll be anxious to come home." My cheerfulness was a lie.

"I hope so," Paul said. "We both miss her."

"Coming for family dinner tomorrow?" I asked, changing the subject.

"Yep. I'm bringing a smoked turkey breast."

"Great," I said. "Have fun with the kiddos tonight." I pushed worrying about Paul aside for the moment.

Three weeks would pass before Pamela returned.

* * *

Minnesotans are extremely proud of their voting turnout, which approaches 70 percent of eligible voters. The 1998 gubernatorial race was hotly contested. As lifelong members of the Minnesota Democratic-Farmer-Labor (DFL) party, all of us Piersons supported party nominee Hubert "Skip" Humphrey III, but this was no typical election. Besides the Republican candidate, Norm Coleman, who was the former mayor of St. Paul, the third candidate entering the race, on the Reform Party ticket, was a former professional wrestler known in his World Wrestling Federation days as Jesse "The Body" Ventura. No one expected him to win.

Despite being extremely busy, our family did our part in the tight race for governor. Mother, Dad and I volunteered at Hubert Humphrey headquarters for two days in the final push, staffing phones and canvassing neighborhoods. Our efforts, however, would be in vain, as he finished third, behind Norm Coleman. To the surprise of many Minnesotans and the rest of the country, the colorful insurgent with a penchant for bright costumes and feather boas had been elected governor. The morning after the election, I listened to a stunned local tell Minnesota Public Radio, "Sure, I voted for Jesse, but I didn't think he would win."

The election resulted in national media coverage. As a former journalist I marveled at how the media machine swooped down on the Twin Cities, interviewing voters and shocked veteran politicians alike. Jesse Ventura's victory speech was looped endlessly on CNN, while the major networks ran stories in the vein of "Mr. Smith Goes to Washington." If nothing else, I hoped this election would remind citizens that, in fact, every vote did count. The next four years were sure to be interesting.

While our state was coming to terms with having a wrestler as governor-elect, Mother decided it was the perfect time for a new family photograph. Like many parents, ours chronicled their evolving family through pictures prominently displayed throughout the house. These photographs depicted the typical stages of life—our young parents as newlyweds, proudly cradling their wide-eyed infants; our active childhoods as we grew into the bad haircuts and clothing of awkward adolescence and mild rebellion; our high school and college graduations, marriages and on into adulthood.

Each of the pictures captured one moment in life's fluid passage. The photographs of Paul and Rachel's life together had slowly been supplanted with those of Paul and Pamela. With the addition of Kaitlin, the process continued of documenting our maturing family.

With most of us working and living in the same community, one might think orchestrating a family portrait would be a simple exercise. Our schedules, however, were usually hectic enough to merit last-minute revisions, especially with the new wrinkle of Pamela living in Rochester.

We finally came together on the blustery Friday evening before Thanksgiving. The photographs were scheduled for 6 p.m. in the great room at Goldenwoods. As usual, we trickled in. Tim and I were always the first arrivals—there was something to be said for being married to a man raised on military time. Jack and Michelle followed with the kids, looking very much like the mythical ideal of the beautiful American family with two perfect children. This guise lasted approximately 30 seconds, as Ruthie and Sam became uncomfortable in their stiff new clothes.

"I don't want to wear this dress," Ruthie complained to her mother as she squirmed in a green satin frock.

"I know, sweetie," Michelle soothed. "As soon as the photographer's done, you and Sam can change clothes."

"You look pretty," I told Ruthie, her blonde hair accented with matching ribbons.

She crinkled her nose. "Dresses are silly. I like overalls better."

Michelle rolled her eyes. "She's a tomboy, no question. If I can keep the two of them clean until after the pictures, it'll be a miracle."

At 6:30 p.m., Paul called; he was still waiting at home for Pamela. "Go ahead and get started," he said impatiently. "I have no idea where she is."

The photographer busied himself taking individual family portraits. By the time those had been completed there was still no Paul and family. We were all getting restless at being dressed up with literally no place to go. Sometime after 7:30 p.m., a frazzled Paul arrived with Kaitlin on his hip.

"Pamela called from her cellphone," he explained, aggravated. "She's 15 minutes away."

With their nanny, Heather, studying for final exams, Paul had spent the last week without any help. He'd dressed his daughter in a burgundy velvet dress, lace socks and patent leather shoes, and while Kaitlin was darling, the stress was clearly taking a toll on Paul.

"Come to Grandma," Mother said immediately, offering a helping hand. "How's my girl?"

We continued waiting. Finally, Pamela pulled into the driveway at around 8 o'clock and blew into the house, her appearance mussed. "I need a drink!" she announced, tossing her red wool coat onto the couch without saying hello to anyone.

"Hello, Pamela," Mother said. "The photographer's been here since before 6 o'clock. Let's get the rest of the pictures taken so he can go home."

Pamela flipped her blonde hair off her shoulders. "Fine, Beverly," she replied tersely. "Give me five minutes to freshen up." She grabbed her purse and headed to the bathroom without showing the slightest interest in either her daughter or husband.

During Pamela's absence, the photographer arranged everyone around the sofa, leaving a place for her to sit. When she returned, Pamela plopped herself down on the couch. Mother placed the baby on her lap. Kaitlin immediately became fussy, her bottom lip trembling, and then she started crying. "Stop it!" Pamela reprimanded and shook the baby hard. Kaitlin's cries got louder.

"I'll take her," Dad intervened abruptly from behind the couch, pulling his grandchild gently off Pamela's lap. In an instant, Kaitlin's face transformed, and she was smiling again. "There's a sweet girl."

Sitting next to me on the couch, a clearly agitated Pamela shifted her weight, jabbing me in the ribs with her left elbow. "Ouch!" I said.

"Give me a break, Kay," she snipped. "I didn't do it on purpose." But as I looked down, I became more interested in Pamela's hands than an apology.

The photographer was telling her that her posture was too rigid. "Just relax your hands," he said and came over to position Pamela's right hand on top of her left wrist. Her left hand was resting on her thigh, and I immediately noticed her slender, bare fingers. No wedding ring. No diamond. Just a shadow of sallow flesh where it should have been.

My gaze worked its way along the couch where all the women had been seated in a row, with the men standing behind. Each of us wore our wedding and engagement rings, which was not unusual. I rarely removed mine.

Mother and Dad took turns holding Kaitlin while the photographer took various shots of our group, until at last it was over. He barely spoke the words "that should do it" before Ruthie and Sam were racing off to the nearest bedroom, tugging at bows and stiff collars.

The photographer stopped abruptly as he was preparing to tear down his lighting. "I nearly forgot; did you want a family portrait?" he asked Paul and Pamela.

"That won't be necessary," she replied briskly, walking toward the bar.

Paul frowned in disagreement. "Pamela, we don't have any pictures of the three of us. I want a family picture."

Her sullen eyes glowered. "Give her to me then," she said, snatching Kaitlin from Mother's arms and dropping her angrily into a chair. I watched from across the room as the photographer called for smiles. Pamela's was forced, as though she couldn't stand being there a minute longer.

Mother had prepared a supper of beef stew for afterward. As we were getting ready to serve, Pamela abruptly changed her mind. "I need to go home. It's been a long week, and I'm tired."

Mother asked, "Would you like some stew before you go?"

"No. I'm not hungry."

"I would like to have something to eat," Paul said. "It's been a long week for me too."

"Fine, then you and Kaitlin stay. I'm going home."

"OK," Paul said wearily. "I'll meet you at home."

Mother filled storage containers with soup and bread to send home with Paul. I couldn't get my mind off her naked ring finger. I silently wondered what the hell was happening.

chapter 11

The next day, Jack had plans to go duck hunting with Ron Baker. It was the final weekend of the season, and they would leave before dawn Saturday, head "up north" and hunt until Sunday afternoon.

Minnesota is a quilt of flat golden prairies, blue rivers and lakes, and dense jade forests amid rolling valleys, providing habitat for numerous wildlife. While the bodies of water are plentiful, in recent years the duck population had greatly diminished, thanks to humans encroaching on natural habitats.

Our maternal grandfather had taught all three of us to hunt for duck and geese when we were young. We learned by shooting clay pigeons at our grandparents' lake home, and eventually he took each of us along on hunting trips. I lost interest after high school and so did Paul. But hunting had become Jack's favorite pastime. The annual trip with Ron was one he looked forward to each year.

It was a sunny and crisp afternoon, and Jack phoned that they were on their way back to Ron's with their kill. Ron had built an animal cleaning shed and smokehouse on his property. When the hunting party was large, and there were a couple of deer or dozens of birds to prepare, Mother and I would join up with the hunters and help clean and dress the meat.

I drove 25 miles to Maple Plain, where Ron had 15 gently sloping acres in the still-undeveloped countryside. He and Jack followed within minutes, accompanied by Ron's golden retriever, who, after a day and a half of hunting ducks, was ready for a well-deserved rest, curling up on the sun-lit porch for a nap.

Ron's butcher shop was outfitted with state-of-the-art equipment. In the center of the room was a stainless-steel island with sinks at each end and all the required knives and cutting boards. Next to the island stood a stovetop for boiling birds, an efficient way to remove feathers. Large rolls of waxed freezer wrap stood ready for packaging freshly butchered meats. Once we were through, the floor would be hosed down and disinfected. Afterward, the room was so clean that a visitor would never know that only a short time earlier, animal parts and blood had splattered much of the space.

Contamination is always a concern with any kind of wild game. Ron was meticulous in this regard—inside the shed we pulled white plastic suits over our clothes and covered our shoes and heads. Pulling my hair into a high ponytail, I tucked it under my cap. Color-coded gloves came to our elbows. In layers of protective gear, I imagined we resembled extraterrestrial creatures from an old-school sci-fi movie.

"We did some field dressing, so the entrails and crop have been removed," Ron told me. "The hearts and livers are in the red cooler."

"How many birds did you get today?" I asked, removing the plastic bag from the cooler.

"Five," replied Jack. "Not the limit but still a good day."

We formed an assembly line with each of us responsible for a specific preparation step. I cut off the wings at the joints, removed the head and passed the carcass to Jack. Sometimes we plucked the pinfeathers; other times we skinned them. On this day, Ron wanted to test a new approach. Jack would pluck three birds, and Ron would dip the other two in a mixture of paraffin wax and hot water. Once the wax hardened, he would scrape the feathers off to determine which method was easier.

After cutting up each carcass, I scoured the knives and cutting boards in hot water, the steam rising into my face, as Jack hollered to me over the noise of the running water.

"Guess who called me while Ron and I were driving north yesterday," he said nonchalantly, as I continued scrubbing.

"You're going to have to give me more hints than that," I replied.

"Paul. He said Pamela had been called back to Rochester—something about being short-handed in the lab."

I turned off the water, drying the knife and cutting board. "It's been three weeks since Pamela was last home. Surely she could have said no."

Jack's gloved hands plucked feathers one after the other as he spoke. "He was definitely upset." Jack paused. "In her brief time home, Pamela was distant. He said it was like she didn't want to be there. On Friday night after they got home from Goldenwoods, she had a couple of drinks and went to bed. Paul gave Kaitlin a bath, fed her and put her to sleep. The only time Pamela really saw the baby was on Saturday morning before she headed back."

This seemed very strange, and the words were flowing out of my mouth before I gave it much thought. "What is going on with her? She was downright surly Friday night. And extremely late—I can't imagine keeping everyone waiting that long. She didn't even seem to feel bad about it." I looked at Ron, standing at the island's end. I was slightly embarrassed to be talking about family issues in front of him. "Sorry, Ron, but it's just so odd."

Ron walked next to me and claimed a feathered carcass, preparing to dip it into the hot wax. "Don't be. I agree—something's up with Pamela."

I was caught off guard by Ron's comment. "What do you mean?"

"Jack's heard this, but Sandy's noticed a change, too," Ron said. "Pamela and Sandy were not just friends, they were best friends, talking several times a day at work and maybe again at home. During Pamela's maternity leave, she and Sandy saw each other all the time, getting together with the kids, going out to lunch, shopping, that sort of thing. Then she takes the job in Rochester. We wanted to have her and Paul over for dinner, so Sandy calls her. Not once or twice but close to a dozen times. And Pamela has never returned her call."

I was bewildered. "That is strange."

"Since Pamela left for Rochester, there's been no contact. Sandy's all but given up, and she's hurt. We did a lot for Pamela, especially during her divorce from her first husband. She was absolutely terrified he would come after her. She lived with us for nearly three months. Sandy helped her get through a tough time."

I had forgotten about Pamela's first marriage. Shortly after their engagement, Paul and Pamela told us she had been married previously but that the relationship had been abusive and short-lived. The scene was a dramatic one, with Pamela tearfully recounting how she'd fled to a battered women's shelter in the middle of the night with nothing but the clothes on her back.

"Paul is concerned that she isn't being honest about this Rochester deal," Jack said. "Obviously, he wants to work things out, but her running back down there doesn't make it easier."

I sliced into another duck carcass. "What was her first husband's name again?"

"Doug Castleton," Ron replied. "He's a contractor in Northfield. While the divorce was in progress, I checked into the guy's business activities. I have to say that Castleton Builders has impeccable references."

Jack was plucking faster, and the feathers were floating lazily to the floor, missing the bin used to catch them. "I only bring this up because Paul called me. I don't think we should mention it. At least for now."

"OK," I nodded hesitantly. A feather drifted toward my station. "You need to slow down there, Jack, or we'll have feathers everywhere."

"Some people save those, too," Ron said.

"Nah, too much work," Jack replied. "I'm getting overly enthusiastic about my job."

We worked as a team cleaning, seasoning and packaging the duck meat. As we worked the rest of the afternoon, I contemplated the increasingly odd behavior of my sister-in-law. What could be so important in Rochester that she would neglect her baby and husband?

chapter 12

DECEMBER 1998

Every year, about a week before Christmas, Pierson Properties held its Yuletide party. The evening was one of the few times we had the opportunity to socialize with most of our employees. I always treated the event as a special occasion for Tim and myself as well.

The party was a sit-down dinner followed by dancing, but the occasion had evolved over the years. In the construction boom of the 1970s, the holiday party had been a swank affair held at a large restaurant in downtown Minneapolis. By the early '80s, with interest rates rising to nearly 20 percent, the party was scaled back dramatically.

During one of the leanest years, when I was home from college, the party was held in the clubhouse of one of our apartment complexes. It was potluck and BYOB. That particular evening, disheartened sales associates, managers and Dad blew off their frustrations by imbibing large amounts of alcohol. Intoxicated agents made their way outside, where they left their imprints in the form of "snow angels" on the front lawn. Jack was 16, having only recently passed his driver's test, but Mother was so desperate for sober drivers that all of us were enlisted to pull drunken employees out of the snow and ferry them safely home.

When the real estate market swung back up in the late-1980s, so did the holiday party, and now, in 1998, we celebrated with a more stylish affair. The party was held at the Crowne Plaza Northstar Hotel, a downtown Minneapolis landmark. The Great Lakes Ballroom had been dressed in twinkling lights and festive tables trimmed in red. A majestic Christmas tree sparkled with white lights towered over the room.

Fulfilling our role as hosts, the three of us welcomed the group with brief highlights of the past robust year. Afterward, Tim blessed the meal and dinner was served. We wanted everyone to enjoy themselves following dinner. But the bar, which had been open before dinner, was now cash-only, in the hope that people would drink more responsibly.

After the meal, the dancing started. Tim and I finished a rousing version of "The Twist" and were in need of refreshments. On our way to the bar, Tim was waylaid by an old acquaintance. "I'll order two Cokes," I said and made my way across the crowded room.

I spotted Pamela at the bar, looking stunning in a black silk and velvet pantsuit, her hair in a French twist. I felt dowdy in Pamela's presence, even in the slim red sheath I had bought for the holidays. Pamela and Paul had spent Thanksgiving with her parents, so we had not seen her since the evening we had the family pictures taken.

Slipping behind her, I was about to compliment Pamela on her outfit when her conversation with the bartender stopped me. "Who told you this is now a cash bar?" she asked testily.

The nervous young man, likely a college student putting himself through school, cleared his throat. "Jack Pierson told me that after dinner—"

"Do you know who I am?" Pamela's sharp words sliced at the flustered bartender. "I own this company, and if you want to keep your job, you'll reopen the fucking bar."

My heart began to beat rapidly against my chest as I placed my hand firmly on her shoulder. "Excuse me, Pamela," I said, coolly meeting her seething gaze. "You don't own a damn thing. And as for the bar, it remains cash-only."

We stood eye to eye, and I could smell the heavy sweetness of the alcohol on her breath. Squarely facing me, Pamela pushed my hand away, spitting out, "Fuck you, Kay!"

"You've had too much to drink," I said, holding my ground, my eyes never wavering.

"Fuck you! I've had two drinks!" she screamed. With a dramatic swoop of her arm, Pamela sent the glasses and an assortment of beer bottles lined across the bar crashing to the floor and stormed off into the crowd. Glass and spilled alcohol were everywhere, but the bartender had taken the brunt of Pamela's fury. Shards of flying glass had left his right hand awash in blood.

I came around behind the bar, grabbing a towel. "Let me wrap your hand and get help." He winced when the towel touched his flesh. "I'll be back."

The music was turned up so loud that only a few curious heads turned as the glasses and bottles met their shattering demise. I scanned the crowd for Mother. Jack saw my frantic face and was instantly at my side hollering above the pounding music.

"What's happened?"

"Pamela just smashed the bar to bits," I yelled, pointing to the bartender, the towel soaked crimson from his injured hand. "We need to find Mom."

"I know where she is," Jack said and disappeared among the swirling crowd.

I swiftly returned to the bartender's side with more towels, trying to stem the bleeding.

Mother, a nurse by training, appeared seconds later, beginning to gingerly remove flakes of glass from the young man's bloody hand. "See if you can find a first-aid kit in the kitchen," she instructed Jack, who immediately took off.

She continued removing fragments from the gashes on the young man's hand. In agony he cried out, yanking back his arm, "Shit! That hurt!"

"Sorry," Mother said, gently reclaiming his spliced hand. "There's a lot of glass in there. What's your name?"

"Dave," he replied, trying hard not to flinch from the sting.

"Well, Dave," she said calmly, "you've got deep lacerations that will require stitches. We're taking you to the nearest emergency room."

The remaining color drained from his face. "But I don't have any insurance," he said, slowly shaking his head. "I can't—"

"It's all right, Dave," Mother said, reassuring him. "We'll take care of paying. But you need to be seen by a doctor."

Jack alerted Dad and Tim of the situation and went looking for Paul and Pamela but found neither. "I'll bet she insisted they go home, but if they're both drunk, we certainly don't want them driving," Dad said.

People in search of drinks were gathering near the bar. Observing the bloody mess, they began inquiring about what had happened. "An unfortunate accident," Mother explained. "The bar will be open in a few minutes."

Accompanied by Michelle and the hotel staff, who began sweeping the floor and cleaning the jumble of glass and beer on the bar, Jack produced a first-aid kit and bandages. "Dad, Tim and I are going to see if we can't catch up with Paul and Pamela before they do something stupid," he said.

Mother began swabbing Dave's hand with alcohol and then wrapping it in a gauze bandage. I clasped his other hand, his nails digging into my hand. "Breathe," I said.

"We're taking Dave to Hennepin County Medical Center for stitches," Mother said.

"I'll come with you," Michelle said.

Jack added, "You'll probably be there awhile. We'll stay here till the end of the evening and make sure everything goes OK."

We were starkly out of place in our beaded dresses and party finery in a hospital. Any emergency room would be awash in crisis, but this was especially true of a county hospital serving a major city on a Saturday night. A continuous parade of cops, relatives, drug casualties, accidents and crime victims fumbled their way through the intricate dramas that had brought them here. In the fluorescent brightness of the emergency room, the three of us kept Dave talking to help take his mind off his pain.

Jack was right that we would not be going anywhere fast. It was past 1:30 a.m. before Dave's hand was sewn up; it required eight stitches. Our night finally ended after we helped him get to his apartment in Dinkytown near the University of Minnesota campus. Mother drove Michelle and me home, and we separated in agreement that we would voice our concerns to Paul and Pamela the following day.

* * *

We dragged ourselves through the leaden motions of church, weary and agitated from the night before. Neither Paul nor Pamela was in attendance. The service seemed longer than usual, and I found myself drifting away from Tim's sermon, unable to concentrate on anything but the previous night's events. How to confront Paul and Pamela needed to be decided. Exhausted from the late night, we chose to eat lunch at a restaurant instead of going back to Goldenwoods. None of us seemed to know how to best deal with the situation.

Within an hour of coming home, Paul appeared on Tim's and my doorstep, with Kaitlin bundled in a pink snowsuit. It became immediately apparent he was upset with me. "You wanna tell me what you said to Pamela last night?" Paul asked.

"What have *I* said to Pamela? Nothing, except to tell her that she doesn't own the company."

We undressed Kaitlin from the snowsuit, placing her on our living room floor with some toys, which occupied her attention. Tension creased Paul's weary brow. "I'm confused," he said, finding a seat on our couch. "Pamela came back from the bar really pissed at you, demanding that we leave. We got into a huge fight in our hotel room."

"No wonder we couldn't find you," Tim said. "We never thought to check the hotel."

Paul was baffled, and I picked up the thread of conversation. "You have no idea what happened last night, do you?"

The sallow color of Paul's complexion indicated he was nursing a hangover; the prominent dark circles under his eyes made them sink inward. "What are you talking about?" he said, trying to control the tremor in his voice.

It was difficult to keep the anger from dominating my tone. "Your lovely wife ripped into the bartender, threatening him with the loss of his job. She said, and I'm quoting here, 'Do you know who I am? I own this company, and if you want to keep your job, you'll reopen the fucking bar.' I told her she doesn't own a damn thing." Paul stared at us dumbfounded. "There's more," I said. "She then proceeded to smash several glasses and bottles of beer across the bar, which cut open the bartender's hand. Mother, Michelle and I spent the remainder of the evening in the Hennepin County ER." I knelt next to the couch, lightly placing my hand on my brother's jittery knee. "Paul, it's clear that Pamela's got a drinking problem that can't be ignored. And so do you."

Paul took a deep breath and began to sob, which distracted Kaitlin from her toys. She gazed quizzically at her father. Tim went to get tissues. I slid in next to Paul, draping an arm over his broad shoulders.

His words trembled. "We're in so much trouble. So much goddamned trouble." Nearly panting, he gasped for a breath.

Tim handed him the tissue box, and Paul regained his composure, wiping away tears. "We're in financial hock and don't have a red cent." He hesitated to blow his nose while composing his thoughts. "This summer, I told Pamela she had to cut back on her spending. Her credit card bills alone are astronomical—clothes, shoes, handbags, trips to salon and spa, you name it. She accused me of withholding money, and we had screaming fights. And she started pulling away."

Paul rolled the tissue between his fingers. "I told her going back to work and strict budgeting were our best options. She resisted at first and then tells me she has this fabulous job offer in Rochester. I was hesitant, but Pamela insisted it would solve our financial straits. It turns out this whole thing was a mistake."

I said, "Where is Pamela now?"

"In Rochester. She left this morning without saying goodbye. Whatever happened last night, she doesn't care."

Tim transitioned to counselor mode. "A new baby, job, financial worries and a long-distance marriage are all stressors on their own. Is Pamela running away from your troubles?"

Paul's burst of cynical laughter startled both Tim and me. "Yeah. And she's also been screwing around."

I slunk against the cushions, remembering Pamela's bare hands before the family portrait and her rapid departure. Still, I was unprepared to hear Paul say this.

Tim asked, "What makes you think that?"

Arms hanging loosely off his knees, Paul looked at the floor. "A couple of months ago, I started getting anonymous notes that Pamela was seeing other men. I tried to ignore them, but they kept coming. Whoever sent them knows her because they were very specific."

He shared the details. The first note said: "Your wife is a world-class slut." Then: "They don't call her 'Slam-Bam-Pam' for nothing." The missives grew more detailed: "Check out the Radisson Plaza Hotel, downtown Rochester, almost any night of the week. Recognize this license number—LKB 725? You should. She always parks at the Radisson." And finally: "You're blind if you can't see that your wife is a gold-digging whore taking you for a ride."

"Part of me is afraid of the truth, but I'm beginning to think our marriage is a charade," Paul said, nodding his head.

"Where were the notes postmarked from?" Tim asked.

"Most were postmarked Rochester, except for one mailed from Northfield."

Looking at the floor, he kept talking. "As much as I didn't want to believe it, I already suspected something wasn't right. I think I need to hire a private investigator to find the truth. If I confront Pamela without any real evidence, she'll explain it away."

Kaitlin babbling happy noises as she explored the terrain of our living room floor was the only sound. I wanted to discuss Paul's drinking problem, but common sense told me that hurling another crisis at him would probably push him past his emotional limits. I would have to be patient.

"The anonymous notes aside, what about the money Pamela brings in from her job? That's not helping?" It was an attempt to convince myself that the mounting trepidation was misguided.

Paul let out a sad laugh. "Are you kidding? Like I said, not a cent. We now have no choice but to sell or lose the house." He was quiet for another moment. "Love bears all things, believes all things, hopes all things, endures all things. Love never fails." The passage read at their wedding. Paul made eye contact with both of us. "Love did fail for me, and not once but twice. My first wife dies from a terrible illness, and my second wife's a liar and a cheater," he said cynically.

"One step at a time. Tell Mom and Dad what you think is going on and see what they have to say." I gave my brother a look of encouragement, knowing my smile was a fragile veneer.

"Don't forget that whatever path this takes, you still have a beautiful little girl," Tim reminded him, lifting Kaitlin's squirming body off the floor. "Even if your love with Pamela doesn't endure, there are still positive things in your life."

Kaitlin giggled as she patted Tim's beard, always a source of fascination for her. Watching his daughter, Paul smiled. "You're right. I can't imagine life without her. But I need to know what Pamela is up to. My gut tells me the notes are telling the truth."

I could feel a horrible sensation in my gut, as though my stomach had been tossed out a 10th-story window and splattered across the pavement.

* * *

Shortly after Paul left that afternoon, Dad called explaining he wanted to meet Paul, Jack and me at his office early Monday morning to discuss hiring a private investigator to track Pamela.

We gathered in Dad's spacious office at 9 a.m., the four of us seated around a cherry wood conference table, while outside the closed office door, his secretary was instructed to hold all incoming calls. I faced the massive bookcase that loomed behind his desk, where family pictures lined the shelves. Portraits of Ruthie, Sam and Kaitlin were at the forefront, surrounded by wedding pictures for the three of us and, farther back, our college graduation pictures.

The photos caught my attention. Faces so young and earnest, so impatient to grow into adulthood and impress. I thought with unease that that future was now here, and it didn't look anything like I imagined. Our first test as business owners was not squabbling over some housing development but preparing to delve into another family member's life. If we threw open the closet and found there were indeed bones rattling around, the situation would be a formidable challenge. If we were wrong, however, and there was some plausible explanation, it would be difficult, maybe impossible, to shut that door again.

"Before we get too far along, I have to put my own reservations to rest," I spoke honestly, the men giving me their full attention. "Instead of hiring a private investigator immediately, shouldn't we determine if these notes are, in fact, true?"

"Pamela has not been truthful," Jack stated forcefully. "Why is she really living in Rochester? We need to look at the broader picture of protecting our family and business interests if necessary."

"I understand that," I replied a bit tersely. "It's just that—"

"You're uncomfortable having Pamela followed, asking someone to dig up 'dirt' on her?" Dad said, finishing my thought.

"Yes," I said, relieved that he understood where I was coming from. "I'm wondering if there isn't a better way to approach this."

Dad clasped his hands together, elbows propped on the conference table. "In 1978, when you kids were still teenagers, we suspected a property manager was dealing drugs out of one of our apartment complexes. To gather sufficient evidence to take to the police, we needed to monitor the activities of this employee. The only feasible way of doing that was by hiring a private investigator."

The memory was hazy, but I vaguely recalled a significant issue with an employee who was eventually fired. "But Pamela is not an employee," I said. "She married into this family."

Across from me, Paul leaned forward. "I'm not entirely comfortable with this either, Kay. But as her spouse, I have a right to know exactly what is going on."

"You do have the right to find out the truth," I agreed.

"The private investigator I worked with in the past has since retired," Dad explained. "But Jack has done some fact-finding."

From his spot at the table, Jack looked at each of us. "The apartment manager over at Lakeview is a former Minneapolis cop. I called him yesterday, and he recommended a former co-worker, an ex-cop named Dan Kinney. Been in the PI business about 10 years and is available to meet with us as soon as tomorrow."

Dad questioned Paul. "Do you think we should get more references or explore additional possibilities?"

He fidgeted anxiously in his chair. "I think we should meet Dan Kinney and go from there. I'll make an appointment."

Before the private investigator went to work, there was the business of getting through the holidays. But two days before Christmas, Pamela revealed to Paul she would not be joining us for dinner and opening presents. "My parents are insisting I bring Kaitlin for Christmas Eve and then have dinner with them on Christmas Day."

"What about inviting your folks to join us for dinner? I'm sure Mom and Dad wouldn't mind," Paul had nonchalantly suggested.

"My mother's cooking Christmas dinner, and if you want to join us, fine. But I'm not coming to your parents."

"OK," Paul said, dejected. "I'm sure Mom and Dad will understand. After all, your parents need to see their granddaughter. Have a good time."

Pamela returned to Rochester for New Year's Eve, and despite numerous attempts to contact her, Paul didn't hear from her until nearly a week later. We hired Dan Kinney to track her, but we would need to be patient as the evidence was gathered, bit by bit, to construct the story behind the lie Paul believed Pamela was living.

chapter 13

JANUARY 1999

Once Dan Kinney went into action, we had to make sure Pamela remained unaware she was being tracked. To that end, Paul's situation remained clandestine, never discussed with anyone but family or any place but in the privacy of our homes.

Business progressed as usual. Employee inquiries about how things were going for Pamela in Rochester were simple to handle, generally casual talk-around-the-water-cooler type of questions.

Jack posed no threat in divulging our secret. With the slightest distress, he was a master at controlling his emotions. I regularly watched him chatting with co-workers about Paul and Pamela as if they were the most devoted couple on earth.

With Paul it was the opposite. I worried he might not be able to keep the truth from Linda. She was not only his secretary; she was also his confidante. But he surprised me. When the new family pictures were delivered, he proudly showed them off, displaying them prominently on his desk. "You have a beautiful family, Paul. I'm sure that makes you proud," Linda told him.

To Linda and others, he talked about the opportunity the job presented for Pamela and her career. On the rare occasions when someone asked if the arrangement strained their marriage, Paul presented his cheeriest façade, explaining that they were willing to work extra hard at their relationship.

But the tenseness of the situation broke through to the surface in late January, as Paul prepared for yearly Home Builders Association meetings in Dallas. He seemed preoccupied and anxious, enough so that Jack and I expressed our concern.

Days before his departure, Jack asked Paul frankly, "Pamela isn't catching on to being followed, is she?"

"No, no, everything's fine. I've got a lot to do to get ready for the meetings, and I don't like leaving Kaitlin alone with Heather for long periods of time."

"Mom or I could take her instead," I offered.

Amid numerous presentation drafts, stacks of books and various clutter, Paul looked lost and adrift, like a tiny craft fending off a ferocious sea. Still, he reassured us, "Everything's on track. I just need to concentrate on my Home Builders presentation."

Jack asked him again. "You're absolutely sure Pamela doesn't suspect anything? You've got to tell us if she knows something is up. Otherwise, it could blow up in our faces."

"I'm preoccupied with Dallas, that's all." Paul left at the end of the month.

While Paul was away, Mother tried to check on Kaitlin and Heather, calling the house to invite them for dinner. I had stopped by the antique shop, where I found her elbow-deep in Styrofoam peanuts, unpacking boxes.

"It's the strangest thing," she told me, removing a vase from a large carton, specks of Styrofoam clinging to her arms. "I've left several messages on the answering machine, but Heather's never called me back."

"She's probably busy. Caring for a baby is a full-time job—you've said it yourself."

Mother adjusted her glasses, wiping the clinging peanuts off her arms. "I hate these packing peanuts; they seem to multiply once you open the box. Anyway, I'm starting to worry."

"What are you worried about?" I asked.

"Twice when I called the house to invite Heather to dinner, a man answered the phone."

"Maybe you dialed the wrong number?"

"The first time I was startled but still asked for Heather. He told me she wasn't there and hung up. I thought that was odd. I phoned right back, and the answering machine picked up."

"It could've been one of those rare instances where you called the wrong number of someone also named Heather."

Diving back into the box, fishing for the next piece, Mother was momentarily silent. "Are you trying to humor me or tell me I'm losing it?"

"Neither. I did that once. Called the wrong number, but the person who answered had the same name as who I was calling. It wasn't until we'd been talking that I realized I was speaking to the wrong person."

She shook her head dismissively. "I know that number by heart, and the display shows the number dialed. Yesterday I called again, and the same man answered. He has a very distinctive low voice. He said I had the wrong number."

"OK, you're thinking the worst, that Heather's got a man staying there while Paul's away," I said.

"What other explanation could there be?"

At a loss for a satisfactory response, I didn't feel like arguing. "I guess I'd address it with Paul when he gets back."

Heather phoned the following morning, gladly accepting Mother's dinner invitation. Seeing that Kaitlin was happy and well taken care of alleviated her concerns, and she never broached the subject with Paul.

For several weeks we entered a holding pattern as the investigator tracked Pamela's actions. Dan proposed devising an organized plan to confront Pamela. When he felt he had gathered sufficient evidence, he and Paul would meet with her.

But life rarely goes along as planned, and in the snap of a finger, the best-laid plans can fall apart. On a cold Friday in February, Jack and Paul were out of the office and I was immersed in writing marketing plans. When my phone rang, I never got out a hello.

"Come over to Paul's house right away and pick up Kaitlin," Jack relayed firmly. I started to question him, but he interrupted. "Pamela's on her way home unexpectedly."

I drove along the freeway toward Woodbury, as heavy snowflakes began to fall. I knew I should slow my speed, but time was of the essence.

The sole car parked in the driveway was Paul's. I was not sure who to expect—Jack and Dan Kinney, at least. I secured Kaitlin's car seat in the back seat. As I did, I spotted a sheriff's car parked about a block down the street, deliberately out of view.

I walked in through the four-stall garage. The gargoyles that had once made me scoff at their ridiculousness now seemed to watch me with an ominous stare. Most of the lights were turned on in the house, and I detected voices. Near the kitchen table and chairs stood Jack and a uniformed man with the broadest shoulders I had ever seen. He was clearly a sheriff's deputy.

"Sorry to call you on such short notice," Jack said without the benefit of introduction, "but Pamela could be here any minute, and we don't want the baby here." His explanation was rapid-fire.

"Where's Kaitlin now?"

"Paul's getting her dressed. A bag's been packed with diapers and all that stuff. Mom's expecting you at her house."

As I listened, I stared down at the sheriff's deputy's shoes. Buffed to a high gloss, the shiny black material distorted the reflection of our faces into the grotesque images of a fun-house mirror. It was exactly how I felt for a few stretched minutes, as though everything was deformed by ultra-slow motion.

Jack sprinted upstairs to hurry Paul, while the deputy and I waited in awkward silence in the pristine kitchen. I glanced around the spacious first level and thought again of how exquisite façades hid many secrets. Pamela had been so particular in the home's design—the commercial appliances, granite counters, custom cabinets, polished hardwood floors and in-home theater system. It was straight from the pages of House Beautiful, only it felt like the picture was about to be torn from the magazine.

Dan Kinney had been on the phone in another part of the house and came over to greet me. "Nice to see you again, Kay. Sorry the circumstances aren't better. A volatile situation has erupted between Mrs. Pierson and her apparent lover, and we feel this is the best time to act. We do, however, want the baby out of the house, as I can almost guarantee it won't be pleasant."

I felt suffocated by the mounting tension. I addressed the sheriff's deputy to keep my mind occupied. "Why are you here exactly?"

"I'm serving Mrs. Pierson with divorce papers," he said, very businesslike. "It's a formality, but I'm also here if there's trouble. Situations like these can turn ugly very quickly."

The sound of footsteps echoed on the oak staircase. Paul carried Kaitlin, with Jack close behind hoisting a brightly colored canvas bag. Paul talked soothingly to his daughter. "Let's go bye-bye with Auntie Kay. She'll take you to Grandma. Such a good girl."

Paul gave Kaitlin a kiss and handed the baby to me without any protest from her. Jack slipped the bag over my shoulder. "Take her to Goldenwoods."

"I know, she's expecting us. Hi, sweetheart," I said, kissing my niece's forehead.

"You need to go," Jack continued with uncharacteristic anxiety. "She'll be here any minute."

Hoisting the baby on my hip, I said, "You'll call later?"

"Yes," Paul said.

Jack's commanding voice was terse. "Just go!"

No one had heard Pamela's car arrive outside. The back door off the garage opened with a slam, banging the wall. "Who the hell are all these people?" The stale odor of cigarette smoke and alcohol trailed after her, her blonde hair falling across her face.

"Why don't you sit down, Mrs. Pierson?" Dan said. He walked over to Pamela, grasped her by the arm, and attempted to steer her toward the kitchen table.

Her voice pierced the air. "Get your fucking hands off me!" She forcibly shoved him away. "Where are you going with Kaitlin?"

The commotion startled Kaitlin into crying, the volume increasing as everyone shouted at once. "Mrs. Pierson, please take a seat. Your daughter is fine," the sheriff's deputy stated firmly, his bulky frame serving as a large barrier between Pamela and me.

"Fuck you!" she shrieked, pounding and clawing at his vast chest like a small, fearless dog taking on a much larger one. "Give me my baby!"

Jack hollered in my direction, "Goddamn it, Kay, get the hell out of here!"

I moved as quickly as I could, Kaitlin's sobs growing more distressed and the heavy bag pulling on my shoulder. Paul said to Pamela abruptly, "Since when do you care about Kaitlin? You go weeks without seeing her or even asking about her."

"My daughter!"

The deputy's calm but authoritative voice followed. "Have you been drinking, Mrs. Pierson?"

The falling snow made the pavement slippery, and I fought to keep my balance fastening my crying niece into the car seat. "It'll be all right, sweetheart. It'll be all right."

I noticed I hadn't closed the front door to the house all the way. Opening the driver's-side door, I heard Pamela's screaming and the sound of breaking glass. The tires squealed when I hit the gas. I was driving too fast for such slippery conditions, but the more distance I put between us and Pamela, the safer I felt. If I got stopped for speeding, I had no idea what I would say. I doubted a family crisis would qualify as an excuse.

Kaitlin calmed as I talked incessantly, as much for her comfort as for my own. My whitened knuckles tightly gripped the steering wheel. "Auntie Kay's here, sweetheart," I said, watching her in my rearview mirror. "Everything will be fine."

Halfway to Mother and Dad's, traffic slowed to a crawl—lines of cars crept along Interstate 94, ribbons of headlights penetrating through a white curtain of heavy falling snow. Kaitlin fell asleep, a blessing. I concentrated on driving, the road conditions steadily deteriorating. The constant "thwack, thwack" of the windshield wipers and the crunch of tires over road salt filled my head. Turning on the radio, WCCO's traffic reporter read a lengthy list of accidents throughout the metropolitan area. "Give yourself extra time, folks, and drive safely," the announcer admonished. I obediently slowed the car further.

I had been driving for well over two hours by the time I reached our parents. My arms were sore and rigid from anxiety. The image staring back from the rearview mirror was a face taut and haggard, far older than my 37 years. I was steeped in exhausted defeat, as though Pamela was sucking all the energy out of me.

PART THREE

chapter 14

The confrontation with Pamela had been fierce, climaxing in her heaving her engagement ring across the kitchen at Paul.

As we feared, he was in dire financial straits. Pamela returned to Rochester, and Mother and I began moving him out of the Woodbury house. He relocated to Goldenwoods, where he would reside indefinitely.

Of no great shock to anyone, Pamela left chaos in her wake. Surveying the jumble of the master bedroom, Paul's belongings strewn everywhere, he shook his head in frustration. "I guess I should be glad she didn't do any more damage."

"Getting your clothes in order will be the easy part," I said, helping to lay pants and jackets across the king-sized bed.

Paul fitted a drawer back into a dresser, his voice heavy with resignation. "My main concern right now is having a temporary settlement drawn up and signed and ending this marriage."

It was clear Pamela had helped herself to anything she deemed to be of value. "She shouldn't have been allowed to be in the house alone," I said angrily. "It looks like she's taken everything of value including the last few pieces of Red Wing pottery."

"Kay, I don't care," Paul responded, wearily slouching fatigued shoulders. "It's just stuff."

I said irritably, "Those things were gifts to the both of you, and you have a right to an equal share."

Mother sided with me. "Your sister's right. We'll need to write out a list of the items she's taken, which we'll present to your attorneys. No-fault divorce does not mean Pamela can walk out of here with whatever she wants."

The three of us returned early the following morning, going room by room to inventory what was missing. She had left almost nothing. Even in the lower-level storeroom, most of the holiday decorations had been taken.

"I'm just grateful I have a place to stay," my brother said. He had set up in Mother and Dad's lower level, devising a nursery in the sitting room adjoining his bedroom. "And I got $35,000 for the engagement ring."

"I'm surprised she didn't keep it," I said, anger curling my words.

Mother and Paul agreed.

* * *

"I never did care for her. She could be so rude, especially at company functions. You'd have thought she owned the place."

"Me neither. As soon as I heard she was moving to Rochester I thought something was up. A married woman with a new baby taking a job and an apartment in another city? C'mon."

I recognized the voices of two longtime co-workers in the accounting department, whispering between themselves in the coffee room. Clearly, they were talking about Pamela. Good sense told me to come back later for a refill, but the pull of fascination was too great, like witnessing one's own entanglement in a gory accident.

"What I don't understand is why they didn't investigate what she was doing down there sooner," one of them said, a spoon clinking against the ceramic of a mug. "I wouldn't have trusted her for a minute."

"Well, I think Paul was in denial. He was always talking about how great the opportunity was for them. I don't think he had a clue."

Leaning forward to hear more, I lost my balance, stumbling over my feet and banging into the wall with a shaking thud.

"Kay!" the women said in alarm.

I was furious at my clumsiness. "You'd think I couldn't walk and chew gum at the same time. Is that a fresh pot?"

"Yes, yes. Just made."

The horrified expressions on their faces made clear they realized I'd overheard at least part of the conversation. "I'm a little low on caffeine, as you can tell," I said, a self-deprecating comment being the best I could do. Too embarrassed to say anything further, they departed the kitchenette in a hurry.

Within days, all of Pierson Properties' employees knew the preliminary details, the dismantling of Paul and Pamela's union becoming a prime topic of gossip. Dan Kinney produced evidence that much of Pamela's life in Rochester had been spent carousing in bars and clubs, meeting and having sex with numerous men, just as the notes had claimed. He also discovered that she had taken expensive trips to Las Vegas and Los Angeles over the weekends she had claimed to be working extra hours.

As proof mounted, it became apparent that Pamela would not separate quietly. Her first ploy was an attempt to win Paul back, using the manipulative tactics that had served her so well in the past. She called him constantly from Rochester, and if she did not find him in the office, she tracked him on his cellphone, interrupting appointments and meetings.

After several days of continued harassment, Paul was worn out. In a session with the family's attorneys discussing strategies of protecting our business interests, Paul's cellphone vibrated on the table. "I just can't deal with another call from her," he groaned, her number displayed on his phone screen.

Big-sister protective instincts kicked in. I would intervene. "Give me your phone," I said briskly, carrying the ringing culprit out into the hall. I would not play nice with my soon-to-be-ex-sister-in-law. "He doesn't want to talk to you Pamela, so stop calling," I said. I found an unoccupied office, closing the door behind me.

"I don't understand why you're being so snippy with me, Kay. I only want to talk with my husband."

"He won't be your husband much longer."

"I think that's for us—"

I cut her off. "Call Paul again and we'll consider it harassment."

The sweetness evaporated. "You're such a bitch, Kay! Stay out of this."

"Stay out of this? What you're after affects our entire family. And remember this, Pamela: Blood always runs thicker than water. Especially tainted water."

"Don't talk to me like that, you fucking bitch!"

"I'll talk to you any way I want."

Pamela was still screaming as I switched off Paul's phone. My breathing was shaky and fast, as if catching each breath was just out of reach. The tinkling of metal distracted my thoughts. I looked at the shaking gold bracelets on my wrists and realized I was trembling uncontrollably.

* * *

By the end of February, realizing her pleas for reconciliation were going unheard, Pamela changed tactics and tried a different approach to get Paul's attention. She threatened suicide and then her mother got involved. Paul and I were waiting for a conference call with Ron

Baker to discuss marketing for a new development. When the phone rang, Paul answered on the speakerphone assuming it was Ron.

"Paul Pierson."

"Paul, this is Annette. I need to talk to you about Pamela," she said, speaking so quickly there was no chance for him to cut in. "Why are you rushing into a divorce? This has all been blown out of proportion."

I moved to the edge of my chair as Paul gave me an exasperated look across his desk, which was strewn with papers and files. "Annette, Pamela was having an affair."

"It didn't mean a thing. Pamela loves you, Paul, but she needs professional help."

Paul tried to keep his composure. "Then she should get professional help, Annette. That doesn't change the fact that I want a divorce."

Annette's voice took on a spiteful edge. "That is so unfair. You know most of this is your fault."

"My fault? I honored my marriage vows," Paul continued, his tone even.

"You pushed Pamela away, Paul. She only had those relationships for the sex."

"Look, I'm not going to argue with you. This marriage is over and that's final."

Annette was relentless, barely letting Paul complete his sentence. "Think about Kaitlin! The stigma of coming from a broken home will haunt her forever! You've got to give Pamela another chance!"

"Listen, Annette, I'm waiting for an important call. My decision is final; I'm getting a divorce."

"If you don't take Pamela back, you'll destroy her life!"

"Annette, Pamela is responsible for her own life. And Kaitlin will be OK. I will be sure of that." He disconnected her call.

"Good for you for standing your ground."

"This isn't the first time I've heard from Annette," Paul said. "She's left several messages on the answering machine, which I ignored. She does not want this marriage to end."

As I listened to my brother describe Annette's attempts to stop the divorce, something occurred to me. Rather than repairing the relationship, her main interest was placing the blame on Paul and shielding her daughter from accountability. I began to wonder what had really happened with Pamela's first husband. It struck me that the answers could be as close as Northfield.

* * *

An idyllic town of 15,000, Northfield was home to two of the best liberal arts colleges in the country, Carleton and St. Olaf. Pamela had graduated from Carleton, but there were other connections—her father, Donovan, was a highly respected English professor at the college. I suspected that other truths in Northfield were waiting to be exhumed. So I decided to drive there one chilly gray morning in early March. As I made my way south on Interstate 35W, I kept revisiting the story Ron had told us about assisting Pamela during her divorce from Doug and our own response when the family heard this sad tale.

No one questioned her side of the story—who would be so callous to challenge a battered woman? At the time we had no reason to doubt her, casting Doug as the villain she made him out to be. Now I wanted to hear Doug's side. If he would talk to me, I thought we might begin to understand more about who Pamela was and what she was after. First, however, I would be engaging in some good old-fashioned research.

Minnesota is dotted with stately Carnegie libraries, and Northfield was lucky enough to have one. I loved the ornate grandeur of such buildings and envisioning Minnesota's robber-baron era.

I arrived at 9:30 a.m., just as the public library was opening. Being the first patron, I had the reference librarian to myself; I explained that I was looking for information on the Annette and Donovan Schaeffer family.

"What kind of information?" the older woman asked, peering over severe half-glasses. Her name badge read "Mrs. Parsons."

I had guessed I might have to explain and slightly fabricate my intent before obtaining any data of value. "My brother Paul is married to Annette and Donovan's daughter, Pamela," I said.

"So, you're family from Minneapolis," she replied, less formal now and smiling.

"That's correct. Kay Pierson-Scott," I said, shaking her hand.

"What exactly are you looking for?"

I decided to just get to the point. "I'd like to find out more about Pamela's first marriage."

"Oh." She nodded. Even though it was just the two of us in the large library, she whispered. "Doug Castleton's such a nice, hardworking young man. It's unfortunate that things turned out so badly."

"When were they married?" From my husband's pastoral experience, I knew how to play the role of confidante well.

"It's been five years now, at least," Mrs. Parsons replied. "What a wedding! The ceremony was held on campus in Skinner Memorial Chapel. You would have thought a princess was getting married. The best of everything."

Pamela had never mentioned her first wedding. "If you could direct me to the town newspaper, I'd appreciate it."

Mrs. Parsons showed me to the section of the library where the microfiche was kept on file. "If I remember correctly, they were married in 1993, at the end of the school year. There was quite a bit written in the Northfield News." After she instructed me how to load the microfiche, a second library visitor asked for her assistance.

As the librarian had indicated, the wedding occurred in May of 1993. The paper carried a full-length picture of the couple on their wedding day, showing a handsome light-haired groom and a gorgeous

Pamela in a voluminous taffeta dress with a crown holding her cathedral-length veil. I thought to myself that "princess" had only scratched the surface.

Next, I scoured the daily record for the divorce-filing date. I had little luck at first. I was using the timeline Pamela had given us—that she and Doug had been married for a year—but I went through nearly 18 months of records finding nothing. On a hunch, I started looking for divorce filings only a few months after their marriage. I found my answer: Doug—not Pamela—had filed for divorce in January 1994, less than eight months after their wedding, citing irreconcilable differences and not abuse.

Recalling her teary confession of an abusive, short-lived marriage, the real story was now coming into focus. Pamela had played the martyr, casting herself as a devoted wife who had been brutalized by her husband, leaving her no choice but to flee to a battered women's shelter in the dead of night. It was no wonder that Mother and Dad had insisted on paying for the wedding after hearing this, hoping a fresh start within a loving family would assuage some of Pamela's pain. Knowing what I knew now, I had an uncomfortable inkling there was more to come.

* * *

On the internet, I located a website for Castleton Builders that listed Doug Castleton as the proprietor. Just outside of town, a wooden sign perched in front of a white metal building announced "Castleton Premier Builders." Gravel crunched under the tires, kicking up dust when I drove onto the lot. The noise must have announced my presence; as the door to the building swung in, I found myself nearly falling into the arms of the strapping man who opened it.

"I'm sorry," he said. "Didn't mean to pull so hard. Can I help you?"

"Yes. I'm looking for Doug Castleton."

Dressed in a long-sleeved plaid wool shirt and well-worn blue jeans, I recognized him from the newspaper photos, but his response was aloof. "Who wants to know?" he asked, giving me a cool stare.

"Mr. Castleton, I'm Kay Pierson-Scott. Paul Pierson is my brother."

His taut face muscles softened. "Oh. C'mon in. Call me Doug. I'll bet this is regarding my ex-wife, Pamela. Did Paul finally start taking my notes seriously?"

I nodded. "I thought it might be you but wasn't sure. Yes, I'd like to talk with you."

"Sure. My secretary's running errands and my crew's out at a site. I've got plenty to say—and the time. Want some coffee?"

"Yes, please. Just black." I gazed around the office, noting the color photographs of Castleton homes displayed on a back wall. "I'm curious about one thing. Instead of anonymous notes, why not just talk to Paul?"

Doug motioned for me to have a seat in a padded vinyl chair across from his gray metal desk. "It was my word against hers, and I could imagine what Pamela had said. I tried to warn your family before they even got married, but I guess I didn't go about it in the right way." He handed me a mug of piping hot liquid with large, weathered hands that obviously were accustomed to outdoor work.

I was confused. "I don't remember anyone saying anything about Pamela before the wedding, except to say what a wonderful person she was."

Stirring powdered creamer into his cup, Doug suddenly looked rather sheepish. "I didn't tell anybody directly, just a couple of anonymous phone calls to your mom's antique shop."

I shifted so quickly in my chair that coffee lapped at the edges of my cup, nearly spilling onto my black wool slacks. I remembered Mother telling me she'd received strange calls at the shop—the caller would hang up before she could ask any questions. "You told Mom that Pamela was not the girl Paul thought she was? That he shouldn't marry her?"

"I wanted to stop her from fucking up someone else's life." Catching himself, Doug blushed in embarrassment. "Excuse my profanity."

"Don't worry about it," I answered, waving my hand dismissively.

"My intent was to save another poor bastard from making the same mistakes I did. Maybe calling your mom wasn't the greatest idea, but I couldn't think of any other way."

With this intel I pressed the conversation forward. "How did you know Pamela was having affairs in Rochester?"

The frame of Doug's swivel chair squeaked as he settled in. "Word gets around. An old friend of mine is a nurse at the Mayo Clinic. She knew Pamela had remarried and taken a job there. Completely by accident, she encountered her picking up men at area bars. She called me, and I went down to Rochester to see for myself. And sure enough, there Pamela was, having sex with some guy in the parking lot." He paused, taking a drink of coffee. "Should I have told your brother face to face? I suppose so. But would he have believed me?"

"Probably not," I acknowledged, dryly adding, "Paul's filed for divorce after confirming for himself that Pamela's been cheating."

"That's a start, but it won't be the end of his problems. There are plenty of things I'll bet you don't know about Pamela."

"OK," I said.

Much like Paul, Doug and Pamela had been introduced through mutual acquaintances. "Pamela knew a great deal about my life and family," he explained. "Northfield's a small town, and if you don't know everybody directly, you're acquainted with someone who does. Pamela was inquisitive, complimentary and a good listener. What guy wouldn't go for that?"

They dated for nearly a year, but the relationship was often volatile, as Pamela proved immensely jealous of Doug's time with anyone but her. "She was very controlling, always pushing for me to make a commitment," he related. "But the longer we were together, the more I was convinced that we weren't good for one another. I should have ended it sooner, but there were also things that appealed to me.

"Even though we were living together I kept holding off, trying to keep my distance while not cutting her off completely. Finally, I decided we really needed to take a break and not see each other for a while. I had to know if I was in love with Pamela or if it was just the great sex," he said bluntly. "I figured if the relationship was the right one, it would work out; otherwise, we could both move on."

As Paul and the rest of us were discovering, Doug had found severing ties with Pamela was not easy. "We had a brutal fight, screaming and throwing things. She accused me of leading her on and trying to sabotage her academic career. The argument got so loud that the neighbors called the police. Pamela was intent on humiliating me and told the cops I had attacked her. She was focused on showing the world what a heel I was for breaking up with her. She moved out, but my problems were far from over.

"Pamela made herself scarce for several weeks, and just as I was becoming interested in another woman, I ran into her at a party. We started talking, and during the conversation Pamela told me she'd been pregnant when we broke up. Rather than tell me at the time, she'd had an abortion.

"Whether or not it was true, I don't know. But Pamela made sure I knew that I had disrupted her life. She laid the guilt on thick. Said she was pregnant, alone, dealing with school, and she'd had to fend for herself. At the time I thought our meeting was coincidental, but I now believe she was stalking me, setting up this story."

Pamela would never be able to prove she had been pregnant, but her ruse worked, and they were soon sharing a home again. Once a couple, she campaigned for a commitment.

"Her devastation over the abortion suddenly disappeared," he said, tapping his fingers against the ceramic mug. "But I was reacting to the guilt, not true love for her.

"She must've sensed that I was becoming skeptical and couldn't risk this opportunity slipping away twice. Within a few weeks, Pamela tells me she's pregnant again. It was another bad scene, hysterical tears, yelling. She's adamant in her refusal to have another abortion, even though I never asked that of her. I'm trying to be rational, and she's screaming that I'm denying her the chance to have our baby."

I shook my head in recognition. "She did something similar when Paul served her with divorce papers. I was there; suddenly she's shrieking for her baby."

"Whenever Pamela is backed into a corner, or she senses things are not going in her favor, she throws a shit fit. I should've recognized the pattern."

"I interrupted you. What happened after that?"

Reaching this apex, Doug's voice grew heavy with weariness, dragging on to its inevitable conclusion. "Essentially, she just wore me out. She and her mother planned the wedding within weeks, and we were married in an elaborate ceremony on the Carleton campus in May 1993. We returned from the honeymoon, and suddenly Pamela's not pregnant anymore. Tells me she miscarried on our honeymoon but didn't want to spoil it for me. Always out to make herself the martyr."

The story was riveting, and I didn't expect him to take it further, but Doug seemed to find talking cathartic. "I really believed I had an obligation to make this marriage work," he continued. "Pamela graduated shortly after the wedding, and I expected her to pursue her career goals. Instead, she takes her time following job leads, until one day I catch her in our bed with a fellow classmate." He paused to catch his breath. "And I slapped her."

There was simply no way Doug could miss the sharp jerk of my body as I visibly flinched.

"I also punched the guy and tossed them both out on their asses," he added. "Unacceptable? No question. But I finally realized the whole thing had been a lie, and the rage I experienced was indescribable." I didn't respond, letting Doug conclude his story. "Pamela told anyone who'd listen that I'd physically abused her from the very start of our relationship. I just kept my mouth shut. I tried to maintain some integrity."

"That's how she presented it to us," I said.

He clasped his large hands behind his head. "She's a master manipulator and a great actress. As the situation was exposed, Pamela was tenacious in her refusal to let the marriage end, even though she'd made me out to be the bad guy. Annette called me, begging for a reconciliation. When that proved fruitless, Pamela showed up at my parents' home. The confrontation with them turned into a real shit show."

"Annette has taken a similar approach with Paul," I offered quietly. "She has made it clear that while Pamela may have been unfaithful, she was not to blame."

"It's never Pamela's fault," Doug said, moving closer to his desk and shaking his head. "What's interesting, at least to me, is that Donovan is this nice guy, teaching Shakespeare at Carleton. But Annette is extremely shrewd, and Pamela's just like her. If I were Donovan, I'd have seen the marriage barely included me and walked years ago. Annette is clearly in control, and she's never made Pamela take responsibility for her actions."

While Doug's assertion was true, in the end he had been able to extract Pamela from his life and family. But there was one distinct difference between him and Paul: Doug had not fathered a child with her, and he seemed to understand this. "I thank my lucky stars every day that there was nothing to connect Pamela and me for the rest of our lives. I could cut her off at the knees and did so without hesitation."

I sat my empty coffee cup on the edge of Doug's metal desk. "Paul's situation is even more heartbreaking. When he and Pamela met, Paul was recovering from the death of his first wife. We thought Pamela was a godsend and were thrilled when they married."

An agonizing groan escaped from Doug's lips. "I'm so sorry. Pamela is the Princess of Darkness, and no one, especially someone as vulnerable as your brother, deserves to have his life destroyed by her."

I glanced at my wristwatch, realizing nearly an hour had passed. "I should let you get back to work. But thanks for your time and the information," I said, rising from my chair.

Doug's swivel chair squeaked when he stood to his full height of well over 6 feet. "No problem," he said, extending a brawny hand. "I wish I'd contacted Paul by phone. And sooner."

"It's just helpful knowing someone else who's had to deal with her," I said.

Doug handed me a business card from the metal holder on his desk. "When Paul goes up against Pamela in court—and he will; she'll want more child support, more money, more everything—let me know. Glad to testify with my personal experience."

As I departed Northfield, I realized the material I had in my possession was ammunition that would be needed for a long-term battle. What I'd learned could be of use to Paul in the financial and child custody case that would most certainly lie ahead.

chapter 15

Even with the facts I had gathered, the divorce settlement would still be laborious. Six weeks after the papers had been filed, there was no temporary resolution. Jack's rationale seemed the closest to the mark. "No doubt she's squandered most of the money she's earned over the last few months, and now Pamela is edging toward panic as she realizes the gravy train that she's become accustomed to has dried up."

We all were getting restless as the battle dragged on, especially Dad, who steadfastly supported Paul's every decision. When Pamela refused to sign the temporary settlement, Dad patiently waited her out. But as the impasse continued, with Pamela still demanding larger sums of money, his tolerance finally ran out.

He phoned Pamela's attorney and left a voicemail. It was succinct and to the point: "I've had a bellyful of Pamela and her demands. Tell her she either signs that agreement, or Beverly and I will use all of our resources to get full custody of our grandchild and put an end to this nonsense."

The threat of involvement by Mother and Dad was the last thing Pamela wanted to hear, and she grudgingly put her signature on the temporary agreement. The divorce would be final in six months, making it late September before the marriage was officially dissolved, and autumn seemed a lifetime away. But numerous details, including child visitation rights and the ever-explosive issue of monetary support, would still need to be resolved, and no one expected those negotiations to be uncomplicated.

There was one bright spot amid all the gloom: The celebration of Kaitlin's first birthday. From the moment Pamela and Paul had separated, everyone, but especially Mother, worked to make the transition into a new environment as smooth as possible.

"The only world this child has ever known is crumbling around her, and I want her to know she's not being abandoned," she made clear. "Her sense of trust has been severely damaged by all the upheaval. Kaitlin needs to know there are people who love her dearly and that she can depend on." Making good on her promise, she hired extra help at Past Treasures Antiques so she could care for Kaitlin at least two days a week, and Michelle would watch her the rest of the week.

As Kaitlin's first birthday approached at the end of March, Mother decided the celebration should be fun and special, so we set about planning a "Sesame Street"-themed party for family and neighborhood children.

Three days before the party, Mother breezed into the company office unannounced. My mother exuded supreme confidence, elegant in a black wool sheath, her London Fog topcoat hanging casually from her shoulders as she warmly greeted the employees she knew around our office. When we were out of earshot, her voice took on an incensed tone, and a scowl creased her forehead. "I need to talk to Paul about Kaitlin's birthday. Is he in?"

"No, he's at the Lakeland Hills development. What's wrong?" She followed me into my office, and I shut the door, attracting the attention of his secretary, Linda, and several others. A closed office door had come to symbolize another crisis brewing in the pot.

"Pamela called me this morning. She must know about our birthday celebration for Kaitlin on Saturday. She's demanding Paul let her have Kaitlin for the weekend."

I walked around my desk, absentmindedly searching for my coffee cup. "She has to be doing this out of spite, since it's not her weekend to have Kaitlin." I spied my cup behind a stack of manila files; it was cold to my touch, and I fed the remaining liquid to the sprawling ivy plant on my credenza. "Paul has Kaitlin 90 percent of the time, and now Pamela is demanding visitation changes?"

"Of course, she's demanding the change to harass Paul and put a damper on plans we've already made," Mother replied, throwing her coat across a chair. "As the mother, Pamela still has the upper hand, and if she wants to make things difficult, she will."

I opened the sliding doors of the credenza, removing a Pierson Properties coffee mug, handing it to Mother. "Paul should be back shortly. There's nothing we can do but wait and have a cup of coffee on it."

We had not finished our first cup before Paul's loud, distressed voice preceded him down the hallway. Leaving my office, we followed his rapid-fire orders to Linda. "And call Bill Johnson and tell him we need to talk about the drainage problem. Today."

Furiously scribbling notes, Linda replied without looking at Paul, "Bill's at his cabin up north, so he might be hard to get a hold of."

"I don't care; we need to get this resolved now."

I sensed Paul's abrupt manner signaled deeper problems. Whenever he was under stress, the tension rose noticeably in his voice, and he rushed on in overlapping sentences. He had not even noticed Mother and me standing behind him. I called out, "Hey Paul, Mom and I need to talk to you for a minute."

Having closed the door halfway, Paul's head jerked in surprise. "I don't have time to talk to you right now."

"It's about Kaitlin's birthday," Mother interrupted, gliding past Linda's desk into the office. "Pamela called me this morning."

I pushed the door shut behind us, Paul retreating behind his desk.

"I've already talked to her, and there's been a change of plans," he spoke anxiously. "We're still having the party, but we're celebrating it together."

"Paul, she has never taken an interest in that child until now," Mother said, incredulous.

"Look!" he growled at the two of us, slamming a drawer shut. "I don't want to hear about this anymore! I'm tired of fighting with Pamela and all of you. I just want this damn birthday party over with, OK? Let's just do what she wants."

"You're gonna regret this," I said, irritated at Paul's spinelessness and his attitude toward Mother.

Paul was infuriated, stomping to the closed door. "Shut up, Kay. Just shut up!" He flung the door open wide, silently waiting for us to leave.

"Think hard about this," Mother calmly whispered in Paul's ear. "If you're this enraged now, I guarantee you it will only get worse."

* * *

The party was rescheduled at a Chuck E. Cheese, which was noted more for its games and attractions for children than its pizza. The shrill glee of the kids pierced the air as they requested brass tokens allowing them entry into rides, video arcades and playrooms. For the adults, this meant being especially eagle-eyed in tracking the paths of mobile children, while trying to stomach pizza having the taste and consistency of cardboard. At the center of the restaurant stood the towering space tube, a contraption of slides and rooms filled to the ceiling with vividly colored balls, into which Ruthie, Sam and several others immediately disappeared.

Exploring the surroundings with her first wobbly steps, Kaitlin appeared overwhelmed by the cacophony of bright lights, music and blasting video games. Since Kaitlin was too little to enjoy the games and rides, I wondered what Pamela's intent had been in insisting on sharing the baby's birthday, except to make Paul and the rest of us look bad and start a round of infighting.

"We're still a family," Pamela cooed to arriving guests, "despite what Paul may have told you."

"Pamela, we're getting divorced," Paul answered with ragged exasperation. Still mumbling under his breath, he turned toward me. "This was a huge mistake."

"Yes," I replied. "You've got to start standing up to her."

It was not the answer Paul wanted. "Don't start, OK?" Paul threw up his hands and shook me off, heading to the table where most of the adults congregated. The evening was already beginning to unravel as Pamela and her friend Lula Faye Simmons, a busty Southern blonde who was the ex-wife of one of our sales associates, moved off by themselves to the smoking section, an ice-cold pitcher of beer between them.

Ron and Sandy Baker had been invited and brought their 14-month-old son, Jake. Sandy felt uneasy—she hadn't seen nor heard from Pamela since she had moved to Rochester. "We think Jake has a crush on Kaitlin," Ron confided as they made their entrance into the organized chaos of the party. "He adores her."

Since she'd learned about Paul and Pamela's split, Sandy also harbored pangs of guilt believing she was partially responsible for bringing them together. Even with assurances from our entire family that no one could have foreseen the future, Sandy dwelled on past events, convinced that Pamela had been trolling for knowledge on Paul's family and history, carefully plotting her attack.

"I wasn't going to come tonight, but Ron insists I have nothing to be worried about."

"Which you don't," I answered. "And the kids have a great time together."

"I'm completely baffled. Part of me thinks Pamela was setting us up, while another part of me nags that it's not right to treat her as a pariah. Maybe I should at least acknowledge her," she said, more to herself than to me. Excusing herself, Sandy walked across the boisterous game room to the table where Pamela and Lula Faye smoked an unbroken chain of cigarettes.

I couldn't make out Sandy's comments, but Pamela's response exploded over the noise. "What's your fucking problem? It's only been nine months!" she spat, blowing a cloud of smoke directly into Sandy's face.

If Sandy voiced any sort of comeback, it was lost among the din. Walking back to our table, her face was flushed, clearly on the verge of tears. Sandy sat with her back to Pamela and choked out the words, "Well, that was a mistake."

I reached over and took her clenched hand. "Pamela isn't worth shedding any tears over. You were only trying to be gracious and civil, and she reacted like the psychopath that she is." Over Sandy's shoulder, I made stinging eye contact with Pamela, who mouthed, "Fuck off." It was the first time I fully realized her psychopathic tendencies.

"Will you excuse me?"

Pamela must have assumed I was planning a confrontation; she forcefully stubbed out her cigarette and tossed her hair as if prepping for battle. Instead, I ignored her and found Paul and Mother. "Let's get this party underway, shall we?"

"Everyone's not here yet," Paul said, shaking his head. "I don't want to piss off Pamela. It's bad enough as it is."

I raised my hand between us. "Pamela's insulting the guests, and she and Lula Faye are on their third pitcher of beer. Let's get this over with before they're completely smashed."

"I agree," Mother said. "This is out of control."

Just gathering the children together to sing a round of "Happy Birthday" took several minutes, as we had to pry them from every nook and cubbyhole.

"Why are we doing this now?" Pamela demanded when she saw the plans were being altered without her consent.

I was about to answer, but Mother intervened. "It's getting late, and people need to get home."

Mother got the party underway by presenting Kaitlin with her first birthday cake, as the group sang "Happy Birthday."

Too small to sense the rigid body language between her parents, Kaitlin sat between them in the high chair, a "Sesame Street" party hat crowning her small head. She accepted the Ernie and Bert birthday cake by tentatively plopping a hand in the middle of it. She was fascinated by the wrapping paper more than the presents and overwhelmed by all the attention and picture-taking.

"I want a picture of all three of us," Pamela announced unexpectedly. A prickly silence descended over the adults, everyone expectantly waiting for Paul to respond.

"No, Pamela. *We're no longer a family*," Paul said with loud emphasis. Pamela was obviously furious. Mother had already started matching coats and children, and we began bidding everyone good night.

It was well past 9 p.m., and Kaitlin had fallen asleep on Mother's shoulder, exhausted from all the excitement and activity. I had been watching the amount of beer consumed by Pamela and Lula Faye, preparing to stop Pamela if she insisted on driving back to Rochester with the baby.

"I'm too tired to keep Kaitlin tonight," Pamela surprised Paul. "You take her."

"Good," Paul answered, relieved. "Do you want me to bring her next Friday?"

"No, you keep her," Pamela said nonchalantly, and with a final drag on her cigarette she and Lula Faye were out the door, leaving the rest of us to clean the party room and pack up the presents.

Michelle had headed home with Ruthie and Sam, while Jack stayed behind to help clean up. "That was a disaster," he said, gathering discarded paper plates and cups.

"I'm sorry, OK?" Paul started whining in a woe-is-me tone, but Mother's angry voice stopped him.

"I don't ever want Pamela overruling our plans again," she said, deftly balancing a sleeping Kaitlin at her shoulder while helping dispose of the trash.

Paul fidgeted in embarrassment, staring intently at his nervously tapping shoe, but Mother would not let him off. Still holding the baby, she grasped his face by the chin with her free hand and looked him directly in the eye. "Next time, you tell your ex-wife she is not welcome."

* * *

The birthday party fiasco kept the saga of Paul's divorce a fresh topic and one of speculation at the office. Enough conversations were overheard for us to know that opinions were being bandied about, and I was reminded of the warning Dad said often as we were growing up: Like it or not, we exist in a glass cage, and every triumph, foible or weakness eventually will become common knowledge among our employees.

I decided to surprise Mother for lunch one afternoon in April in an attempt to put some distance on the situation. The brick building housing Past Treasures Antiques was one of many specialty shops, restaurants and other businesses and offered a dramatic view of Wayzata Bay and Lake Minnetonka. I arrived with sandwiches and found Mother unpacking several boxes that lined the front counter. "Hey," I said as the chiming of the bell heralded my entrance. I could see the sleek silver coif of Mother's hair bobbing just below the counter. "Thought you might like company for lunch."

As she rose to greet me, her fury was evident. I placed the food at a table, removing my coat, and Mother made a sweeping gesture over the partially opened boxes. "Pamela must think we're fucking idiots!"

I can almost count the number of times I've been speechless, but having never heard my mother use the word "fuck," I stood there open-mouthed, staring at her as the rage spilled forth. "I've just been to the Antique Attic in Rochester, and guess what I found?"

I still said nothing, shocked by Mother's outburst. From amid wads of crumpled newspaper she removed a blue-tinted pitcher with a lily motif. "The basin's in the smaller box," she directed briskly.

I peeled back the tape, opening the second box and removing the basin, setting it next to the pitcher on the counter. "Pamela must've needed the cash," I said, able to finally speak.

Mother stepped back from the counter, arms tightly folded across her heaving chest, reiterating, "Clearly she thinks we're stupid! I should have suspected something when Thelma from the Antique Attic called me. I mean, Pamela was living in Rochester, so it was convenient for her. But it never even dawned on me."

My head ached at the incoming stream of bad news. "Pamela screwed Paul out of most of his worldly possessions. How much did Thelma pay for this?"

"Well, Thelma never overpays for anything. She gave her $1,300. It wasn't until she saw Pamela's driver's license that she recognized Pierson as the last name. That raised a flag, and yesterday she called me."

"What's in the other boxes?"

"Ten other fairly expensive pieces. A couple of cookie jars, a cherry band pitcher and some Nokomis vases."

"All the stuff she insisted on taking to make her new apartment 'homier,'" I said.

"I wonder if she planned to sell it all along or if she's just desperate for cash," Mother said, a bit calmer now. "I suppose it doesn't matter."

I took a deep breath and slipped a comforting arm around Mother's waist. "Tim and I kept those discarded wedding gifts in our basement for months, maintaining that Pamela would eventually want them back. I feel like we've really been duped."

Mother sighed deeply, giving my hand a squeeze. "Don't beat yourself up. She's not worth it."

We stood there amid the clutter of the boxes and wads of paper, silently clasping hands, looking over the array of pottery.

"I need to eat something," Mother announced.

"That I can help you with," I said, taking the sandwiches from the bag. "I've even brought us some dessert."

"Good. I hope it's chocolate."

"Brownies," I said, taking the first bite of my sandwich. Both of us hungry, we concentrated on our food for a few moments. "How much did Thelma charge you for repossession?"

"She was very fair. I paid what Pamela had sold them for." Mother paused to take another bite of food. "Now I wonder whether we should tell Paul."

"We should," I said emphatically. "He'll wonder what happened to all the Red Wing pottery, and he'll find out sooner or later. I don't think anything Pamela does will surprise him any longer."

Mother poured Coke into her glass, the fizzy soda crackling over ice cubes. "I'm probably being overly protective of Paul. I feel like we're constantly barraging him with bad news."

"Well, we are," I said. "But not telling him won't make it go away."

chapter 16

MAY 1999

It was several months after asking Pamela for a divorce that I noticed Paul was hightailing it out of the office by 5 p.m. at least three days a week, something he had never done in the past. When I questioned Jack about it, he was his usual evasive self.

"Can't say that I've noticed any difference in Paul's routine. Maybe he can't leave Kaitlin at day care past a certain time. But if it bothers you, why not ask him?"

I should have known it would be a waste of time to query Jack, and I let the matter drop. I was attempting to schedule an early evening meeting for Paul and me the following week when the matter surfaced again.

"The only time that Ron Baker could meet with us to finalize the marketing plan for the Riley Heights development is the Wednesday before the Memorial Day weekend at 5:30. That work for you?"

Paul was shaking his head. "No. I have a standing appointment on Mondays, Wednesdays and Fridays. There's no other time?"

I tapped my pencil in frustration against the calendar I held in my lap. "We're running out of time here. We don't have a fall launch without a marketing plan. Can't you be a little more flexible and change your schedule?"

Paul fidgeted with his glasses, taking his time before finally facing me squarely. "I'm in AA, Kay, and I've been going to meetings at least three times a week. I've been attending this one for about a month. I'm really comfortable with the people, and right now I don't think I'm in a position to miss any meetings."

Seeing Paul's contrite face before me, a swell of emotions washed over me. I felt rather dense that I had not caught on, yet I was relieved that Paul had taken it upon himself to acknowledge his problem. Once his admission soaked in, however, I realized I was also upset at having been cut off from the process, which in turn made me ashamed of my pettiness.

"That's wonderful news, Paul. What meetings are you going to?"

He inhaled a deep breath, happy in releasing his burden. "I've been going to the ones sponsored downtown at Harbor Lights. There are meetings every night, but I've committed to those three."

I felt the creasing of my brow. "Wouldn't it be better to attend meetings closer to home?"

Paul smiled, knowing what I was thinking but too embarrassed to say. "You don't think I belong at the Salvation Army mission?"

"Well," I said, trying not to sound condescending, "what do you have in common with the people at that location?"

"You mean, just because I have a job, a family and a roof over my head? Kay, the only thing that separates me from these guys is luck. Just like them, I'm an addict, I'm broke, and without Mom and Dad I'd be out on the street, in the very same situation they're in."

Slumping in my chair, I followed my brother's every word. I had forgotten an important point: Drug abuse harbors no prejudice or class distinction, no bias toward age or sex. Chemical dependency is a destructive force of equal opportunity, and it had taken Paul's gut-level honesty to remind me of this fact.

"Oh man, Paul. I was being a narrow-minded bigot, and I owe you an apology. If these are the AA meetings that are the most beneficial to you, then that's what's important."

"It's OK. But I do believe I could be any one of those guys, and I need to remind myself of just how little separates us," he said with a weighty sigh. "I never want to forget that."

Paul's face softened, the most relaxed I had seen him in a long time. It struck me that I had neglected another point. As a pastor's wife and recovering alcoholic I was forgetting that the kinds of people Paul was referring to were the same downtrodden souls Christ had surrounded himself with. I silently berated myself; I was in no position to judge.

"Let me talk to Ron and see if we can't come up with a better option," I said at last, zipping my leather calendar case closed.

"I'd really appreciate any flexibility they could give me."

We rose from our seats. Paul shifted some papers across his desk, and the only sound was our steady, rhythmic breathing. I walked to the other side of the room and gave Paul a hug. "I'm really proud of you. This is a decision you won't regret."

There was a tremor in his voice. "Thanks, Sis," he said, engulfing me in a tight squeeze. "Your support means everything to me."

* * *

The signing of the temporary divorce settlement had really been only the beginning of the end. In constructing the case against Pamela, Dan Kinney brought forth taped conversations between Pamela and her current lover, plus sordid photographic evidence. While the information could not be used in a no-fault divorce state, it would be helpful in the custody fight.

Our attorneys suggested that all of us be present to hear and see the evidence Dan gathered. The lawyer in charge of the case, Jay Dobson, felt that since Pierson Properties was peripherally involved in the final settlement, we needed to view this information firsthand.

We met on a bright June morning in Jay's sprawling offices on the upper floor of a gleaming glass tower in downtown Minneapolis. As I admired the view, it struck me that it was almost three years ago to the day that Paul and Pamela had been about to embark on what we hoped would be a lifelong partnership. It all seemed so long ago, more like a dream than reality. Sadly, I turned my attention to the dealings at hand.

"Just so everyone understands—some of what you're going to hear is pretty crude. If it's too much, let me know," Dan said. He set the small tape recorder in the middle of the circular table and switched it on.

The word "hello," spoken by a male with a deep, husky voice, began the conversation. We understood this to be Billy Watts, an Army recruiter and felon whom Pamela had met in a Rochester bar.

"Wanna fuck?" was Pamela's blithe reply.

"You get rid of your old man?"

"Yeah, the millionaire's gone 'til Friday night."

"Meet you at your apartment?"

Pamela sounded slightly irritated. "No. We'll meet at my house on Tuesday, unless you can't get off work."

"I've got comp time." Billy hesitated momentarily. "What about your daughter? I don't want no kid around."

"That's what nannies are for. We've got the whole place to ourselves. We can fuck in every room."

Billy inhaled loudly, clearly relishing her offer. "Fucking in every single room. Mmmm." He paused abruptly. "You're sure your house is a good idea? We almost got caught last time."

"We got caught when I was sucking your cock in your office, you idiot." Pamela stopped unexpectedly, her tone less confident. "Tell me that was the best blow job you ever had."

Billy laughed nervously, lowering his voice to a near whisper. "Baby, you were fucking incredible."

I looked around the table, the awkward expressions of embarrassment present on everyone's faces. Just as I was about to suggest we stop, Dad intervened. "I think we've heard enough."

Dan switched off the recorder, and Jay began laying out the proposed final divorce settlement. "Even with this kind of evidence we need to be cautious. What Pamela ultimately wants is a stake in Pierson Properties' businesses. To avoid that, my suggestion would be to give her a substantial monetary settlement."

"So, Pamela's essentially rewarded for being a horrible wife and mother," I said, making no effort to hide my disdain. "Paul does nothing and loses everything, while she gets paid for history repeating itself."

"I don't care about the material stuff," Paul emphasized. "I just want to get on with my life."

"You can't let Pamela get off so easy," I said again. "Her ex, Doug Castleton, can attest that sleeping around, lying and twisting facts are all things at which she is very adept."

Jack had been silent, soaking in the discussion. "We have to look at the broader picture, Kay," he said, his piercing eyes aimed solely at me. "Giving Pamela a financial settlement is a lot less painful than waging a court fight to protect our business interests."

"And don't forget the child-support issues," Dad added. "That alone makes this situation much more complicated than what Doug Castleton experienced."

Apparently, no one got my point, and I felt dejected. "I understand all that," I responded tersely. "But why hand Pamela a big, fat settlement when she destroyed the marriage? And as far as child support, Kaitlin is just a bargaining chip. Pamela doesn't want Kaitlin; she wants money, and there's not enough of it in this world for her."

Jay shifted in his seat, turning to face me. "Which is why it's most imperative we keep Pamela away from the business by providing a settlement that will be acceptable to her."

"No amount of money will ever be acceptable! Doesn't anybody here but me get this? Once we give her any sort of financial support, it will never end." I realized too late I was nearly shouting.

Paul's growing agitation manifested itself as he absentmindedly fiddled with his glasses. "I just want Pamela off my back. Give her what she wants and be done!"

My frustration was audible, the hissing sigh through my lungs loud and long. "Fine. I give up."

Dad stepped into the role of mediator. "Think about it this way: We don't want to back Pamela into a corner over money, because there's no telling what she'll do. Everyone understands what you're saying, Kay, but Kaitlin is also a priority."

"Are we going to take some proactive steps or just talk about it?" I said, my hands falling limply to my sides.

Dad shot me a look of stern annoyance, one I had not witnessed since childhood. "Kay—"

Jack averted a family argument by interrupting. "There are a couple of different things we can do. First, give Pamela a substantial monetary settlement, similar to alimony, to keep her away from our business interests. Second, with the child-support payments, keep tight tabs on expenses, being vigilant the money is used only for things Kaitlin needs."

Jay cut in. "As I've said, I think it's in your best interests to make her comfortable. That will create difficulties in Pamela coming back for more money."

"I dunno," I replied, still skeptical.

"Don't be so negative all the time," Paul said, the curt tenor of his voice growing louder. "I have a daughter who I want to make sure is taken care of."

There were many responses I could have made, but I chose to keep them to myself. I was losing this battle, and it was not worth continuing the fight. When discussions turned to how much the financial settlement should be, I found myself tuning everyone out. Some figures were tossed about—$500,000, $750,000, even $1,000,000. Coupled with all the material possessions Pamela had come away with, I just did not want to hear it. Nothing concrete was decided that day, but I knew eventually Pamela would get her money.

chapter 17

The summer months remained the busiest time of year for the business, and the home buying and property management areas continued to gain momentum as the decade ended. On top of finalizing Paul's divorce, Pierson Properties, like companies all over the world, was working through the Y2K dilemma. To avoid the possibility of our computers crashing as the millennium rang in a few short months away, new compliant computers were purchased. The added expense and installation only increased everyone's anxiety.

It was mid-July when my new computer arrived, and problems loading the software caused me to fall behind in completing a marketing brochure launching our newest apartment complex, Willow Woods. Jack requested changes in the design; after several days lost dealing with IT issues, I was eager for his input on the revisions. He was engaged in conversation on the phone. Rather than intrude, I walked out into the lobby, where I came face to face with Pamela.

"What are you doing here?" I asked, the curt words tripping out of my mouth before I could rein them in.

"I don't know why you're always so rude to me, Kay," she said with an arrogant flip of her hair. "I have an appointment."

"With whom?"

Caught in our crossfire was the receptionist who, while incredibly proficient, liked to gossip, and Paul's situation provided ample opportunities. I realized too late that this conversation was apt to be repeated, as the receptionist followed every nuance like a fierce match of tennis.

"Terry Rasmussen's showing me some apartments, as if that's any of your business," Pamela said.

After all the time and money expended moving Pamela to Rochester, and the discovery of her true life as an adulteress party girl, I didn't bother concealing my disbelief. "You're leaving your job with the Mayo Clinic?"

Pamela's body gave off mixed signals. Her posture stiffened, but she flashed her sweetest smile. The receptionist hung on every syllable, as Pamela tossed back her hair with that damn flip. "I'm moving back to the Cities to be closer to Kaitlin," she replied loudly, her voice honey sweet. "I've accepted another job at a lab in the east metro. I had to take a cut in pay, but it's worth the sacrifice to spend more time with my daughter."

My better judgment prevailed. Rather than fire off what would surely be a snide reply, I simply said to the receptionist, "Would you please tell Mr. Rasmussen that his 2 o'clock showing is here?"

"Certainly, I'll buzz him right away," she replied, punching the extension. Pamela's chilly stare met mine, and our conversation ended in my crisp statement: "Terry will be with you shortly, Pamela. Congratulations on the new job." I smiled, without waiting for her response. I briskly entered Jack's office, where he had finished his call.

I closed the door and leaned against it, my hands positioned behind my back, clasping the brass knob. "What the hell is she doing here?"

"She, who?" he asked in what I was sure was one of the few times he'd been caught unaware.

"Pamela," I said, the jagged words spitting out.

"You are really mad, aren't you? Have a seat."

I refused to budge, rigidly remaining at my post. "What. Is. She.

Doing. Here?" I asked again, each word forced and deliberate.

"Kay," Jack said in the kind of endlessly patient parental tone he used with Ruthie and Sam, "she's here to see an apartment."

"You knew she was coming?"

"Terry Rasmussen told me."

"Jack, I'm telling you, if Pamela rents a place from us, it will be nothing but trouble. I wouldn't wish her on our closest competitors."

He threw up his hands. "Hey, I wish she'd rent with anyone else but us too," he replied sincerely. "But we can't discriminate, Kay, you know that. That's all we'd need, for Pamela to say Pierson Properties refused to rent to her."

I knew the law but found this an ominous development. "She will absolutely drive the staff nuts," I said.

"She hasn't actually rented anything yet."

Leaning back, my head knocked against the wooden door. "Where's she looking at apartments?" I said at last, gazing up at the swirling plaster patterns of the ceiling.

"Willow Woods."

"Shit!" I abruptly realized that I had left the new copy at the receptionist's desk. I jerked my head forward, meeting Jack's eyes beyond his desk. "I was bringing you the revisions when I ran into her. Let's finish this. I know what our legal obligations are, but you'd better hope she lives somewhere else. Otherwise, she will make our lives a living hell."

"Let's see what happens. If she makes unfounded complaints or is a bad tenant, then we can take measures to evict her," Jack said diplomatically. "But otherwise, Pamela can live wherever she wants."

* * *

On the July afternoon that Pamela was viewing apartments, Paul was out of town on business. When he returned two days later, I fully expected him to be outraged. While I had pegged the correct emotional response, I had grossly miscalculated to whom he would direct his anger.

"Goddamn it, Kay, why do you always have to antagonize Pamela? Can't you just be civil to her?"

"Be civil to her? Paul, are you out of your mind?" I was nearly screaming at him, standing stiffly behind my desk, my fingernails digging into the wood. "This is the ex-wife who's attempting to screw you and the rest of us out of everything we own, remember?"

"I don't give a damn about that," he replied, clearly infuriated. "Every time you talk to her, she calls me, pissed as hell. It's like you go out of your way to make her mad! Instead, you just make more trouble for me."

Furious words spurted from my mouth. "I will not be blamed for Pamela's deviant behavior! As far as her calling you, don't take her calls! Stand up to her, Paul! Stop this vicious cycle of always giving in to her."

"You—you have no idea what it's like dealing with her," Paul stuttered.

"Oh, I know exactly what it's like fighting with Pamela. But I won't let her roll over me, Paul, and neither should you." I moved from behind the protective barrier of my desk, confronting my brother at close range.

His clenched fists were reddening. "That's so easy for you to say! You don't have a baby caught in the middle. Pamela can make things extremely hard for me, especially with custody issues."

"God help me, Paul, if you don't stop handing Pamela every goddamned thing she wants, I'll strangle you. You weren't the one catting around Rochester. She deserves to pay dearly for her sins!" I yelled.

"You are so goddamned sanctimonious and vindictive! Whenever things don't play out the way you think they should, you get pissed!

Stay out of my life!" A whoosh of air blew into my office as he opened the door; the shelves of the bookcase rattled as he slammed it forcibly shut.

"She's affecting all of our lives!" I screamed after him, but Paul was storming down the hall and out of the building, leaving my words to fall on the ears of nervous employees huddling once again in the hallway.

I sat down hard in my chair, the depth of my fury exhibiting itself in short, terse breathing and the shaking in my hands. Stinging tears sprang from my rage, and I remained alone at my desk, oblivious to the concerned faces drifting past my office. For the first time, I genuinely believed Pamela's real intent was not just monetary; it was the destruction of our family. At that moment, I knew she was succeeding.

* * *

As Tim and I were finishing supper that evening, Mother called, asking if either one of us had heard from Paul. "I haven't spoken with him since he stormed out of my office," I replied flatly.

"I heard the two of you had quite an argument," she answered. "You really need to avoid those kinds of confrontations at the office. It just sets everyone to talking about our personal affairs."

Mother's apparent willingness to hold me responsible only revived my ire. "Paul initiated it. He's crazy to think I'd ever kowtow to Pamela."

"Well, I don't want to start another disagreement. If you hear from him, call me please." There was a lengthy silence at my end. Mother was asking, "Kay, are you still there?"

"Yes, I'm here. It's Wednesday, so he's probably been delayed at his AA meeting."

"I know he has AA, but he's usually home by 7:30. If he's running late or has a change of plans, he always calls to let us know."

"Meetings can be pretty intense and run long," I said, trying to shed my irritation and be helpful. "Is Kaitlin asleep?"

"Yes, I put her to bed about 8:30."

"If Paul's not home in the next hour, call us. We'll just have to wait."

As I hung up the receiver, I felt a guilty tinge of responsibility. "I hope Paul hasn't done something really stupid over this fight," I said to my husband.

"Sounds like you had a pretty nasty row."

"Nasty doesn't quite do it justice," I said, shaking my head. "Paul is furious with me for being rude to Pamela when she unexpectedly came into the office. And you know what? I don't care. I stick by my gut feelings that Pamela is setting us up for more trouble."

"You do need to be wary about how you approach her," Tim replied, always the diplomat. "Pamela isn't the one that looks bad."

The circular clock hanging over the sink read 9:15. I heard the distinct tick-tock, which I never noticed unless I was running late or worried. Although Tim disapproved of my smoking, it was a habit I picked up when I first got clean, and I always came back to it like an old friend when stressed. This was one of those moments. I kept a pack on hand for such emergencies. I found them buried in a dresser drawer and carried them outside onto the front porch. I did my smoking here on a wrought-iron bench, thinking, processing and slowing down. I puffed vigorously, watching a luminous pearl moon rise in the still-light northern sky. Nervously contemplating where the hell Paul might be, I swore I could hear the annoying ticking of the kitchen clock.

My deepest fear was that our quarrel, coupled with Pamela's constant assault, had sent Paul spiraling into abysmal despair. Going on a bender would be the last thing he should do, but from experience, I knew it might well be the first.

At 9:45, the phone clattered to life, and I grabbed the receiver without a hello. "Is he home?"

"No, Paul's downtown," Mother answered, her distress replaced by distinct anger. "He's absolutely three sheets to the wind, and your father's on his way to get him. Can you and Tim meet them and bring back Paul's car?"

"Yes," I said, barely able to speak. "Where is he?"

"On 11th Street, one block off Nicollet Mall. Given the shape he's in, the location could be wrong. But I told him to turn off his car and stay put until your dad got there."

"Shit!" I shouted as I slammed the receiver into its cradle. "Paul is smashed, somewhere downtown. We need to go help Dad bring him home."

We drove the 20 minutes to downtown Minneapolis, and I vowed that I would gladly put Paul out of his misery when I got my hands on him. "Enough is enough. He needs professional treatment. Tomorrow, we confront him and check him into an inpatient program."

"Let's get the whole story first," Tim said, far too reasonably.

Downtown, crowds of people were enjoying the summer evening in several outdoor cafés along the mall, and strains of classical music drifted across the block. I realized Sommerfest was in progress at Orchestra Hall, a celebration of the warm weather featuring German delicacies and nightly entertainment. The fading notes wafting through the air indicated the performance was ending. I hoped Paul had listened to Mother and had not ventured far. Searching the crowd anxiously, we passed a mosaic of faces, but none were familiar. Several minutes passed before Tim caught sight of Dad's taupe Mercedes pulled alongside the curb near the WCCO television building. Maneuvering our car next to Dad's, I noticed Paul's dark blue Jeep Cherokee parked crooked and pointing the wrong way along a one-way street. We spotted them out on the sidewalk, Dad supporting his wobbly son and attempting to walk.

"Hey, Sis!" Paul greeted me with a slobbering grin and a hard slap to Tim's back. Drunk, but keen enough to sense I was fuming, he made a clumsy attempt at regaining my good graces. "Oh, Kay, don't be upset. Let's not fight anymore. I had a very bad day, so I went and had a little drink," he slurred his words together, making a shaky gesture with his thumb and index finger to represent the "little drink" he'd had.

"You're lucky the cops didn't pick you up for a DUI," I snapped. "You'd get disbarred. Give me your keys."

"Here," Dad said, placing the cluster of keys in my outstretched hand.

"I'll help you get him into the car, Bill," Tim said, as he took Paul by his other arm to steady him.

Weaving back and forth, barely able to stay upright, he was still trying to make up. "Oh, I hate it when you're mad, Kay. Let's be nice." It took both Dad and Tim to keep him from toppling over.

"C'mon, sport," Dad said, guiding Paul toward the open back door of his car.

At the Jeep's door, I saw one wheel had jumped the curb, stopping inches from the base of a parking meter. The more I thought about the stupidity of his actions, the more my rage intensified. No quarrel was worth putting his life and that of his child in jeopardy. Starting the engine, I was ready to engage in hardball tactics and force Paul to face reality. I brought the wheel to the street with a loud thud and made an illegal U-turn, following Dad's dim taillights with Tim close behind.

A few minutes behind the others, I parked Paul's car in the garage. He was giving Mother, Tim and Dad a stammering explanation when I entered. Paul advanced, arms open wide, for a hug of forgiveness. "Sis-sy!" he said slowly, drawing the word out, but I stopped him.

"Where the hell have you been?" I said, the flat of my palm meeting his bulky chest.

Realizing his attempts at reconciliation were fruitless, Paul stared at me hard, his hazel eyes wet and glistening. "Let's not fight anymore," he said forlornly, slowly shaking his head.

"Should I make some coffee?" Tim asked.

"No," Mother interjected quickly. "We'll just have a wide-awake drunk. Bed is the best place for him."

When I protested, Dad slipped an arm around my shoulder, guiding me toward the great room, out of earshot. "Your mother's right, Kay. He passed out once in the car on the drive home."

"We can't just ignore this."

"We're not going to ignore anything," Dad said in a firm voice. "But Paul isn't worth a damn in this condition."

"Fine," I said irritably. "At least tell me what happened."

"After you and Paul fought, he went to his AA meeting and celebrated three months' sobriety. Afterward, he went straight to the nearest bar."

"Damn it! I knew this would happen."

Tim joined us. "A good night's sleep will clear everyone's head and put this into perspective."

"Exactly," Dad agreed. "Be here at 8 o'clock for breakfast."

"OK," I said. "But I want to discuss serious treatment beyond AA. Some drunks can succeed with only AA, but we all know Paul isn't one of them."

"Your mother and I agree. Tonight, however, is not the time to discuss it. Come prepared to make recommendations on the best treatment options tomorrow."

* * *

Sleep eluded me. While Tim slept through the night, I was wide awake, the argument with Paul replaying inside my head like an endless video loop. Even smoking failed to have its normal relaxing effect. Listening to the song of chirping crickets, I alternated between anger and tears, feeling as if flawed genetics had tainted Paul and me forever, leaving us unable to handle life's problems without a crutch, whether it was a drink or a cigarette. I wondered if Paul's situation with Pamela, with all its pressures and demands, would ever be rectified. I understood interacting with her was infuriating, and she was keenly aware of Paul's weaknesses and how to provoke him. But the fact remained that we would be forced to interact with her until Kaitlin reached adulthood.

Dawn crept over the horizon before 5 a.m. I had immersed myself in rehabilitation research for hours. When Tim awoke at 6:30 a.m., I was sitting in our study at a desk covered by neat stacks of materials on chemical dependency, the room warmed by the early morning sun. "You didn't sleep at all, did you?" he said, handing me a fresh cup of hot coffee.

"Thanks. No. My adrenaline kept pumping, and I never got tired. There are so many things to say to Paul. While he is ultimately responsible, there are factors he has little control over."

"You're more levelheaded than you were last night," Tim smiled.

"Yes. Being angry and alienating Paul instead of helping is the last thing I want."

"Don't be afraid to use a tough-love approach," he advised. "Regardless of genetic predisposition, Paul needs to understand and accept that alcohol and any other drugs cannot be a part of his life."

I showered quickly, and we were at Mother and Dad's before 8 o'clock. The aroma of coffee and freshly baked cinnamon rolls drifted through the house. We found Mother in the bright kitchen, dressed in a loose-fitting tunic and slacks, adding icing to the still-warm rolls. "Good morning," she said, her smile weary. "Either one of you get any sleep?"

"I couldn't; there's too much to consider," I replied. "Is Paul awake?"

"Yes, but I don't think he slept much. He's nursing a throbbing hangover. Tim, the coffee's just about made. I even have half-and-half this time," she said, gesturing toward the small carton on the counter.

"You and Dad giving up on the fat-free stuff?" I asked, removing two mugs from the cupboard.

"No. It was all I could find at the supermarket at 3 a.m."

"Looks like everyone except for Tim's been up most of the night. Paul say anything after we left?"

Mother finished frosting the rolls, reclaiming her mug. "There were many contrite tears," she said, leaning against the granite counter. "Paul has a problem that we must address. But we are all going to have to learn to deal with Pamela in a more diplomatic or constructive manner."

"It's hard to be civil or tactful when she's pulling out all the stops and constantly playing the victim. 'I took a pay cut, but it's worth the sacrifice,'" I mimicked.

Mother filled all our mugs with coffee, handing the cream to Tim. "She said that?"

"Yes. And loudly. In the reception area, so the entire company probably knows by now."

She did not reply, looking beyond me into the great room where Paul had appeared, clean but unshaven, in jeans and a white polo shirt. "Hi," he said, the word barely audible.

I said, "How're you feeling?"

"Slow," he replied in a voice thick with phlegm. "Real slow."

"Do you want something to eat?" Mother asked.

Paul walked into the kitchen to where Tim and I stood sipping coffee. "I'm so sorry ..." he began, but the sentence was unfinished. His arms enveloped me in the quivering hug of someone ashamed yet terrified of what the future held.

"I won't stand idly by and watch you destroy yourself," I said, pulling back from the embrace and searching my brother's anguished face. "You're worth more than that."

The door from the garage opened. Dad and Jack came into the house. He had collected Jack, dropping Kaitlin off at their house. Jack crossed the expanse of the kitchen, reaching Paul and grasping his shoulder. "Feeling OK?"

"A little queasy," he acknowledged, "but it's my own fault."

Ceramic mugs clanked together as Mother set them on the oval table, and I carried the coffee pot and the folder of treatment information into the dining room.

"Coffee for everyone?" Paul shook his head "no" and we gathered.

Dad was the first to address Paul, realistic yet authoritative. "You no doubt realize after last night that AA alone is not enough to keep you from drinking. As your family, we feel it's in your best interest to discuss and settle on other alternatives." Paul nodded his head in mute acknowledgment. "Your sister has some thoughts on possible treatment programs."

Torn between coming across as the know-it-all recovering addict and being too soft, I faced Paul across the cluttered table. I cleared my throat, taking a quick sip of coffee as if seeking fortification. "Given the similarity of our drinking patterns, and the added factors of attempting to deal with Pamela, the pressures of your job, and essentially being a single parent, I believe the best choice for you is entering an extensive inpatient treatment program. Hazelden offers—"

"No. No. No." Paul voiced his rejection to this idea adamantly. The conversation already was being met with resistance.

"Let Kay at least finish," Dad said, commanding Paul's attention. "She knows what she's talking about."

"I can't be at an inpatient facility," he said emphatically.

If Paul wanted a battle of wills, I had the stamina to take him on. "Listen, Paul, I'm not going to bullshit you. You have a serious chemical dependency problem that requires attention at one level, but you also need psychiatric care to learn how to constructively approach your ex-wife, instead of always appeasing her. Hazelden has inpatient programs covering both."

His voice was on the defensive, nearly whining. "I know I have a problem, OK? But I'm not going into a treatment center far from home and Kaitlin."

Dad came between us, fixing Paul with a parental look that said, "I am only going to say this once." He shifted his body so that he and his son were eye to eye. "We will make certain that Kaitlin is taken care of, Paul. Your sister's right, you have a problem that Alcoholics Anonymous alone cannot solve. Hazelden is in Center City, which is only an hour away."

Paul remained awkwardly silent, and I wondered if he was going to shut us all out, in the same way he had done when Rachel died. Frustration mounting, I laid out the scenario. "It's true that we can't force you into a treatment program, Paul. But think about this: If inpatient treatment is the worst thing that happens to you because of drinking, you're truly fortunate. Why risk injuring someone or, worse, killing someone—events you can never take back—when you can stop the cycle before you destroy your life? Just answer me that."

Tears sprang to his red and puffy eyes, but he said nothing. Out of the dense silence, Tim's voice was reassuring. "Don't discount your sister, Paul. She's walked this road, and I can attest to how lucky we are. Had Kay not agreed to enter a treatment program and stopped drinking, we wouldn't still be married. In a very real sense, it was either me or the alcohol, not much different than the choice before you."

Instinctively, I reached for Tim's hand, feeling the soft stroking of his fingers against my palm. Paul seemed genuinely surprised by this revelation. I finished our story. "That's right. Tim said, 'Either you get treatment, or this marriage is over.' Did he play hardball? You bet. But getting and staying sober gave me my marriage and my life back, which was far more important than the fact that I'd never drink again." I stretched my hand, placing it on Paul's knuckles, which were clammy to my touch. "Take the chance on sobriety before you're forced to solve this."

He wiped away a tear on his sleeve. "It's not that I don't want treatment, because I know I'm a drunk. But an inpatient program is out of the question. There are other options I'm willing to try."

Not satisfied with this answer, I said, "Like what?"

"I'm willing to enroll in an outpatient program and get counseling. But I won't be locked away, leaving Kaitlin to wonder where her daddy is and let Pamela use this against me."

Jack spoke. "I think you should take some time off from work. With all you're going through, there's enormous strain. You need to step back and focus on your treatment."

Paul again shook his head. "I want everything to remain as normal as possible. I can perform my job and join an outpatient program."

"Jack's right, Paul," Dad said. "The three of us can handle anything that comes up in your absence. Your health and well-being should be your priority."

Paul was emphatic that the structure of an outpatient program would be enough, a decision that left me feeling thwarted. With heavy cajoling, we convinced him that he would have to cut back on business if there was even a chance of this succeeding. If he were futile in reclaiming his life and keeping sobriety, his predicament would invade our lives even further.

Paul's insistence on familial support was my only consolation. I consented to being the person who would attend most of the program with him. But I needed him to know I would not cut him any slack. "I'll go along with this," I said. "But if you screw up, start blowing me off or start drinking again, I will do everything in my power to see that you're institutionalized. Believe me, I won't care how much you hate me or how deafening your protests are. You've got one chance."

"And your father and I will back up Kay 100 percent," Mother said in the same stern tone that had put the fear of God into us as children. "We'll try this on your terms, but one slip-up and you're in lockdown so fast you won't know what hit you."

Paul's expression was one of mounting fear. I hoped he was afraid, because if he was not, he would never grasp that he stood to lose more than just himself—he could also lose the family he so desperately needed.

chapter 18

We settled on an intensive outpatient program in Minneapolis. For me, accompanying Paul on his daily ritual into the world of chemical-dependency treatment was worse than I thought. It was like a delayed flashback, the sticky sweat and tremors haunting me long after the initial experience. In cramped rooms filled with the ever-present aroma of brewing coffee, we told our stories—the alcoholic forklift operator whose supervisor sent him to drug treatment each time he sacrificed another body part; the cocaine-addicted teacher making his sixth attempt at rehab; the teenager responsible for killing two classmates while driving drunk. The goal was the same for everyone—ending another day clean and sober.

Bolstering Paul's fragile self-esteem almost every night was difficult, especially given my own long-dormant feelings. Anger, dread and resentment washed back over me as if those emotions had only been buried in the short term rather than being truly exorcised. *Once an addict, always an addict.*

The attitudes of drug counselors tended to rub me the wrong way. I often found them to be condescending and humiliating. Most were, themselves, former abusers, and years of sobriety taught me that they too possessed the same dysfunctional flaws that program attendees had. But I was at a different point in my own recovery now. This time, I was compelled to call them on it. I recognized in Paul the initial acceptance of everything the counselors regurgitated, but by the end of the program, he was pushing back too.

Still, the process drained me. Every session lasted four grueling hours. We sat in a semicircle listening to addicts and their families recount stories of abuse, tragedy, loss and, in the best cases, redemption. Each night, Tim poured me into bed while my complaint remained the same: "I can't do this one more day. It's too familiar, too ugly, too devastating."

His response was forever consoling, always uplifting. "Yes, you can. This is the one concession Paul agreed to. You're not only giving support but showing him that he doesn't have to throw his life away."

"Yes. I can do this for Paul."

Day after day, following long hours of marketing strategies, campaigns, meetings and phone calls, I witnessed my brother expelling demons, weeping distraught tears, unraveling lies, and seeking to discover some semblance of who Paul Pierson was and who he hoped to become.

Jack, Mother and Dad attended sessions when they could, coming together to work through this not just as Paul's problem but as ours collectively. We heard traumatic stories of families torn apart by physical or sexual abuse, financial devastation, lost jobs and broken lives. Our family was far from perfect, but those stories shared by other families gave us pause. I never forgot how lucky we were.

In late September, Paul completed the program. All of us were exhausted. Now the difficult task of remaining sober began. As a former abuser, I knew as well as anyone the pitfalls and temptations littering any life of recovery. Statistics indicate that after a year, on average, only a quarter of alcoholics remain sober; for abusers using multiple substances, as Paul had on occasion, the rates fell even lower. We would be there offering support, but only he could control his fate.

* * *

Days after Paul's graduation from treatment, the divorce was final. The end of his marriage could help Paul maintain his new state of sobriety, certainly. I still believed Pamela should receive no financial support whatsoever, but Jay Dobson was adamant that making her financially comfortable would protect our business interests in the long term.

Jay cited other reasons for a larger financial settlement. Although Pamela rented an apartment from Pierson Properties, she shied away from the new, upscale and more expensive units of Willow Woods. Instead, she signed a lease for an older unit in East Bloomington, which she noted was way below her living standards.

"Money is tight for her," Jack informed me after the lease was signed. "Pamela's credit report came back with an OK rating but not great. She's got large credit card debt, putting Willow Woods out of reach."

"I still think this is a bad idea."

"As one of our tenants, we can indirectly monitor if Pamela has loud parties, constant traffic or unpaid bills and keep an eye on Kaitlin. There are definite advantages."

That fall Mother and Dad felt good enough about Paul's progress to keep plans they'd made a year earlier to tour Australia, which had been a lifelong aspiration. They departed the country in early October and would be gone five weeks. Michelle would care for Kaitlin when she wasn't teaching English at a local community college. The remaining days, Kaitlin would be at day care.

A week into Mother and Dad's trip, I was sick with a cold. Just when I thought I had it beat, it threw me reeling back to square one. I finally gave in to some well-deserved rest at home. Laid out on the living room couch under a quilt, I had the TV on and was watching a raucous guilty-pleasure talk show that everyone talks about but swears they never see. This was something about husbands and boyfriends accused of cheating and agreeing to undergo a lie detector test on national television to prove their innocence to suspicious wives and girlfriends.

I was more involved than I realized, as loud pounding on the front door startled me. Trudging off the couch, through the living room bay window I observed Michelle standing on the porch. I opened the front door to a brisk fall day. "Hi," I said hoarsely. "Making calls to the sick? C'mon in."

"Sorry, Kay. I know you're not feeling well. But I need advice."

Out of the bright afternoon sunlight, I could see the worry across my sister-in-law's face. "Have a seat," I said, clicking off the television. "I'm past being contagious, just tired." As soon as I finished speaking, I launched into a lengthy coughing jag. "With a terrible cough." Taking a long drink from a glass of juice settled my throat. "Can I get you something?"

"No, no, I'm fine," she said, waving off my offer and settling in an overstuffed chair. "I won't keep you. I just went to get Kaitlin at day care and was told that Annette had already come for her."

Propped up on the sofa, I asked, "Why would Annette be taking her?"

"I don't know. Here's what really upsets me. The head teacher told me that Annette made it clear she won't be bringing Kaitlin back anytime soon. I have no idea what's going on."

Lying against the pillows, my head felt as though it weighed 400 pounds. "Have you talked to Jack?"

"I called him on my cellphone, but it went directly to his voicemail. I tried Paul and got the same thing."

My head was throbbing as I slowly scrolled through the week's schedule. "What is today?"

"Thursday."

"At 1 o'clock they had a meeting regarding some land we're

interested in purchasing, I think at Jay Dobson's office." Grabbing the portable phone off the coffee table, I dialed Jay's law office. After I was put on hold and shuttled from person to person, Jack finally got on the line.

"Hey. What's up?" he asked.

"Michelle went to get Kaitlin at day care but was told she'd already been picked up by Annette, who wouldn't be coming back. Has there been a change of plans?"

"Not that I'm aware of. Hold on."

I could hear voices muffled by Jack's covering of the receiver. Cradling the phone against my shoulder, I told Michelle, "This was not part of the plan."

Jack came back on. "Tell Michelle to go on home. We'll have to make some calls and figure out why and where Annette has taken Kaitlin. Something's not right."

I switched off the portable phone. "They don't know anything. Jack said to go home."

Michelle ran a hand through her long auburn hair, emitting a heavy sigh. "I'll bet Pamela's behind this. Why else would Annette take Kaitlin?"

I thought about this for a moment. "Leverage?"

"Sure. She wants more money."

"Except that this would be kidnapping."

"Pamela would find a way out of that."

As Michelle was preparing to leave, the phone rang again. "Hold on, this might be Jack. Hello?"

"Kay, I am so sorry to bother you, but it's important!" Linda Petersen's voice was frantic. Lowering her words to a whisper, she said, "The Bloomington police are here, and they want to talk to Paul."

Michelle sat down on the couch, knowing instinctively this was not good news. "He's with Jay Dobson. Did you try there?"

"They've already left. What should I do?"

Jack and Paul were en route back to the office, so Linda needed to remain composed. "Offer them some coffee and—"

Linda cut me off in mid-sentence. "Wait ... Jack and Paul are here."

"When you get the chance, have Paul or Jack call me." Switching off the portable, I told Michelle, "The police are looking for Paul."

"What? This is surely Pamela, up to no good."

I shook my pounding head, at a loss to understand what was happening. "It must be a doozy if she's gotten the police involved."

* * *

In the evening, at the end of an exceedingly long day, Jack, Michelle and Tim gathered in our living room to hear Paul explain his quandary.

"During that late-summer warm spell in the last week of September, Pamela called me, complaining the air conditioning unit in the apartment was on the fritz," he relayed solemnly. "I told Jack, and a maintenance crew from our office removed the unit, had it repaired and returned it in a couple of days."

"It may have been our fastest repair ever," Jack interjected. "The on-site manager is terrified of Pamela because she complains so much," he said, giving me a knowing glance.

"While the air conditioner was being repaired, Pamela and I had a terrible fight. She wanted money for a cellphone, Timberwolves tickets and items for Kaitlin. When I told her no, she accused me of neglecting Kaitlin and a whole bunch of crazy stuff." Paul stopped talking, staring at his shoes. "Pamela kept hammering away, and I finally got so pissed that I told her if she didn't stop hassling me about money all the time, I was gonna ..." He hesitated and swallowed hard. "Kill her."

Tim, Michelle and I gasped in unison.

"Paul—" I started.

Jack interrupted, "It gets worse."

"I forgot about the fight, the air conditioner was reinstalled, and I went about my business." Pausing, he slowly shook his head. "Then today, the Bloomington police inform me they're investigating my threat to kill Pamela because she's become mysteriously ill."

"What?!" I said, bolting upright on the couch.

I caught my breath, Jack continuing the conversation. "Pamela is currently in the intensive care unit at Fairview Hospital, under police guard. She says she's having symptoms associated with carbon monoxide poisoning and that the air conditioner has been tampered with. Both the Bloomington and Edina police are involved."

Michelle shook her head in disbelief. "And they just believe her story?"

"When Paul threatened to kill her, Pamela was taping the conversation. With that 'evidence,' she has convinced her attorney and the police that Paul is a serious threat to both her and Kaitlin's safety. Annette has taken Kaitlin into hiding on the pretense of protecting her from Paul."

Tim soaked this all in, before asking Jack what I had been thinking. "Isn't eavesdropping a federal offense?"

"In most states, no, not if one of the two parties knows the conversation is being recorded," he explained.

Paul's voice filled with woe as he cradled his head in his hands. "I know I shouldn't have threatened her. She just keeps badgering me all the time, and I couldn't take it anymore."

"What about getting the air conditioner looked at?" Tim asked.

"Tomorrow morning at 10 o'clock the unit will be disassembled in the presence of one of the officers assigned to the case," Jack said.

"I definitely want to be there," I said.

Paul gave me a perplexed glance. "You're sick."

"I'm not dead; I just have a cold."

"Paul's right, Kay," Jack said. "The maintenance shed is the last place for a person with a cold."

"I want to see for myself that the air conditioner has not been tampered with."

Michelle and I locked eyes. "I'll pick you up at 9:30," she said.

Reluctantly giving in, Jack waved off his annoyance with a hand. "OK, OK. But you're not going to see anything exciting."

* * *

I bundled myself in a bulky oatmeal-colored wool sweater paired with jeans to ward off the crisp chill of the October morning. On the drive to the maintenance shed, Michelle and I exchanged theories of how, or if, Pamela was really ill.

"At first, Jack disagreed, but I think she has made herself sick," my sister-in-law explained. "When he thought about it, it made sense."

"She's a lab technician. She would have the knowledge to infect herself with something," I concurred.

"Exactly. Plus, in her new job she's exposed to dangerous viruses. She could infect herself with a virus that, while not lethal, could still make her quite sick and show up in initial tests."

"I'm willing to bet that once the air conditioner is cleared, she miraculously gets well before any diagnosis can be made."

When we arrived at the maintenance building, Jack was waiting out front, along with a tall, angular man sporting a thatch of copper hair. "This is Detective Sanders with the Bloomington PD. My wife, Michelle, and my sister, Kay."

"Nice to meet you," the detective answered, with a firm and hardy handshake.

Introductions exchanged, we made our way into the activity of the building, where our senior maintenance man, Jim Thompson, had set out the air conditioner on a yellow plastic tarp spread over a worktable. "This everybody?"

"Yep," Jack said. "We're it."

"Paul not coming?" I asked curiously.

"No. He's meeting with his attorneys."

Jim rolled up the blue sleeves of his maintenance uniform, exposing burly forearms, and began disassembling the air conditioner by removing the front. "What I'll be focusing on is the compressor of the unit, the drip pans and evaporator coils, looking for bacteria that could make someone ill."

"You won't find any," Michelle said confidently, zeroing her gaze in on Detective Sanders, "because Pamela is making this up."

Jack shot her a look of irritation that said, "Don't say anything in front of the police," but I found myself appreciating her willingness to vocalize what we'd both been thinking.

Reaching the compressor deep in the guts of the unit, Jim used a penlight to demonstrate as he clarified his findings. "You can see that the compressor isn't flaking or cracking in any way." Shining the light on the drip pan and evaporator coils, he continued, "And the drip pan and evaporator coils are clean. Like I said, people can get sick from mold and mildew in air conditioners because the drip pans and coils are a breeding ground for bacteria."

"That's correct," Jack confirmed, standing to the side. "What Jim is referring to relates to allergies and respiratory infections. Pamela may have an infection, but it's not from this air conditioner."

Detective Sanders, who had been taking copious notes of everything Jim said and did, ventured a question to us three. "You claim your ex-sister-in-law is fabricating these allegations. Why do you say that?"

"Because Pamela is pure evil," Michelle replied irritably.

"The divorce, custody and financial issues remain points of

contention," Jack offered diplomatically. "Pamela is constantly pushing Paul for more, especially where money is concerned."

Addressing us again, Detective Sanders tapped his pen on the pad of paper. "Why would Paul say he wanted to kill her? There's a tape with him making the threat."

"Pamela is extremely cunning and manipulative. She knew what buttons to push to get him to say exactly what she wanted him to say."

"Is it even legal for her to tape-record phone conversations in the first place?" Michelle asked the detective, her arms tightly crossed over a brown suede jacket. "It's so easy for her to twist words into something they're not."

"I don't make the laws, ma'am. That's something you need to ask your legislator."

Detective Sanders' pen scratched against the paper, and I wondered if he was noting our hostile comments for reference. Flipping the notepad shut, he directed his comments to Jim. "I'll need to take some Polaroids of the unit and various pieces for labeling."

"No problem, Officer," Jim replied.

Detective Sanders turned to face Jack. "Thanks for your cooperation. This may help shed some light on an otherwise unpleasant situation."

"No problem, Detective," Jack said, shaking his hand. "We want this resolved as quickly as possible."

"Ladies, thank you for your input as well," Detective Sanders said.

"You're welcome," I replied. Jack held the door for us as we made our way out of the building and into the sharp autumn air. "I told you there would be nothing to see," Jack said, casually eyeing Michelle and me.

I disagreed. "Oh, there was plenty."

"Unfortunately," Jack said, "Pamela still has the upper hand."

* * *

"Jack's right, you know," Michelle said, steering the Ford Explorer out of the maintenance parking lot. The tires kicked out a brown cloud of gravel dust. "That tape isn't the only problem."

"Which means?" I said, digging deep into my leather purse for a tissue.

"Even after we prove no one was trying to poison her, it will play out like I said. She will suddenly get well before a firm diagnosis can be made. Then we're left with a taped threat, which is still a threat."

Wiping my raw nose, I considered her statement. "Well, we could go see for ourselves just how sick Pamela really is."

"Great idea. But you're sure all this running around isn't wearing you out?"

"I'm up for this challenge."

Thirty minutes later, we stood in the lobby of the hospital, inquiring where we might find Pamela Pierson's room. Scrutinizing us over multicolored speckled reading glasses, the receptionist checked a computer screen. "Mrs. Pierson is in ICU on the fifth floor, but no visitors are allowed."

"Even family members?" I asked.

"No visitors" was the brisk response. "You'll have to come back once she's out of the ICU."

My hand at Michelle's back, I guided us toward the doors. "Thank you," I said pleasantly. Outside, traffic whooshed by on France Avenue, a few blocks from our office. "C'mon," I said, "there's a smaller entrance at the end of the block. There's no receptionist there."

"You're sure?" Michelle asked tentatively.

"Yes. Just act like you know where we're going."

On the fifth floor, we avoided the nurses' stations, gravitating toward a waiting room full of fatigued relatives reading dog-eared magazines. I assessed our surroundings while trying not to appear as though we were loitering, glancing up and down the hallways. "If there are armed guards posted outside her room, they'll be easy to spot."

"If someone asks where we're going, ask for the women's restroom," Michelle proposed.

"Got it."

We ventured along the main hallway, strolling the curve of the corridor. A few feet ahead, a lone Edina police officer stood his silent sentry. He looked to be about 35 years old and well over 6 feet tall. His taut muscles filled out the uniform; his sculpted face was devoid of emotion.

"When we get to her room, walk slower. Maybe we'll catch something from the door."

The two of us chatted quietly, ambling by the partially closed door and the officer, who was enduring what must have been a boring watch. As I strained my neck past the sliver of open doorway, a professional but firm voice startled both of us. "Can I help you, ladies?"

Michelle spoke, stuttering her response. "Uh ... yes ... um ... we're looking for the ladies' room."

"You walked right by it," the officer responded, catching me looking into the room. "Unless there's been a modification in orders, this patient isn't receiving visitors. You'll have to leave, but you can let the nursing station know you were here to visit."

Noting the officer's name tag, I smiled and extended my hand. "Good morning, Officer Swanson. My name is Kay Pierson-Scott, and this is my sister-in-law, Michelle Pierson. The woman you're guarding is our former sister-in-law, who was married to my brother Paul." The officer didn't interrupt, and I kept talking. "We understand Ms. Pierson is claiming someone poisoned her. We have strong proof her allegations are false."

His voice was courteous but firm. "I'm sorry, ladies, but you can't be here." Suddenly, a deep guttural moan came from Pamela's room.

"C'mon, Kay," Michelle said anxiously, tugging at the sleeve of my sweater.

"OK. But no one is trying to kill Pamela Pierson."

The wailing grew louder, and a nurse came jogging toward us.

"Pamela, are you in pain? What do you need?" she asked, entering the room, and in the brief instance before the door shut, I could see Pamela, pale but awake, tubes winding out of her left arm.

The officer was standing behind us, leading us away from the room. "I'll escort you to the elevator. I understand this may be emotional, but I don't want to see either of you here again or you'll be looking at loitering and trespassing charges."

I pushed the elevator button, the doors opened, and I stood facing Officer Swanson. "I realize you're just doing your job," I said.

He watched the doors slide shut, a ghost of a smile on his lips. Michelle sagged in the corner. "I am so sorry, but when he started asking us questions, I panicked."

"It's OK," I said, fishing in my bag for another tissue. "We've done our best to give the police real facts. We can only hope they follow up."

"I know one thing for certain," Michelle said, patting my arm. "We cannot tell Jack we were here."

"He'll unquestionably think we're making things worse," I replied.

* * *

In the time it took for us to leave the hospital and drive back to my house, Pamela had been well enough to contact her attorney, who phoned Paul's lawyer with threats of a harassment suit. When he found both Michelle and me later that afternoon, Jack was not as angry as we anticipated. "Pamela heard you two and started moaning in agony?"

"It was so contrived. As soon as Kay told the cop that no one was trying to poison Pamela, she started groaning and pushing the emergency call button," Michelle replied, brushing back a stray wisp of hair.

"It was all for show so that Officer Swanson would think she was in genuine danger."

"I'm not disagreeing. But Paul is frantic because there are people—powerful people—who do believe her," he said earnestly. "Pamela has also put the idea into her lawyer's head that you and Michelle were there to do her harm."

I rolled my eyes in disbelief. "Does Pamela's attorney really think I'd introduce myself to a cop if we were planning to hurt her? I will gladly speak to her lawyer."

"As much as I agree, Pamela has an amazing ability to manipulate the truth. I've come to believe it's her vicious gift."

Jack's observation that Pamela's talent lay in her capacity to twist the facts to her advantage struck me, as we had seen her exploit even the sanest of people. As Michelle had predicted, Pamela circumvented a damning situation by miraculously recovering in 36 hours. Her attorney backed off too, and while that was positive, there was still Paul's tape-recorded threat.

* * *

Instead of challenging Pamela's story and near-instant recovery, Paul's divorce attorney, Jay Dobson, refused to pursue the matter further, including the issue of the custody agreement being violated when Pamela's mother took Kaitlin from day care. Once Pamela's attorney dropped the idea that Michelle and I meant to injure her, Jay believed the whole matter should be forgotten. Even worse, Annette had essentially kidnapped Kaitlin, and Jay's acceptance of Pamela's tearful pleadings of ignorance as a "misunderstanding" released both her and her mother from any liability.

In the days after, Michelle would tell me, "Jack was willing to let

Jay give Pamela what she wanted in money to protect the company. But letting her get by with blatant disregard for the custody agreement has him really steamed."

"It should," I answered. "We lost an opportunity to put a stop to this nonsense."

"What's really sad is that this stuff with Pamela affects all of us," she said wearily. "Jack and I started talking about if we ever got divorced, and he made it clear he'd fight me down to his last dollar for the kids."

"Like you would ever take Ruthie and Sam into hiding."

"That's not the point. It's a residual effect of the circumstances. You actually begin looking at how you would react, regardless of how outlandish the circumstances may be."

It was sad but true. Irrespective of how diligently we tried to not lower ourselves to Pamela's level, her malevolence was tainting our own lives, the seepage so subtle that by the time anyone realized what was happening, the stain had already begun to spread. Paul's death threat worsened the situation.

Paul's visitation rights were restored before Mother and Dad's homecoming from Australia. In early November, we met with Dad and our lawyers to bring him up to speed. In the 20th-floor conference room of Jay's law offices, I was again captivated by the view that stretched across downtown and the mighty Mississippi River. There, bridges and old flour mills gave a hint of Minneapolis' past as a vibrant mill town where General Mills and Pillsbury had their origins.

Listening to Jay, I was struck by how easily he had accepted Pamela's explanation. "If she didn't realize she was in violation of the custody agreement, we can't really pursue this."

"She knew what she was doing!" I interrupted. "She pleads ignorance because it has worked for her before."

"Pamela certainly seemed surprised and upset at the misunderstanding," he said, startled at my outburst.

"Jay, she accused Paul of trying to kill her and tried the same ploy accusing Michelle and me of having nefarious intentions."

Dad watched our exchange without comment, but I could almost see the information being filed away like data on a computer. Within hours, Dad suggested Jay was no longer the man for the job. He strongly recommended that Paul hire new legal counsel for the approaching custody hearings, which were certain to push everyone to their limits. The next level of the battle had begun.

chapter 19

I would have passed over the story in the Metro/State section of the Minneapolis Star Tribune that Thursday morning, had Dan Kinney's name not caught my attention. Only a couple weeks after Pamela claimed to have been poisoned, life had returned to its hectic pace. In the article, the Minnetonka police, while searching for illegally taped phone conversations, had raided Dan Kinney's private investigating business.

Hurriedly scanning the piece, I read Tim crucial bits over breakfast. "Minnetonka police were tipped off by a former client, claiming Kinney was using illegal means to tape conversations. While searching Kinney's office, the police discovered other tapes that roused their interest, and they obtained a second search warrant. Those additional conversations have also been confiscated."

Tim's cereal snapped and crackled as he filled the bowl to the brim with milk. "Either a lot of people cheat on their spouses or eavesdropping is a bigger business than I thought."

"Think of all the people who've confessed to committing adultery to you."

"Nobody's ever admitted to wiretapping their spouse's phone."

"Not to you, anyway. But I have a sinking feeling this doesn't bode well."

By the end of the day, we learned that the second group of taped phone calls the Minnetonka police had found so interesting were, in fact, those between Pamela and her then-lover Billy Watts, the Army recruiter and convicted felon. The evidence in question was the same collection of tapes Dan had us listen to at the law office, providing Paul the proof that Pamela was committing adultery.

What none of us knew until the Dan Kinney story appeared was that Paul had not been truthful in his version of events—he had omitted crucial details. It opened my eyes to just how hard it is to know how people will behave when rapt with fear. Sometimes they perform tremendous acts of courage; other times, when forced to make a split-second decision, it's the wrong one.

We learned just how much Paul neglected to tell us as a more detailed account appeared the next morning under a headline heralding "Three men face charges of wiretapping." The story would be read countless times. "A Minnetonka-based private investigator and two of his clients face felony charges accusing them of conspiring to illegally wiretap telephone conversations of the clients' estranged wives. Dan Kinney, 50, a former Minneapolis police officer who owns a private investigator's business; Roger A. Larson, 37; and Paul C. Pierson, 33, all face charges of conspiracy to illegally intercept wire communications."

I met Mother for lunch at her antique shop later that afternoon to commiserate about this new development. The fading remnants of autumn cast a warm golden glow over the shop as the low sun streamed through the front windows. Spreading out our food on the table, Mother reminded me of a conversation we engaged in when Paul attended the Home Builders meetings in Dallas. "Remember, I called Heather at the house, but a man kept answering the phone telling me I'd called the wrong number. I thought it was Heather's boyfriend, but it turned out he was Pamela's boyfriend." Now the pieces were starting to fit.

In reading the story aloud to Mother, the scenario depicted was far more disparaging than we thought. "According to prosecutors," the article relayed, "Kinney and Pierson allegedly used the contents of the conversations to discover Pamela Pierson's whereabouts and the identity of people she was involved with." I folded the paper, sliding it across the table. "The recordings of Pamela were obtained illegally. And he didn't say a damn thing to us."

The creasing of Mother's brow showed the pained resignation of a parent forced to watch her child endure a terrible mistake. "Here's the worst part—if the case goes to trial and Paul's convicted, he'll be a felon and be disbarred."

"Jack's livid," I said. "When Paul was preparing to leave for the Home Builders meetings, he was acting strangely—disoriented and overwhelmed. He asked Paul point-blank if something was wrong, and Paul said no. Paul is a lawyer and should know better."

Mother rose from an antique oak chair to fetch napkins. "Besides being upfront with you and Jack, he should've told your father. Your dad would've told him in no uncertain terms that it could not be done without a judge's approval."

"Pamela's a cheating psychopath, but now the spotlight is on Paul breaking the law. He looks like a complete maniac, stalking his wife," I said, fretfully hearing my fingers tapping over the newsprint. "If only we could turn back time and erase her entirely from the Pierson family history."

Mother placed the napkins and tableware between us. "Based on what we know about Pamela, my gut reaction is that Paul's in more trouble than he knows."

No one was prepared for the attention Paul's alleged crime generated. As soon as the story became public, our phones rang incessantly for the entire day as worried friends, family and employees called to express their outrage and sympathy.

It would be months before the wiretapping case was tried, allowing plenty of time for gossip and rumors to smear my brother's reputation.

His rash decision might cost him dearly and provide Pamela with the advantage she needed to access the material possessions and financial support she was after all along.

chapter 20

Once the wiretapping story broke, it was difficult to get the day-to-day workings of the office back to some semblance of normalcy, but Pierson Properties could not be ignored. All the repugnant details that drove Paul to install the wiretaps were rehashed by employees over coffee in guarded murmurs, and they began referring to the disarray of his life in the terms of the soap opera "As the World Turns." The sad truth was that the chaos was indeed taking on the proportions of bad melodrama.

Before we knew it, the holidays were upon us and the office gossip had subsided; it was replaced by a festive air of decorations and strings of greeting cards festooning offices, which helped lighten the mood.

Paul brought Kaitlin to church for Christmas Eve services and opening presents at Mother and Dad's. He agreed to allow Pamela to take Kaitlin to her parents for Christmas Day. But after the holiday, to no one's surprise, Pamela lost all interest in her daughter, disappearing through the first week of the new year just as she had done the year before.

While many planned big parties for New Year's Eve that year, our plans to ring in the millennium were subdued. A gathering of 200 or so parishioners was coming together in the church basement to share a potluck supper. I arranged to bring a dessert, and as I finished frosting a chocolate sheet cake, I watched TV from my kitchen as the millennium began to roll in across the world. At 6 p.m., CNN broadcast the new century arriving in London as Big Ben tolled and dazzling fireworks exploded over the Thames. I felt a sense of anticipation of better things to come. I creased foil around the edges of the cake pan as Tim slipped behind me, putting his arms around my waist as we observed the festivities.

"Now that Paul's divorce is final and he's finished treatment, there's a lot to celebrate. We can all move forward and put the disappointments of the last few months behind us."

"But the real millennium doesn't begin until next year," I said, giving his slender arm a loving squeeze. "You told me so yourself."

"We won't quibble over the true calendar. Today it's seeing those numbers turn over that people look forward to. Paul, as well as the rest of us, can view this new century as the ultimate clean start."

I turned to face Tim, my arms draping around his neck. "Well, he's certainly starting off right. He's got the daughter he adores with him, and he's spending the evening with the Bakers. I'm optimistic that Pamela will find someone else to expend her hostile energy on, and we will become a distant memory." He pulled me close for a kiss.

Our evening was low-key, but we had fun. "Happy 2000!" banners were strung across the room, and balloons would fall from the ceiling at midnight. Everyone wore silly "2000" glasses and hats, Prince's song "1999" playing over the speakers. As we counted down to midnight, someone flicked off the lights, playing on the fear that had been drummed into people for more than a year—fear that a Y2K disaster would strike at the stroke of midnight. It did not, and we drove home after 1 a.m. with the world we left behind in 1999 still humming along in the 21st century.

We had plans with the rest of the family to spend a cozy New Year's Day at Goldenwoods. The sun glistened on newly fallen snow, and ice skaters, braving the cold, glided across the gleaming surface of Lake Minnetonka. Comfortable on the sofa and pillows in front of the big-screen television to watch my alma mater, the University of Wisconsin, play Stanford in the 86th Rose Bowl, I was not planning to digest anything more substantial than football scores and high-calorie goodies.

"There's something I need to tell you," Paul said as Ruthie, Sam and Kaitlin noisily played with their Christmas toys on the floor.

"If it's about work, it'll have to wait until after New Year's. My brain is still on vacation."

Plopping an overstuffed pillow on the floor next to me, Jack said, "Paul wants this to come from him. It's not that big of a deal."

I rolled my eyes. "This sounds serious," I replied, not interested in having this conversation.

"Not necessarily," Paul said, now blocking my view of the television so I was forced to pay attention. He took a deep breath, making me suspect it might be a big deal after all. "Pamela is buying a house through us, and the closing's on Wednesday of next week. When she comes into the office, try to not agitate her, OK?"

I stared at Paul's anxious face in paralyzed silence before finding the energy to rise from the floor in exasperation. "Don't tell me—she couldn't find a house with any other real estate agent in town."

"She started working with one of our agents," Paul said.

"Don't even give me the details," I said, annoyed. "She just had to come to us, and we couldn't discriminate. After all, you tried to *kill her*, so of course she'd want to buy a house through us."

"Kay," Paul began slightly perturbed, but Jack interrupted.

"How about being a little more accommodating, OK? Kaitlin will have a more stable environment when she's with Pamela, and we won't have the maintenance issues."

"No, this time the roof will just cave in."

"Do you always have to be so negative?" Paul griped. "Jack's right. There are some positives here."

Football and relaxation were suddenly now the furthest thoughts from my mind. "You guys just don't get it, do you? It's Pamela, for chrissake."

"Hey!" Jack raised his head with a stern parental look. "Watch your language in front of the kids."

"Sorry," I said flatly. I moved to within inches of Paul's face, lowering my voice to a whisper. "Where'd she get the money for the down payment? Annette and Donovan helping her out?"

Paul's face scrunched in uncertainty. "The divorce settlement was over a million dollars. She could pay for it in cash if she wanted."

I'd done a better job of blocking out the details of the settlement than I'd thought, having no recollection of the financial windfall Pamela had walked away with. I was far too annoyed to pursue this conversation; Paul's final words trailed after me as I departed the room.

chapter 21

"I can't keep track of all the men in Pamela's life," I told Jack. We were sitting in his office, taking a few minutes to catch our breath after a lengthy marketing meeting.

"Me either," he said. "But I'm not surprised."

"And this is an acceptable environment for a child not even 2 years old? I can't believe a judge in family court won't take that into consideration."

"Well, Paul's doing plenty to enable her behavior," Jack replied testily.

"What's that supposed to mean?"

"Shut the door." Jack cocked his head toward his office entrance.

I rose from my chair and quietly pushed the door closed, so as not to attract the unwanted curiosity of employees. I reclaimed my seat as Jack removed a manila file folder from his desk drawer and carefully laid out copies of what appeared to be an assortment of bills. Sitting at the edge of my chair, I leaned over the top of the desk, waiting for him to explain.

He selected a small pile of invoices and handed them to me. "These are cellular phone bills for a phone Pamela purchased. She got it by telling the sales clerk she was Mrs. Paul Pierson and to send the bills here care of her husband. It happened several months ago, and Paul's been paying them ever since."

Jack moved the first pile aside, choosing another. "These are credit card bills for gas, Dayton's, Target and VISA. But this one takes the cake," he said, placing a final invoice on top of the stack. "Here's a charge account Pamela opened at Kinko's Printing by claiming that she was a Pierson Properties employee who works directly with you."

Jack waited for my shock to register. "I thought you'd appreciate the irony in that one. I only found out because a new employee in accounting got suspicious and questioned the Kinko's invoice. Paul's apparently been having Linda pay the other bills on the q.t. for a while."

I did not know what to say or think. I moved the folder closer and flipped through the stacks of bills, which listed hundreds of dollars in charges at locations throughout the Twin Cities. The questions were tumbling through my head so fast it was hard to know what to ask first. I closed the folder, my nervous fingers tapping. "What on earth would possess Paul to pay Pamela's bills through the company—or at all, for that matter?"

Jack's chest heaved, and his fingers beat against the folder. Even in a crisis, he would not say much, but it seemed an eternity before he said anything at all. "I think," he said, drawing each word out, "that Pamela has something damaging on Paul, something that he believes is detrimental, and this is how she gets what she wants."

I sat back in the chair thinking. Then it hit me—so obvious I was almost embarrassed by its simplicity. "He must have been dealing drugs," I said plainly. "Remember in treatment, Paul admitted to using cocaine. They weren't just drinking, and the drugs had to come from somewhere. Even if he wasn't dealing, Pamela could say he was involved."

Rage slowly built on Jack's face, culminating in angry steel-blue eyes. "That's as good a guess as any," he said, "but I'll tell you one thing; this bullshit stops, and it stops now." His fingers patted a faster rhythm on the folder. "Pamela seems to think we owe her, and it keeps accelerating because she knows Paul's afraid of her."

I was at a loss. "How do we put an end to this once and for all?"

"I've already instructed Linda to cancel the credit cards, the phone, the works. I assumed you'd agree."

"You are correct," I said, ragged with exhaustion. I pondered the problem before us. "What's our next move? We can't just cancel all the credit cards and think she won't notice. Pamela will be incensed. Paul has to understand that paying any of her expenses on the company's dime won't be tolerated, no matter what he's done."

I expected Jack to respond; instead, his eyes drifted over my shoulder and beyond, as Paul's loud, jittery words tumbled over themselves, the door flying open as he barged into the room.

"Can one of you go pick up Kaitlin? I've got a 5 p.m. meeting. I'm already 15 minutes late, and I've canceled on this guy twice. It's across town, and I don't have time to get her."

"Sure," I said, giving Paul's flailing arm a sisterly pat. "I'll get her. Is she at day care?"

"No, she's at Pamela's, and I need you to take her home to Mom."

Since the New Year's revelation, Paul and I had tiptoed around the topic of Pamela, avoiding any mention of her. The day she closed on her house, I stayed away from the office, knowing I could not force the artificial civility that would be required of me.

Today, however, I believed I could encounter my former sister-in-law without open hostility. "I'll take care of it," I said.

Paul seemed to be pulling his body in different directions at once, part of him running out the door, another fumbling with his topcoat, and still a third firing off directions. "You know where Pamela lives, right? Ninety-first and Portland in Bloomington; the address is 9119."

"Paul, I'll find it. Go to your meeting."

I stood for a minute in the doorway, partially closing it again. "He's scared to death of Pamela. He can't stand up to her, so he pays off her bills instead, believing that will keep her from harassing him. We need to finish this conversation."

"We will, but not now," Jack repeated. "The house is on the corner; you can't miss it."

* * *

The yellow-and-tan brick bungalow was situated in the same neighborhood of East Bloomington as Pamela's old apartment. This was the older part of a suburb that had taken root in the early 1950s, just as suburbia was exploding across America. I found the one-story rambler with no trouble and parked in the narrow, snow-packed driveway behind a van I did not recognize.

It was February, the dead of winter, but the last measurable amount of snow had fallen a week ago. I was annoyed that the driveway hadn't been shoveled and I was forced to slog over the slippery walk and up to the porch. On my first ring of the doorbell, no one answered, so I pushed the button again. The door came open with a whoosh.

"Yeah?" An angular male face was framed in the screen door. I stood on the cement stoop, chills tingling across my back. I wasn't sure if they were caused by the cold or abrupt fear. I didn't answer right away. "What do you want?" the gravelly voice asked again.

I stared into eyes like muddy brown pools, peering at me from the doorway. His greasy brown hair was combed back into a pompadour. The dark goatee and mustache gave the sharp contours of his face a demonic appearance.

"Hi," I finally forced the word out. "I'm here to pick up Kaitlin Pierson."

"Hold on." The door slammed shut in my face, and I stepped back off the icy concrete porch, my heart hammering inside my chest. The male voice yelled, "Hey, Pam! There's some woman here to pick up the kid!"

Clapping my gloved hands together against the cold, I wondered how long I would have to wait. The temperature could not have been more than 10 degrees, and in a few minutes, I would be chattering with cold. I quickly decided that my being outside in the cold was a better option than being asked in.

When the door flew open, I expected to see Pamela. Instead, the male visitor stood alone, holding Kaitlin. "Here!" he said, thrusting my niece into my arms, along with a stuffed toy Elmo and a diaper bag. The sleeves on the dirty blue shirt he wore were rolled up, exposing protruding veins in muscular forearms. As he handed the baby to me, I caught a glimpse of a black-and-red skull tattoo.

"Hi, sweetheart. How's my girl?"

Kaitlin said, "Go bye-bye?" in a tiny singsong voice.

The door slammed shut, leaving me to balance Kaitlin as I struggled back along the snow-covered sidewalk to my car. I placed her in the car seat, the stench of stale cigarettes filling my nostrils, and I realized that Kaitlin's clothes and hair reeked of it. "Bye-bye," she said and smiled at me.

I brushed her cheek. "Yes, we're going bye-bye." On closer inspection, I noticed stains on her pink-and-white snowsuit and the matted texture of her dirty brown hair. "And as soon as we get to Grandma's," I announced, "we're giving you a bath."

* * *

"That's Pamela's current boyfriend, Robert something," Mother confirmed as we peeled off Kaitlin's dirty clothes and placed her in the bathtub full of warm, sudsy water. "I don't know much about him, except that he's rude and my granddaughter is always filthy when I pick her up."

I shuddered. "He gives me the creeps."

"I thought Paul had mentioned him, since he and Pamela are living together."

"He probably did. But there's a constant stream of men in Pamela's life. It's exhausting to keep track. Plus, I just don't care."

Kaitlin splashed happily in the water. Mother reached for a yellow plastic duck, squishing the soft sides together to make the toy squeak. "Quack, quack," Mother said with a smile, and Kaitlin squealed in delight. "That always makes her laugh. Quack, quack," she said again.

"I'll take her clothes and start a load of wash," I said, scooping up the grubby pile.

"Wash her snowsuit, too, would you? God knows the last time it was cleaned."

I started the washing machine and sorted through the diaper bag. Most of Kaitlin's clothes were covered with old stains, and everything smelled of cigarettes. I tossed all her clothing into the wash. Something began to bubble up. I was disgusted that Pamela saw Kaitlin as nothing more than a meal ticket. Even worse, I hated imagining my precious niece being exposed to the kind of people her mother had been associating with.

The washing machine kicked into the beginning of its cycle, and it occurred to me that at not quite 2 years old, Kaitlin was too little to understand and verbalize to us how her mother cared for her or the kinds of people she was spending time with.

Added to this mounting concern was my unfinished conversation with Jack and how we would confront Paul on his hidden expenditures. Mother was still talking to Kaitlin upstairs, and I knew neither she nor Dad would be pleased that Paul had again let Pamela threaten him. I had the vague outline of a plan. Now all I had to do was get Jack on board.

* * *

"Surprise is crucial," I explained, "because Paul won't have time to frame any excuses. He can't be trusted right now, and if catching him off guard doesn't force him to tell us the truth, it will be easier to determine if he is lying. But we need a remote location."

Jack suggested the clubhouse at one of our apartment complexes that was under construction. "There are some issues with the workout room that we've been discussing, so it's legitimate," he said. "Crews aren't currently working on the site, so it would give us privacy."

No one had informed Paul that all of Pamela's accounts had been canceled yet, which meant we would have to move quickly. Jack told Paul to meet him at the construction site early the next morning, asking him to bring a copy of the blueprints as part of the ploy.

Jack and I arrived at the clubhouse together in a single car. The February sun was brilliant against the mounds of snow; light streamed in through the windows. There were a couple of metal chairs, so we unfolded them and used a couple of sawhorses and a piece of plywood as a makeshift table where we placed the manila file folder.

A car engine alerted us to Paul's presence. Fumbling with the blueprints, he made his way inside to where the two of us stood waiting. Stomping the snow off his shoes, he looked up and was startled to see me. "Kay, what are you doing here?"

Jack smiled, motioning for him to come in and sit. "There's been a change of plans. Kay and I have something we need to talk with you about."

Paul started to protest, "But I thought—"

"Forget it," Jack interrupted. "We have more important things to discuss." There was no heat in the clubhouse, and the three of us sat in a semicircle, huddling in our heavy coats and gloves. Jack handed him the folder, saying tersely, "Kay and I would like you to explain these."

Paul slowly flipped through the bills, his discomfort increasing with each one. "These are some items Pamela asked me to get for her. If you're worried about my paying the company back—"

"That's only one of our concerns," Jack interrupted. "Start at the beginning. What the hell would make you think that paying any of Pamela's expenses was appropriate, not to mention that she's passing herself off as your wife. That's fraud, Paul."

"Well, I ... I ... you don't understand."

"No, we don't," I said, standing up. "Covertly paying the expenses of your ex-wife, who's trying to destroy your life, is insane. It's like you're afraid of her and think that paying for things she has no right to have will keep her off your back. But it won't."

"You don't know what dealing with her is like."

"Yes, we do," Jack said, sitting forward in his chair, hands dangling off his knees. "We've been dealing with her just as long as you have. We have had this conversation before, Paul, and both Kay and I have dealt with Pamela. But you need to come clean, because not only is what you're doing incredibly stupid, but you've also violated our trust. This business is not owned solely by you."

I knelt on the cold concrete floor, placing one hand on Paul's jittery knee. "Pamela is obviously holding something over your head. Whatever you've done or think you've done does not merit this kind of behavior. We love you. We want to help you. Please tell us the truth."

Puffs of Paul's breath came in short bursts in the cold air. His knee jiggled incessantly, and I could see his eyes widen in fear. He opened his mouth to speak, and only a few dry words squeaked out. "I ... this isn't ..."

Still kneeling next to him, I held his quivering chin in my gloved hand. "Paul, when you were married, were drugs being dealt out of the house?"

"No. No, nothing like that," he said, shaking his head. Paul inhaled deeply, his cold breath hanging in the air. "Pamela did cocaine, and I used once in a while; I'll admit to that much. But she didn't really start using heavily until after she moved to Rochester." He stopped to catch a breath and looked me in the eye. "I've been clean since treatment, which I'm sure you're wondering." He paused again, taking another breath. "It's not one particular thing she's holding over me. It's just that ... it's just that she never fucking quits. If I don't give her everything she wants, she threatens to take Kaitlin. Says that I'll never see her again."

From behind me, Jack said, "Anyone else threaten you?"

"Yeah. Her boyfriend, Robert Carter. He's told me he'd break my neck."

"When?" Jack asked urgently.

"I dunno. It's happened more than once."

I said, "Over the phone or in person?"

"Over the phone."

"And you didn't record it?"

"No, I—"

"Jesus Christ, Paul," Jack said, shaking his head in dismay. "You know you can tape it if you're on the call. You've got to document this. These are bona fide threats, and we can press charges."

I began pacing the floor to keep warm. "You have to keep track of any threats. This is extortion, Paul."

"You'll want to know I've canceled all the credit cards, the cellphone, the gas," Jack cut in. "You need to be prepared for the worst, because she'll be pissed when those cards are declined."

Paul sat silently, the constant shaking of his knee the only sound as it bounced the metal chair. He finally said, "When were the accounts closed?"

"Yesterday. We wanted to make a plan before you heard from her," Jack said, clapping his gloved hands together, "because you will."

I paced back and forth between my two brothers. "From now on, you've got to tell us everything that's going on between the two of you. As your business partners, all of this affects us, too."

Paul shrugged his broad shoulders. He stared at the cement floor, unable to make eye contact. "I know this was stupid, OK? I'm sorry. I just wanted her to stop."

"But she didn't," Jack responded forcefully. "You've made the situation worse. You think she threatened you before? She'll really try and put the heat on now." He cleared his throat in the increasingly cold air of the clubhouse. "Let me make one thing crystal clear—if you ever pay a bill of Pamela's again, Kay and I will take the necessary legal action to remove you from the company. If you think I'm bluffing, go ahead and try me." Jack paused for an icy breath. "Sure, a court fight would be acrimonious, but believe me Paul, Mom and Dad will back us."

Jack's harsh words registered in Paul's wounded face. "I understand," he said, trying to regulate the tremor in his voice. "I'm not trying to destroy the company. I can take out a loan and start paying the money back."

"We're not going to ask you to reimburse the company," I replied. "We want a vow of good faith that this will never happen again and that when Pamela or anyone else makes threats, we have evidence to go to the authorities."

"When she starts screaming about those closed accounts, you tell us. Every call or physical encounter is logged from now on. Maybe it's better if you don't talk to Pamela directly for the foreseeable future. She does not scare Kay or me."

Paul choked back tears, and my heart began to swell as his face wore the frightened expression of a little boy, not a man of 33. "I'm so sorry," he said again. "I agree I shouldn't be dealing with her right now."

"Please, Paul. Let us handle Pamela," I replied.

Rising from his chair, Jack extended a conciliatory hand. "You are still going to have to say no to her. Otherwise, this will never end."

Confronting Paul had been painful, but using company funds could not be ignored. As we left the clubhouse, I thought about Jack's comment—that if we did not start protecting ourselves and taking Pamela on ourselves, she would never stop. I began to wonder if the reality would not end up being much darker, an evil none of us could fathom.

* * *

The end of the day would not come before Pamela was on the phone demanding to speak to Paul. He alerted me she was holding on line three. I braced myself for what was sure to be a fierce confrontation.

I pulled a mini tape recorder from a drawer, switched it on and answered on the speakerphone, "Kay Pierson-Scott."

"I don't want to talk to you," Pamela hissed. "I'm calling for Paul. I need to talk to him right now!"

"I assume this is regarding the credit cards you've been using," I said succinctly. "All those accounts have been closed."

"This is ... this is none of your fucking business. I want to talk to Paul!"

"Credit cards that you have no right to use are most definitely my business."

"This is between me and Paul!"

"We owe you nothing," I continued resolutely. "The credit cards, the cellphone, the gas ... no more, Pamela. And by the way, the Kinko's account you opened using my name is also closed. You've committed fraud, and I will most certainly be seeking legal counsel."

"How dare you! You and your fucking family will not destroy me! I know what you are, Kay! I know what you all are! And you'll hear from my lawyer!"

"I'm sure we will. In fact, here's our attorney's number so we can get things rolling." I rattled off the digits. "We're not afraid of you, Pamela. Whatever you're holding over Paul, we'll find out."

"Fuck you!" she screamed and slammed down the phone.

The call ended just as I expected—rancorously. I rewound the tape and checked the recording. "This is between me and Paul!" It was a bit scratchy, but I got every word. As soon as I hung up, Paul was at my desk.

"What'd she say?"

"Jack's contention that she'd be pissed is an understatement. Pamela wants to talk to only you, and she'll be relentless," I said, probing my brother's hurt face.

"Look, I'm sorry, OK?" Paul replied in exasperation. "I didn't mean for this to get out of hand."

"I know you didn't. But the bottom line is that giving in to your ex-wife will always get out of control." I held up the small tape in the palm of my hand. "Starting with this, everything goes through our lawyers."

chapter 22

APRIL 2000

In my dream, the phone was ringing incessantly, but I was having difficulty searching out the noisy intruder. It seemed to fade as I got closer, then jingled gleefully from some distant hiding place as I hunted to no avail.

My world was shaking violently as I recognized Tim's soft but urgent voice. "Kay! Wake up. It's your mother."

"Tell her I'll call her tomorrow" was my groggy response. It was Saturday, and I just wanted to sleep in. I pulled the duvet over my head and heard his muffled voice—something like "I'll make sure she sees the paper."

I was already drifting back to sleep, but Tim was annoyingly persistent. "C'mon, sleepyhead; there's big news about Pamela's boyfriend in the paper."

Still half asleep, I said, "Good. Maybe he offed her." As I lay among the warm covers, my terrycloth robe landed across the foot of the bed.

"It could be in our favor" was all he said before I heard the thump-thump-thump of his slippers on the stairs. The door alarm beeped; it was switched off. I heard the front door open—he must be retrieving the paper from the porch—and quickly slam shut from a burst of early April wind.

By the time I slogged my way downstairs, the aroma of coffee filled the air. Tim looked up from the Minneapolis Star Tribune. "Pamela is keeping company with dangerous men," he said, the paper skimming across the table. The headline immediately had my attention: "Men charged with alleged pandering."

Sunlight streamed into the breakfast nook, and I settled against the white slatted back of the chair and started reading. "Two Minneapolis area men arrested Friday for allegedly soliciting a 16-year-old girl for prostitution and several sex offenses are awaiting charges.

"The men, Robert James Carter, 29, of the 9100 block of Portland Avenue South, and Daniel E. Burke, 28, of the 3100 block of Dupont Avenue South, were being held in the Hennepin County Jail on $500,000 full cash bonds, according to Chief Deputy County Attorney Lynn Carlson."

I felt sick, and the dropping of my stomach seemed unstoppable. Tim brought full cups of coffee to the table. "No wonder he gave you the creeps," he said, pointing to the next paragraph.

"Among the allegations contained in court documents filed in the case are that Carter had threatened to blow up a car belonging to a Hennepin County prosecutor, with whom he was angry after being thrown out of the prosecutor's office. Authorities said on Friday that police conducted search raids on Carter's home, vehicle and a vacant property he owns, as well as the home of Burke's parents."

The coffee was clearing the cobwebs from my head, and I absorbed each sordid detail. The paper's account went on to say that the 16-year-old in question had told her probation officer in September about a series of events set in motion the previous summer when, as a runaway, she had made her way to Minneapolis. Meeting Robert through a friend, he offered to get her work as a prostitute but not before having sex with him as a form of initiation.

The article recounted that on and off, over the next few months, Robert employed this girl, then 15, as a prostitute downtown, on Lake Street and in parts of north Minneapolis. In November 1999, Robert contacted her with various moneymaking schemes involving acts of bestiality, including having sex with a dog for $1,000, which she refused.

The teenager alerted her probation officer, and the authorities taped subsequent meetings between her and Robert. In those taped conversations, he and the friend discussed the girl having sex with a drugged woman while being videotaped and several other blackmail schemes.

From the moment I first glimpsed Robert's face, I was terrified. These were unbelievably repulsive acts, and the only consolation was the arrest of Robert and his friend after they connected with the teenager and drove her to another "job," which involved an unidentified man in the case, who had been seeking the services of a prostitute. The unidentified male was an undercover cop.

Once arrested, the depth of Robert's threat was made explicit with the additional items confiscated from him during a search by police: 3 grams of methamphetamine, $1,000 in cash and a loaded 45-caliber handgun.

I folded the paper and passed it to Tim. "So far, I don't see how this helps us. Just realizing that Kaitlin's been in the same house with him makes me sick."

"If they can implicate Pamela in any of this, Paul's worries about a custody fight would be over."

Savoring a long drink of coffee, I took back the paper, slowly rereading the article as my fingers mindlessly tapped against the crisp newsprint. "It leaves plenty of room for her to weasel her way out of a tight spot," I said finally. "I'm not making any predictions. We always seem to lose where Pamela is concerned."

* * *

In the hours after the lengthy criminal history of Robert Carter was detailed in the local papers, our family floundered, not at all sure what we should do. While Paul met with his attorneys to request an emergency custody hearing, the rest of us held our collective breath.

We pored over Robert's illustrious career, beginning at 19 with his arrest for robbery at a north Minneapolis adult bookstore. For that gambit, which also involved blackmail, he was sentenced to three months in jail on a reduced misdemeanor charge. In the years that followed, Robert always seemed to be in trouble, perpetuating any number of schemes involving drugs, sex and blackmail.

It was the reporting of two unrelated incidents that served as the impetus for Paul to pursue an emergency custody hearing. Robert was a peripheral figure in two murder-suicide cases that entailed the deaths of six people. In a 1995 case, a woman identified as Melanie Brown obtained a protection order against him. A short time later, she killed herself, the 2-year-old daughter that she and Robert had together, and another daughter from a previous relationship.

If this were not enough to cast a threatening pall of suspicion over Robert, the following year he was charged with a felony for allegedly providing a handgun illegally, which was used in a suicide pact between a 26-year-old woman named Lynette Lee and her 28-year-old boyfriend Scott Wills, both of Minneapolis. As part of the apparent pact, their 3-year-old daughter was also killed. Robert pleaded guilty to a misdemeanor.

Six people were dead, three of them children. The only common denominator among them was that they all had known Robert. Pamela was scraping against the underbelly, a steep plunge for the woman who had once demanded the best of everything.

* * *

Saturday's 6 p.m. newscasts all led with the arrest of Robert Carter and Daniel Burke, with no unsavory aspect ignored as reporters laid out the charges against them. Normally, prostitution would not be cause for such coverage, but the death threat Robert made against the Hennepin County attorney and his apparent willingness to carry it out sharpened the story's edge. News reports indicated that police also seized a live hand grenade from Robert's vehicle during their search.

At 10 p.m. we were transfixed again, but the ringing of our phone interrupted the broadcast. I answered the call, never getting a word out. "Turn on KSTP," Mother commanded. "They've got Pamela on video."

Flipping to Channel 5, we saw Pamela being led from her house by police, a coat shielding her face from the camera. She could try to hide, but the home's street address was prominently displayed in the background as a reporter discussed the scope of the raid. On the surface it looked like events were finally falling in our family's favor, but I reminded myself we were dealing with no ordinary person.

By Sunday morning, Paul's attorney had succeeded in obtaining an emergency custody hearing for the next day. The thought of returning Kaitlin to her mother that evening cast anxious gloom over nearly everyone. The entire family would meet to discuss what, if any, options we had. The hours slipping by like sand through a sieve, there would be precious little time to devise a plan.

We gathered at Goldenwoods immediately following church, congregating in the great room while the children occupied themselves downstairs.

"With bail set at $500,000 cash, Robert won't be going anywhere fast," Jack reasoned as some of us settled into sofas and chairs, Michelle and I sitting cross-legged on the Persian rugs carpeting the hardwood floor.

I made it known that I was not nearly as convinced. "True at the moment," I said, "but bail can be reduced tomorrow at the preliminary hearing."

"Not likely," Dad said. "The threat against the county attorney is serious; plus, the number of weapons confiscated gives credence to a higher bail. Factor in Mr. Carter's criminal history, and I don't believe that's our primary concern."

Mother waved past the current track of conversation, setting out a tray of snacks. "All I care about right now is the welfare of my granddaughter and whether we return Kaitlin to Pamela."

Dad said, "At this point, Pamela has not been implicated in any of her boyfriend's activities. We may have no other choice."

"But they were living together," I protested vehemently. "How could she not know?"

Michelle entered the kitchen, returning with the coffee pot, offering refills. "Pamela can say she had no idea what he was up to. God knows playing ignorant has served her well before."

Impatiently squirming on a sofa, Paul said, "I don't want Pamela accusing me of violating the custody agreement, yet I'm not willing to just hand Kaitlin over to her like nothing's happened. I'm damned if I do and damned if I don't."

Ever the mediator, Tim questioned him. "Does Pamela know of the hearing tomorrow?"

"Not that I'm aware of."

"Then my advice is to let her have Kaitlin as usual."

On the sofa, Mother visibly stiffened. "I have a real problem with handing my granddaughter over to that woman. If something should happen to Kaitlin, we will never forgive ourselves."

The arguing continued unabated, voices raised loud enough to attract the curious attention of Ruthie and Sam, who wanted to know if we were "fighting."

"They're just talking noisily," Michelle gently explained. "Like you guys when you're playing a game."

Worn out from playing with her cousins, Kaitlin toddled upstairs and fell asleep next to Mother, one red Elmo slipper still on, the other temporarily misplaced. Watching this blissful child asleep, oblivious to the turmoil of which she was at the center, I was gripped by the kind of clammy terror one experiences in only the most forbidding circumstances. Mother was right: If we made the wrong decision, our regret would be intolerable.

At 5 p.m., the debating still furious, the phone rang. Physically and emotionally exhausted from all the discussion, I answered without a second thought. "Piersons.'"

"This is Pamela. I'm coming to pick up Kaitlin at 6 o'clock." Her tone was blithe, as if nothing were amiss. Hearing her voice, my hand clutching the receiver dropped to my side. The conversation subsided and we could hear her shouting, "Is anyone there? Hello?! Say something, goddamn it!"

"Just a moment," I said and stuffed the receiver into a nearby drawer so not to be overheard. "Well, what's our decision?"

Our hushed faces searched each other for the solution no one seemed to have. Dad ended the silence, unruffled yet forceful. "I think Tim is right; we go ahead and give Kaitlin to her mother as planned, without letting Pamela know anything out of the ordinary is afoot. Unless someone else has a better idea."

The first sound to be heard was a deep and pained sigh escaping from Mother's lips; she was noticeably unhappy with this choice. Paul, nervous and twitching, his hands clasping one on top of the other, said quietly, "As much as I hate to let Pamela have her, it's the best of equally bad options."

Jack seconded the opinion. "I agree," he said as Dad carefully monitored each of us for a dissenting response.

"OK," I replied. "It's not what I was hoping for, but I'll go along with it."

Michelle and Tim both responded with silent nods of their heads.

Everyone's attention focused on Mother. Her rigid arms folded crosswise and eyes rimmed in red told us exactly where she stood. "I'm sorry," she said, "but I can't agree to this, no matter how bad the alternative might be."

"Mom ..." Paul went across the room, enveloping her in a hug, but she broke free, her open hands pushing him away.

"I'm outvoted, and I understand that," she said. "I just want to voice my opinion."

Pamela's muffled screaming distracted us, so loud that we heard her even with the receiver in a drawer. "All right, then," Dad said, giving us one last glance before retrieving the phone. Pamela's tirade was now clearly audible. "You can pick Kaitlin up at 6:30," he told her coolly.

"Six o'clock was the agreement," she protested, and Dad said again, "Six-thirty. We'll be waiting for you." There was no goodbye. He hung up, turning to face all of us. "This won't be easy, but when she gets here, I don't want any shouting or name-calling. Surprise may be the only thing we have going for us tomorrow. Everyone has to be civil."

Mother and Paul set about getting Kaitlin dressed, while I took charge of packing her clothes and diaper bag. Dad, Michelle and Tim began clearing away the food, and Jack went downstairs to help Ruthie and Sam put their toys away. As everyone went about their business, the mood was one of quiet trepidation. This might be the best decision in the end, but it did not make us any less miserable.

The doorbell chimed at precisely 6:30 p.m. From the upstairs window, I could see a shiny white Camaro, the sports car Pamela had traded the Volvo for as she was shedding the last vestiges of marriage. I could hear the low hum of the engine running. I finished packing

Kaitlin's things, hearing her singsong voice ask, "Go bye-bye?" I hoped the handoff to her mother would not be as traumatic as it often was.

The front bell rang a second time, and I realized that no one was rushing to greet Pamela. We had made our decision, but no one was happy with the outcome.

With a click of the lock, the front door opened, Dad greeting her. "Hello, Pamela. Beverly is bringing Kaitlin down."

I heard Kaitlin's soft chatter as Mother carried her into the foyer. From the top of the staircase, clutching the diaper bag, I noticed everyone had drifted into an arc, the stark image of a pack of wolves cornering its prey. Pamela was unfazed. She stood by the door and gave her blonde hair her signature arrogant flip.

Mother silently passed Kaitlin to her. Realizing she was about to leave the warm, familiar surroundings of Goldenwoods, the baby's bottom lip trembled, tears beginning to well.

"It's all right, sweetheart," Paul said, quickly coming over to comfort his child. "Mommy will take good care of you."

"Da-ddy!" Kaitlin said in distress.

"Sweetie, you'll go with Mommy, OK?" As I listened to Paul, I thought that he did not sound very convincing.

"You're fine," Pamela told the baby sternly, jerking her body in the opposite direction of Paul. Kaitlin continued to cry and twist and reach for her daddy.

"It might be easier if I come out to the car with you," he offered.

Dad curtly intervened. "You'll have Kaitlin back here Wednesday evening?"

Pamela surveyed the semicircle of our pack, multiple sets of steely eyes studying her intently. For the first time, she may have detected the depth of our abhorrence, but she maintained an aura of nonchalance. "Say around 6 o'clock?" she replied.

"Make it 5 o'clock," Dad answered firmly.

Her face hardened visibly. "I work until 5 o'clock," she said evenly, but Dad was unmoved.

"One of us will gladly pick her up from day care," he replied.

Pamela's eyes made one more sweep around the room. "Fine," she said, moving to open the door while steadying Kaitlin on her hip. Paul grabbed the handle and followed them outside. Without a word, Dad, Jack and Tim trailed behind into the moist chill of the April evening, no one bothering with coats.

Jack pulled the door shut and Mother turned toward me, her tears coming fast and furious. She had been stoic up to that point, but having to give Kaitlin over to Pamela was devastating. I hugged her close. Michelle offered her a tissue.

"Thank you," she said, removing her glasses and wiping away glistening tears. Mother stood between us, fixing us both with a gaze so fervent and fierce that I fought the urge to recoil from her hold. "If anything happens to that baby," she said, her voice quiet yet laced with bitter loathing, "I swear to God Pamela won't see another day."

PART FOUR

chapter 23

Robert Carter was arraigned Monday morning along with his cohort, Daniel Burke. The day had dawned cold and sunny against icy blue skies, and our family was restless, yet too tired to sleep or concentrate on anything but the most mundane of activities.

Paul and Dad set an early morning appointment with a new attorney, Bob Rolfson. Pamela had no indication of his request for an emergency custody hearing, and no one dared crow about the benefits of catching her unsuspecting. We had witnessed what we thought might be advantages crumble away before.

Jack and I arrived at the office together; our plan was simply to offer no comment. Linda immediately inquired where Paul was, and Jack appeased her curiosity by relating only part of the story. "Didn't he tell you he's meeting with his new legal counsel this morning? I'll bet he just forgot. He'll be in this afternoon," he said, offering a charismatic smile.

I had plenty of work to do, yet the reality of concentrating long enough to accomplish anything was remote. Through the morning, I found myself glancing at the wall clock every few minutes or toying with my watch to check the time. No amount of phone calls or interruptions could distract me, and I eventually moved myself into the conference room. I removed my wristwatch and put it in my pocket, focusing on writing copy for a brochure.

Just past noon, my brothers joined me. Paul had always worn his emotions on his sleeve, and normally I could decipher his moods before he spoke, but this time I could not decode what he was feeling.

I shuffled my papers into a neat stack. "Was the hearing granted?" I asked, both of my brothers seated across from me.

Paul laughed nervously. "I feel like I'm living that old joke: 'I've got good news, and I've got bad news.'"

"Start with the positive," I said.

His hands folded before him, Paul got to the point. "Well, Bob Rolfson has confirmed that the activities of Robert Carter have been viewed by the judge as extremely dangerous. He'll continue being held on a $500,000 cash bond for felony pandering and weapons charges. At least he'll have to raise the full half-million to be released."

I exhaled audibly. "And the not-so-good news?"

"We didn't get an emergency custody hearing. The judge didn't view the situation as urgent, so no hearing until Thursday."

My body felt like a balloon deflating. I wasn't sure how much more of this I could take. Every time we thought things were starting to go in our favor, there was someone else who believed otherwise. "What was the judge's rationale?" I asked.

"Though the judge in criminal courts feels he is dangerous enough to keep in jail on an unusually high cash bond, family court doesn't feel he is a threat to Kaitlin."

"Especially now that he's in county lockup," Jack said.

This seemed odd. "When the police searched Pamela's house, they didn't find evidence connecting her with Robert's crimes?"

Paul shrugged his broad shoulders. "They removed the answering machine on which she says, 'Robert and Pamela aren't home right now,' so she can't deny he was living with her. But whether they confiscated anything like illegal drugs or weapons, we don't know."

"Does Pamela know about the custody hearing?" I asked.

"Her attorney was on the phone to Bob Rolfson while Dad and

I were meeting with him," Paul said, his voice growing heavy with disappointment. "Pamela claims the charges against him have been trumped up and have nothing whatsoever to do with her," he said, slowly shaking his head.

"Of course she did," Jack replied facetiously.

"Her attorney brought up the Dan Kinney investigation too," Paul added. "Their angle is that our family has waged a continuous campaign to smear her reputation. Like someone with such great character would be living with a pimp."

I sighed and cupped my cheek in a hand. "Is there nothing we can do?"

Jack cocked his head at me. "Nothing. Man, Sis, you hate waiting for anything." He smirked. "Unless a miracle occurs and Pamela gives up custody."

Paul agreed. "And that is not going to happen," he acknowledged. "Dad wants to let the custody issues go through the attorneys. It gives Pamela less of an opportunity for personal attacks."

If there was one of my personality traits that tested me again and again, impatience was its name. Jack was being honest, but it felt like infinity would pass more quickly than those three days.

* * *

The story in Tuesday morning's paper focused on Robert Carter's long criminal past and law enforcement officials' elation at collaring him. He was being charged with three counts of felony pandering covering the arrangements he had made for the 16-year-old runaway to work as a prostitute; two other felony charges of possessing a weapon while pandering and carrying a concealed weapon; and finally, a misdemeanor alleging he had sex with the girl, who was a minor.

I found myself reading and rereading the articles, haunted by the fact that so many people, who all knew the same man, had wound up dead. Six seemed like an exceptionally large number, and I could not fathom why the police or district attorney was not examining these cases for every possible scrap of evidence.

The former journalist in me kept bubbling up. Obvious questions kept exploding in my head. I wondered why someone at either paper wasn't asking them. Who were the victims? How did Robert Carter know them? How had they died and when? Moreover, why were the authorities not interested that out of six dead people three were young children? Investigating a story like this could make a reporter's career, and in a sense, I was sorry I had left my career in media. The reservations would not stop coming, so I decided to try to discover the answers for myself.

The Southdale library was closest and one of the largest in Hennepin County. What I found tended to be small stories providing sketchy details, buried deep in the Metro/State section of the paper. Those facts gave credence to the idea that, at least in terms of newsworthiness, the victims had not registered much at all.

At the time of her death in the winter of 1995, Melanie Brown had filed two restraining orders demanding Robert Carter stay away from her and her two children, a 5-year-old named Violet and Anna, the 2-year-old whose father was Robert. When Melanie and the children were found dead in their garage, apparently by asphyxiation as they sat locked in a car, the deaths were ruled to be a murder-suicide. The investigation determined that Melanie had probably killed her children and then taken her own life. Although she had been treated for depression, her family remained shocked by her actions, viewing the term "murder" as much too harsh.

Melanie was working as a nursing assistant at Regions Hospital in St. Paul when she died. She was planning to go back to school and become a registered nurse, had her depression under control and appeared to have overcome the challenges burdening her life. Everything seemed on the upswing—the one exception was her difficulties with Robert being the father of Anna. Her family acknowledged those complications and that Melanie feared for their safety.

Had Melanie been so terrified of him that she became convinced death was her only protection? When questioned by the Minneapolis police, Robert revealed no grief for either his child or her mother. Her complaints were on record and a restraining order in effect at the time she died, yet police viewed him as only a peripheral figure in Melanie's life.

Less than a year later, the three deaths in October 1996 were equally chilling, and Robert was charged with his first felony. Here too, I thought the police were too quick to rule the deaths of Lynette Lee and her boyfriend, Scott Wills, as a suicide pact, especially given a gun belonging to Robert had caused their deaths.

Local papers reported that Lynette obtained the firearm from Robert, who was listed as owning a security business. Three days later, the bodies of Lynette, Scott and their 3-year-old daughter, Tanya, were found in Lynette's car. The vehicle was discovered in the western suburb of Shakopee, on the grounds of the Canterbury Park racetrack. What about a lovers' triangle in which an angry confrontation escalated into murder? If the child had been a witness, she too would be killed, leaving Robert the opportunity to give the scene the appearance of a murder-suicide. There also was the deserted location of the racetrack, shuttered for the season, and the fact of no witnesses.

Robert served a year in Stillwater prison for providing the weapon, pitifully little time considering the loss of life involved. No one interviewed at the time would say so publicly, but I wondered if because all the people involved were poverty-stricken—people whose priority in life was merely to survive—the authorities chose to write off both episodes and concentrate on crimes involving "productive" members of the community.

Robert's menace escalated in threatening to kill a county attorney, deemed a most worthy member of the community, and the police snapped to attention, pouring huge amounts of resources into cornering him. As I perused the news accounts, it occurred to me that the rest of his criminal history was mentioned only as an afterthought.

I was so enthralled by the scenarios and missing pieces that I seriously contemplated investigating further. There were interviews with family and friends of the victims, police who worked on the cases, people who knew Robert and a host of others whose lives might have crossed with his. I feared that delving into these discarded stories—now cold as winter starlight—to search for what I perceived to be the truth might cause more harm than good. Our efforts had to be on protecting Kaitlin. Any thoughts I had about mislaid justice were silenced.

chapter 24

Jack was not kidding about my possessing no patience. By Wednesday, it felt like the days were playing out in slow motion, the hours dragging by, minute by minute, in the endless interval leading up to this custody hearing. I needed a distraction and caffeine, so I headed for a favorite spot, Caribou Coffee. Leaving the bustling city outside, I entered the building, its décor offering a retreat reminiscent of a comfortable log cabin tucked deep into the northern Minnesota woods.

As I waited for my order, I heard someone shout my name from across the crowded shop.

"Kay!" It was Michelle, waving a slender hand above the crowd of business professionals and artisans. At a corner table, she sat next to her mother, an attractive and elegantly dressed blonde woman.

I joined them at the small table surrounded by cozy furniture. "Hello! What brings you to the coffee shop on this Wednesday afternoon?"

"Shopping," the two women responded in unison. "You remember my mom, Jeanne," Michelle said, making quick introductions.

"It's been a while," I said, shaking her outstretched hand. "Nice to see you again."

"We were just discussing something you may find very interesting," Michelle said. "You know my mom is an alderman on the

Richfield City Council. It turns out she's had personal experience with Robert Carter."

Instantly intrigued, I was all ears as Jeanne shared her story. "I recognized Mr. Carter's picture in the paper," she explained. "I realized that not even a month ago, the City Council had been asked to consider a proposal concerning his obtaining a liquor license for a vacant building he was planning to purchase and open as a dance club. One of our concerns was that the property is located off 66th Street, a part of town we're trying to revitalize."

"Here's the best part," Michelle casually interrupted. "Guess who his partner in this endeavor is?"

"I recognized Pamela," Jeanne continued, "and I of course knew that she and Paul had divorced. Pamela was introduced as Mr. Carter's business partner, and she was not at all shy about throwing the Pierson name around, claiming she had both the financial means and experience to run such an establishment."

"That's news to me," I said, sharing my disbelief with both women. "What happened to their proposal?"

"We turned it down," Jeanne confirmed. "As soon as we started investigating Mr. Carter's background, we discovered his felony convictions, so of course he can't be involved with an establishment that serves alcohol." She paused, taking a sip of her coffee. "Even if he weren't a felon, it's not the kind of business we want in town."

"Now that he's in jail, I don't think you'll have to worry about Robert Carter opening up shop in Richfield," I said, taking a long drink of my beverage.

"It's unfortunate that Pamela is still using your family's name," Jeanne said. "I'm not sure the other council members realized she wasn't part of your family until I told them. Her whole presentation emphasized having access to great amounts of money."

I cringed, stirring my coffee with a swizzle stick. Michelle asked, "Why is she still allowed to use Pierson as her last name?"

"I guess because of Kaitlin and paternity issues," I answered.

"Well, she milks it for every cent it's worth," Jeanne said, her voice taking on the tone of a seasoned politician. "Have Paul find out if he can legally get her to revert to her maiden name; otherwise, you have no idea what she's telling people. Unless they've followed the news, no one even knows she and Paul are divorced."

As we chatted, I realized I hadn't told Michelle about my research on Robert's criminal history. Sharing coffee with her and her mom seemed the perfect time to reveal my findings.

"I've done some investigating on those murder-suicide cases Robert was connected with," I said. "I'm curious to know why the district attorney hasn't pursued them more vehemently. There are six people dead, including three children. All had ties to Robert, either personally or through his businesses."

Michelle's eyes widened. "Do you think he killed them?"

"I don't know that he killed them, but he was definitely involved," I said. "Murder-suicide pacts are not that common, and to have one person involved with two seems highly suspicious."

Jeanne was quiet, deep in thought. "I agree. And now that I think about it, Robert had a relative who was involved with one of the police departments, but the name has completely slipped my mind."

Michelle swept a stray auburn hair away from her face. "It's almost as if the DA is afraid to pursue these cases against him."

"Earl Carter!" Jeanne blurted with a snap of her fingers. "I remember now. Earl Carter was either Robert's uncle or possibly father. He was a Minneapolis police officer, and in the late '80s he was fired. The charge was corruption, I think, but the bottom line is that Earl sued the Minneapolis Police Department for unfairly dismissing him. He never got his job back, and eventually the department paid a settlement, but only after he dragged it through the courts."

"That explains why the DA wouldn't touch Robert with a 10-foot pole," I said.

"And then some," Jeanne added. "No DA worth his political hide is going to get caught up in that kind of case."

"This keeps building into a more complex narrative, with so many disparate people connected to one another," I said, sifting through those very events in my mind. "Does your mom know about the wiretapping mess Pamela is dragging us through?"

"Oh, yes," Michelle said.

"Michelle mentioned that Paul was in trouble for recording Pamela's phone conversations, even though they were still married. Meanwhile, she records everyone else's conversations. It's definitely a law that needs to be reviewed."

"What I've wondered is how the Minnetonka police came across those tapes in the first place. It was almost as if they were looking for them."

Jeanne said, "It was a raid, if I remember correctly."

"Yeah," Michelle recollected. "But Kay's got a point. The search warrants the police obtained didn't involve Paul. They had to come back with a second warrant later."

"Hmm," was all Jeanne said, but I could almost see her writing mental notes to herself.

Michelle sat against the wooden chair, her penetrating eyes registering skepticism. "There's a story for you, Kay. How did the police 'just happen' to stumble across those tapes?"

I shook my head. "No, my reporter days are over. My life is in a completely different place now."

Seated diagonally from me, I saw a sparkle in Jeanne's vivid green eyes. "It never completely leaves your blood. It's the same with politics. Listen, I've got contacts in all the police departments, and I can find out what really happened with Earl's firing. It might provide your family with new or useful information."

"If it's not too much trouble," I replied.

"I'll have some answers in a day or two," she promised.

* * *

Dawn inched over the horizon into Thursday morning, and I had been awake for hours. I sat on the front porch in a fleece jacket with a fresh pack of emergency cigarettes, watching the smoke curling up against the cold gray of an early spring sky. I cycled through my routine of smoking, pacing, smoking, pacing—cloaked in dread at what this day might bring. The hearing was tremendously important to Kaitlin and Paul's welfare. But I couldn't shake the feeling that with the judge's opinion that no one appeared to be in immediate danger, there was only the slimmest chance of success. I was terrified of what Paul might do if we lost.

I toyed with the idea of joining Paul at the hearing, yet there was the risk of coming across as the overprotective big sister, which wasn't always appreciated. Instead, I went to the office as if it were an ordinary day. The latest ads for the Sunday paper were due to the Star Tribune by noon; a deadline would keep me occupied.

Deep into concentrating on the ad layout on my computer screen, I jumped at the knock on my door. Rotating in my swivel chair, I was surprised to see Dad, whose office was at another location in the western suburbs. "Sorry, Dad—I didn't hear you. Want something to drink?"

"No thanks, honey," he said, sitting down. My father was still strapping and handsome at 68, only a touch of gray at his temples. He held part of a rolled newspaper in his hands. I knew instantly what the conversation would entail. "I've had my limit of caffeine for today," he said and pointed to the ad layout on my computer screen. "Good, you're working on the Sunday ads—exactly what I want to talk to you about."

He unrolled the Pierson Properties ads from the last few weeks of Sunday papers, and I did my best to squelch my rising irritation. "I know we've had this conversation before," he began, "but I still don't understand why you're wasting so much space. You're paying good money for the ads, so why not fill up the page?"

"I understand and appreciate what you're saying about getting our money's worth. The other side of it, however, is that too much material makes our ads look crowded and confusing."

He shrugged his shoulders. "I can find exactly what I'm looking for."

"Yes, because you already know which houses are being listed. The average homebuyer doesn't want to be overwhelmed. We need to make it as easy as possible for prospective buyers to find the properties they're interested in. That means ads that are well designed and simple to follow."

Dad moved closer to the desk, making a sweeping gesture over the ad pages spread in front of us. "I don't have a problem with easy-to-find, but there's a helluva lot of extra space here. Jesus, Kay, the margins must be 2 inches wide."

"One inch," I said defensively. As I watched my father still speaking, I heard nothing. It was like looking at a television with the sound turned off; some things I could decipher, while others made no sense. We were arguing about white space, while Paul was begging a judge to allow him to keep his daughter safe.

Our debate went back and forth for over an hour, and as we were struggling toward another tenuous compromise, Paul tapped on the partially closed door. The hearing was over, and Dad and I had completely lost track of the time.

Sticking his head halfway in, he said, "Hi. Let me get Jack, and I'll tell everybody at once."

I looked at my father, prepared to end this impasse. "Thanks for bringing your concerns to me, Dad. Why don't we continue this tomorrow?" I suggested.

"There's no need," he replied with a smile. "In my opinion, too much space is a waste of money. But it's just that—my opinion. You and your brothers run the company now, and I'll respect whatever decision you make."

I was still in shock from his candid pronouncement as Jack and Paul began crowding into my office, pulling in chairs. I wondered if Dad's intention had never been to change my mind at all, but to provide a diversion to release the two of us from the stress of the moment.

No one said a word, the air heavy with anticipation. Paul then quickly came to the point. "Well," he said quietly, "the judge refused to alter the custody agreement."

My eyes darted first to Jack, whose staid face betrayed no emotion, then to my father's brow, crinkled in concern. "And the reason?" Dad asked.

"The judge did not believe there was enough evidence to indicate that Pamela is involved in any of Robert's activities."

I asked, "Even though they were living together?"

"Yes. Pamela agreed to let the Bloomington police do the search, and they found nothing."

"She can argue that she didn't know," Jack said derisively.

"Exactly," Paul said. "Screwed by Pamela again."

"This is not exactly good news," Dad said. "But it forces us, and especially you, Paul, to change our approach. From now on, every child custody arrangement between you and Pamela has to be documented."

"I know, Dad," Paul said, his face starting to fall. "But it's very hard."

"I realize it's been difficult," Dad answered. He adjusted his glasses, his unwavering gaze focused on his eldest son. "But we shouldn't expect things to get easier just because Robert's in jail. If Pamela feels at all threatened or backed into a corner, she'll keep upping the ante. We tried and failed. Kaitlin is still our main priority."

This was not the outcome we wanted, yet Dad was right in insisting that we had to be on our toes. The sense of dejection that hovered over us felt oppressive as we came to terms with yet another setback.

Jeanne called as I was leaving for the day. "Turns out Earl Carter is Robert's uncle. Earl was charged with essentially shaking down neighborhood merchants for a protection fee, which was not looked kindly upon, especially by the merchants. When the Minneapolis police went to fire him, he sued, saying he'd been framed. It was a long, ugly battle, and Earl eventually got a small settlement but was never rehired. I'll fax you the articles if you want."

"Sure," I said, but I was distracted and listening only half heartedly. I rattled off the fax number, ready to finish this conversation.

"Oh, and before I forget, I talked to some of my contacts over at the Minnetonka PD," Jeanne continued. Musical tones were signaling my computer shutting down. "Each one told me the same story—that an officer on the force had an affair with Pamela Pierson. And it was rather public."

What else is new? I thought cynically.

"What's curious is that the officer in question was part of the team that raided Dan Kinney's detective agency."

Suddenly it felt as if someone had put my head in a slingshot, pulled it back as far as it would go, and, without warning, let it snap violently forward. "I'm sorry, Jeanne. What did you say?"

If she knew I had not been paying attention, she was too gracious to say. "Pamela apparently had an affair with a Minnetonka police officer involved in the raid on Dan Kinney's office. Your hunch that the police came looking for those tapes may not be far off."

My breathing became forced; my heart pounded so loudly I was certain Jeanne could hear it. "You don't know his name, do you?"

"Charles Dayton, like the department store family but no relation. Fifteen-year veteran on the force. His supporters think he's a committed officer, but his detractors call him a loose cannon. Had one suit for alleged police brutality brought against him but was cleared by Internal Affairs." Like a true politician, Jeanne had researched the opponent well.

Still, there was a downside. "We'd be hard pressed to prove that Charles Dayton knowingly went into Dan Kinney's office looking for those tapes," I said.

Jeanne was matter-of-fact. "True. But I'd hold on to this information. Charles Dayton is married, but apparently the affair was common knowledge, which means there are potential witnesses."

And potential for blackmail at the hands of Pamela, I thought. It was easy to fathom her threatening to bring their relationship right to his wife's doorstep if Charles Dayton did not readily participate in whatever plan she devised. I thanked Jeanne for all her help, and she told me she would be in touch if any new information surfaced.

The tally of Pamela's targets was growing, and there appeared to be no end in sight. Pamela seeped into people's lives like water into pottery made from porous clay. I wondered how many more lives she would ruin, or if the reality was that she would not stop until she had marred everyone around her.

chapter 25

The sounds of birdsong, increasing warmth and fresh flowers heralded the onset of spring. Paul was in the process of purchasing a new house, after living with our parents for more than a year. It still seemed ironic that he would spend months scraping together the financing, while Pamela used her hefty settlement to finance her own house and her latest Bonnie and Clyde schemes. It was impossible not to be bitter, and it took tremendous strength on my part not to project my anger.

Paul and Kaitlin's new home was in one of the burgeoning subdivisions—a development that consumed him in the months after Rachel's death. Now well established, Rolling Meadows offered easy access to the Twin Cities, yet it was still far enough out to give residents the flavor of country living, an environment he felt would be ideal to raise Kaitlin in.

Other changes were occurring in Paul's life as well, as I was about to find out. We met with managers to update everyone on projects or problems twice a month. Often lengthy and occasionally raucous, we had a policy during such meetings of switching off all cellphones and refusing outside calls. But during a passionate discussion on one of our partnerships, a knock at the conference room door interrupted us. "Sorry for the intrusion," Linda said quickly, "but Paul, I have Lisa Campbell on the phone."

From the end of the conference table, I saw his dark eyes brighten as he excused himself. Next to Jack, I leaned sideways and whispered, "I thought interruptions were forbidden. Who is Lisa Campbell?"

Never taking his attention off the manager who was giving his thoughts on the partnership situation, he gave a knowing smile. "The girl Paul's been dating," he whispered and then plunged back into the conversation without missing a beat. "I think the Thompson partnership is one worth maintaining, and here's why ..."

I, however, found myself fighting to stay centered on the discussion. Who was Lisa Campbell? How long had she and Paul been dating? Was it serious? Why was this the first time I had heard anything about her?

Paul returned within a few minutes, and I thought about whether there had been a difference in his behavior in the past months. Even with the upcoming wiretapping hearing dangling in front of him, he seemed much more upbeat. I attributed the healthy attitude to his finally buying his own place, getting sober and having some money, but clearly these facts were only part of the picture.

I found myself nursing hurt feelings that I had been left out of the loop. Once the gathering was adjourned, I pummeled Jack with questions. "How'd he meet her?"

"Through his lawyer," he replied in his trademark concise fashion.

"And?" I said, making a circular motion with my hand for him to keep talking.

Jack laughed. "Kay, she works for Bob Rolfson as a paralegal. They met at his office."

"Have they been dating long?"

"A couple of months."

"And she knows all the gory Pamela details."

"I would imagine."

"Is it serious? Are we going to be introduced?"

"I already have. In terms of a family get-together, you'll have to ask Paul."

"You know, extracting water from stone is easier than getting information from you," I said in exasperation. "I'm your sister, not some stranger off the street."

"Ask him yourself," Jack said, giving me the smile that made most women swoon but made me furious.

* * *

Paul was forthcoming when I approached him later that day. "Why all the secrecy?" I asked, trying to disguise my irritation.

"We've been dating for a few months. I didn't want to rush her into meeting everybody. We can be a pretty intimidating family."

"We are not!" I protested. "We can be a little boisterous, but overall I'd say as families go, we're a lot of fun. And besides, Jack told me he's met Lisa, and I think it's only fair you introduce her to all of us." Paul ran a hand through his hair, contemplating my request. "It would be nice to get to know the woman who's obviously become an important part of your life."

"You should see her with Kaitlin, Sis. Lisa adores her, and she's content to spend time with both of us."

Paul's confident declaration was enough to vanquish any doubts. "When can we meet her?" I said, placing a hand on his shoulder, giving him a sisterly shake. "We want to share in your happiness, Paul."

"I was thinking about one of our Sunday meals."

"That's perfect." As I stood in front of my brother, I could feel a shadow pass across my face and my tone turn decidedly more serious. "Jack tells me she works with Bob Rolfson, so I'm assuming she knows all about Pamela. How does she feel about that baggage?"

He draped an arm around my shoulder. "This is probably the best way it could've happened. Lisa knew me as a client first and was privy to everything that was going on between Pamela and me. With anyone else, I'd have to explain at some point that I was divorced."

"And that she's the ex-wife from hell," I said.

He laughed nervously. "Something like that. Lisa knows what she's getting into upfront, and she seems comfortable with all of it."

"Then all the more reason for us to meet her."

* * *

Paul announced he would be bringing Lisa for family dinner later that week. It was early May, and Kaitlin had stayed overnight at Goldenwoods with Mother and Dad so Paul could attend a friend's wedding.

Mother immediately began assigning tasks as our group arrived. She was on a mission, having us clean off the sun deck and bring out the umbrella tables, striped padded deck chairs and chaise lounges in preparation for summer. The large wood deck stretched across the back of the house and overlooked a vast expanse of plush green lawn leading to a sandy beach along the still-chilly waters of Lake Minnetonka. Mother declared it was not too early to begin the outdoor season with a hamburger cookout.

In the kitchen flattening hamburger patties and finishing a leafy green salad, Michelle and I were also charged with keeping an eye on Kaitlin, who'd become a very curious and mobile toddler. Jack, Tim and Dad played catch with Ruthie and Sam, and their shouts and laughter drifted up from the yard through the open French doors off the great room.

"Juice! Juice!" Kaitlin said, pointing to the cupboard where her cup was kept.

"What do you say?"

"Peeese."

I gave in, but reluctantly. "Only half a glass or you'll spoil your dinner." I poured out some apple juice, screwed on the cap and handed her the bright plastic cup. "Has Jack said what Lisa is like? All I know is she works for Bob Rolfson."

My sister-in-law raised an eyebrow. "Are you kidding? I didn't even know she existed until Friday."

The front door opened, Paul calling from the entryway, "Hello! Anybody home?"

Kaitlin left her cup on the floor and started running toward the sound of her father's voice. "Let's go see who's at the door," I said and dutifully followed behind my 2-year-old niece. In the entryway, I encountered Paul helping a petite young woman out of her bright spring coat.

"Hi, Sis," he said in greeting. "Lisa, this is my sister, Kay. Kay, Lisa."

"I've heard so much about you," she said, proffering a slender hand. "It's nice to finally meet."

"Yes," I said brightly. "Welcome!"

Lisa's expressive brown eyes peeked past my shoulder. "Hi, sweetie," she said, stretching her open arms. I saw my niece's eager face, small hands clasped to her strawberry mouth in recognition. Kaitlin ran to her, Lisa scooping her into her arms. "How's my favorite girl?"

"I'll take the potato salad," I motioned to the huge bowl they had brought.

"Did you miss us?" Paul repeated happily, smooching his daughter's rosy cheek. "We missed you."

"Yes," she responded shyly. The three of them stood together in the foyer, the clear spring sun catching the red highlights of Paul's and Kaitlin's dark hair. I carried the bowl into the kitchen, noticing that Lisa's coloring was remarkably similar—her hair was a deep, warm brown. This cheerful trio looked like they belonged together, as if they were already a family.

"Paul, is that you?" Mother called. "I'm putting you in charge of the hamburgers."

"Hi, Mom!" he responded, and the three of them came into the brightness of the expansive room. Michelle joined us and introductions were exchanged.

"Let me get your father and everyone," Mother said, heading back outdoors, the threesome at her heels.

Michelle and I were setting out dishes, silverware and glasses for the buffet-style meal. "She's very pretty," Michelle said, holding the tray of hamburgers. "And Kaitlin obviously loves her. I'm going to see if we can get these hamburgers on the grill. I'm starved."

"Me too," I agreed. "It's so nice to see Paul happy and enjoying himself. He deserves it."

We learned Lisa was a Minneapolis native with three sisters. Her dad was an insurance company executive, and before long we realized that we knew many of the same people. She was charming, bright and in the process of shaping her future. After graduating from the University of Minnesota with a degree in political science, she had worked for a state legislator.

"Politics was fun—for a while. The hours were long and the pay terrible, so I decided to get some incredibly useful skills. I've always been interested in the law," she explained. "I went through a paralegal program, and in this job, I get experience of the legal field. I'm planning to take the LSAT in the fall."

"Lisa would make a terrific lawyer," Paul enthused. "Child protection issues are a specialty she's thinking about." It was evident their common interest in law had helped bring them together.

"We'll see how I fare. Law school would be a huge commitment, and I want to be sure the timing is right."

We felt wonderfully comfortable around her, and Lisa did not seem at all cowed by us or the constant racket and activity. Ruthie and Sam were drawn to her, asking her to play games with them. She obliged, engaging in several rounds of tag in the backyard until nightfall was on the horizon. Lisa insisted on helping Paul get Kaitlin ready for bed, giving her a bath and dressing her in Bugs Bunny pajamas. My niece cuddled in her lap, Lisa reading her stories until the baby drifted off to sleep.

When the three departed, I already felt Lisa would be a great addition to our family—and the rest of the family agreed. It wasn't just my brother's happiness that made her such a good fit; it was also her obvious love for Kaitlin. As all of us knew, any woman who would knowingly walk into the kind of harrowing situation that existed between Paul and Pamela and still want to be a part of his and his daughter's life had to be a very special person.

chapter 26

On a stifling July day, the kind where the humidity presses so hard against your lungs that every breath is labored, Jack and I drove downtown to the Hennepin County Courthouse and made our way to the 10th-floor courtroom for Paul's wiretapping hearing. We found seats behind Dan Kinney, Roger Larson, Paul and their lawyers, the fluorescent glare of the stark lighting giving everyone's skin an unnatural yellow tinge. Dad had real estate commission meetings, and Mother simply could not bear to watch it.

From behind, Paul appeared skittish, nervously fidgeting with his glasses and hands. Before the hearing got underway, Jack and I went over to give him some last-minute support.

"Here we go," Paul said as soon as he saw us. "Wish me luck."

"Don't let them intimidate you, Paulie," Jack counseled, using his childhood nickname. "Relax and tell the truth."

Almost standing on tiptoe, I kissed Paul on the cheek. "Don't forget that we love you no matter what happens."

As we stood talking, Pamela entered the courtroom wearing a form-fitting navy-blue suit, with her attorney, Phillip Mattson, at her side. Catching sight of Jack and me, she smirked her disdain, but I didn't avert my resolute gaze. Nor did Jack.

The formal voice of a bailiff announced: "All rise!" Everyone stood as the judge entered the chamber.

As one of the main witnesses for the prosecution, Pamela was the first to take the stand. "I began to suspect my phone was being tapped in January 1999, when Paul, my estranged husband, confronted me about things I had only discussed over the telephone with a friend."

"What kinds of things did your husband confront you about?" an assistant district attorney asked.

"Places I'd gone and the people I'd met. If I made plans with someone, Paul already knew about them."

"How many times did this happen?"

"About four times."

The cross-examination of Pamela progressed. She explained that she began taping her own phone conversations after the Minnetonka Police Department contacted her regarding the wiretapping allegations under investigation.

I was vigilantly hoping the defense could poke holes in her story, exposing the inconsistencies and clarifying why Paul was trying to protect his child. What bothered me most was that she referred to Paul as her "estranged husband," when, at the time, he was not.

Then the prosecution asked to play a portion of one of the tapes Pamela had made in February 1999, just after Paul had filed for divorce.

Paul's voice, tinny but recognizable, filled the space. "I tapped the phone while I was in Dallas at the Home Builders meeting because I wanted to confirm that you were having an affair. You're getting yourself involved in a mess. I don't want that felon Billy Watts around my daughter."

I held my chin in my hands. I could see the back of Paul's neck reddening, his shoulders stiffening, the anger welling up. What came next made him look even worse. "You need to get those tapes back from the police," he said. "This isn't about me. It's about two cops. You knew Dan Kinney was an ex-cop. Now he's pissed off a Minnetonka cop whose wife hired him to prove he was having an affair."

"It's not like I wanted the police involved. But it's out of my control," Pamela replied in a snotty tone—the tone she always used when absolving herself of blame.

"That bitch," Jack muttered, thrusting his body forward to the edge of the chair. His intense gaze worked over Pamela as she nonchalantly flicked back her hair.

Sitting in that stuffy, cramped courtroom, it felt like Paul's life was disintegrating in front of us. At this point, damage control was out of the question. It didn't matter if Pamela had manipulated Paul into incriminating himself. What counted was that he was on tape committing a crime for the entire world to hear.

I could not stand to look at her face. Instead, I scrutinized her blue-suited figure. My eyes traveled down her shapely, crossed legs to her right ankle. There was a tattoo—letters spelling something out. Pamela continued talking, and I became obsessed with the writing on her ankle. My eyes on the tattoo and my ears on her testimony, I tried to decipher what it spelled.

Pamela's next accusation wasn't one we had been privy to. She was claiming that Paul changed his story about how her calls had been tapped. Paul first told her that Dan Kinney installed the wiretaps prior to Paul leaving for Dallas in January, but then he later altered the story, saying Dan instructed Paul on which equipment to buy and how to do the monitoring himself.

I was still fixing on her ankle. As Pamela finished her testimony, rose from the witness stand and strode back across the room with another haughty toss of her hair, I was finally able to make out the two words on her ankle clearly. "Foxy Lady" was written in script in black, accented by a red rose and green thorns wrapping around the base of her ankle.

After her testimony, the district attorney wanted to explore why Paul wiretapped the phone in his own home. *Because his former wife is a liar and a cheat*, I thought.

There seemed little sense in sitting through further testimony of how Dan apparently obtained illegal eavesdropping equipment for his clients. As Roger Larson's wife was called to the stand to build on the prosecution's case, Jack gently tapped Paul's shoulder and motioned goodbye. Paul limply waved his hand in reply.

"Maybe we should stay," I whispered. "It's only going to get worse. He could probably use the moral support."

Removing a business card from his wallet and pen from his pocket, Jack scribbled, "Do you want us to stay?" and handed it over Paul's shoulder.

Glancing at the note, Paul indicated no. We silently left the courtroom. Neither of us said anything in the elevator, and we walked wordlessly through the crowded courthouse lobby and into the glaring sun.

Outside, the air was noisy with traffic and thick with exhaust. Jack and I walked through the park that surrounded the red granite and glass towers of the courthouse. Amid the steamy asphalt, glass and skyscrapers, the park was a welcoming green space, a shaded oasis where office workers could enjoy an alfresco lunch, read or simply watch the world rush by.

Downtown seemed overly crowded, and I realized that Paul's hearing corresponded with the annual Aquatennial Festival celebrating summer and the lakes that dotted Minneapolis—glistening jewels left over from the Ice Age. Tonight was the block party, and though it was early afternoon, crowds were already making their way to Hennepin Avenue, the starting point of the festivities.

We continued through the square, Jack removing his linen blazer and tossing the jacket over a shoulder. "So, how do you feel about having a felon for a brother?" He had fallen into a darkly humorous mood.

"That seems to be Pamela's effect on men."

"Christ, Paul and Robert could be prison-cell neighbors."

"There's irony for you, and she walks away unscathed." My body shuddered; even in the muggy heat I felt chills, causing moist droplets to slide down my back, sticky against my A-line cotton dress. Walking along the crowded sidewalk, past hot-dog vendors, inline skaters and professionals seeking a quick bite to eat, I said, "Did you see Pamela's tattoo?"

"No, guess I missed that. Where was it?"

"On her right ankle. It says 'Foxy Lady.'"

"That doesn't surprise me. She thinks very highly of herself. And she's great at self-promotion."

* * *

The next morning's paper brought the whole story public on the front page of the Metro/State section, with a headline announcing, "Testimony in wiretapping case." Every humiliating detail was printed. The story again referred to Paul as Pamela's "estranged husband" at the time of the wiretaps, including nothing that indicated they had been, in fact, married.

I read the author's byline, letting out a melancholy laugh. The reporter was Margot Paliulionis, a high school classmate of Jack's. I had taken piano lessons from her mother for several years as a child. Her name had not caught my eye initially, but Mother assured me later it was the same person.

"If it were Olson or Anderson, it could easily be someone else. But Paliulionis is not exactly a common name in Minnesota," she said.

"Her story makes it look like Paul was stalking Pamela. Even in court, his attorney didn't correct Pamela when she referred to Paul as her estranged husband. We should contact Margot and set the record straight."

"Well, the story's already been published," Mother replied in exasperation. "The best we could get would be a correction. Those are buried where no one reads them."

* * *

The prosecution won its case, and Paul would face some type of punishment, regardless of how unfair we thought the wiretapping laws might be.

"It makes me livid that Paul could face possible disbarment and imprisonment for listening to the conversations of his wife in his own home," Michelle commented a few days later. "Pamela was having an affair, and he was not only trying to prove that but to protect his child." Paul was proud of his legal background, but especially of following in Dad's footsteps. Publicly stripping him of his license would be the ultimate humiliation.

"Recording phone calls without one of the parties knowing is illegal in most states," I said dryly. "Paul made a critical error in not getting a judge's approval."

Bob Rolfson petitioned for a pretrial diversion at once. In exchange for community service and a fine, the charges would be dismissed and expunged from Paul's record. In the waning days of August, he was accepted into the diversion program, where he would perform 100 hours of community service. He was assigned to the Minneapolis City Planning Department, where he used his expertise in real estate law on city-initiated projects.

He would still be working full time, and the community service would occur throughout the fall over a period of several months. None of us felt this was any sort of victory, but Paul, at least, seemed relieved that he could work his way through the wiretapping allegations with a strong chance of clearing his name.

chapter 27

In October, after six months in the Hennepin County Jail, Robert Carter's pandering trial was heard. I diligently followed the trial in the news, hoping he would be locked up indefinitely. The day the verdict was to be announced, I felt a strong need to hear it in person.

No one knew where I was going, and I updated my voicemail message saying I was off-site for the rest of the day. The courtroom was on the 17th floor, another nondescript room where justice—or, at least, one hoped justice—was meted out. I seated myself in the last row, where I could observe the proceedings unnoticed.

A few minutes before 10 a.m., Robert and a tall, silver-haired man I presumed to be his attorney entered the harshly lit courtroom. Robert wore a cheap, ill-fitting gray suit, a white dress shirt open at the neck and no tie. I assumed that counsel suggested he make a good impression on the jury, but he twitched in continual discomfort. He sported the pompadour and goatee that accentuated his pointed chin and hollow cheekbones—Mephistopheles in the flesh.

The jury entered from a side door; a small crowd rose to its feet at the entrance of the judge, an African American whose bald head and regal bearing gave him a no-nonsense aura. Completing his explanation of what was occurring, the judge asked the jury, "What say you?"

The forewoman, a heavyset woman with an Ethel Merman voice,

stood reading the various charges, followed by the jury's verdict for each one. On all counts, Robert was found guilty, but no emotions crossed his face. As each guilty verdict was read, I could hear the mumbling and rustling growing louder.

Unexpectedly, one of the spectators sprang to his feet. My eyes were fixated on the burly older man in the row behind Robert, large ham-hock arms folded across a heaving chest. From the picture Jeanne had sent, I recognized it was Robert's uncle, Earl. The younger man next to him—who I guessed was Robert's brother, judging from the same prominent nose and sharp features—was shouting and pointing a rigid finger at the judge. "This is bullshit! He ain't done nothin'! Your system is rigged!"

Earl lurched forward, fists clenched, his muscular frame lunging toward the judge. "You better watch your back! I ain't afraid of no goddamned judge!" he snarled. The fearless judge locked eyes with his menacing assailant, making no move to retreat to possible safety. Forcefully pounding his gavel, the judge commanded, "Order!"

The first bailiff reaching the younger Carter took a punch to the face. Frantic screams pierced the crowd. Law enforcement officials swarmed the courtroom with billy clubs in hand. Earl jumped into the fray, slugging his massive fists. The bailiff fending him off was quickly joined by another. They moved to restrain him and elevated their clubs to deflect the oncoming punches. Deputies forced the younger Carter to the floor. His face smashed against the carpet and hands clamped into handcuffs behind his back. He was unceasing in his muffled threats. Two more bailiffs wrestled with Earl, who hollered over the din, "You won't get away with this! I'll have your ass!"

My heart was racing. Then, amid the bedlam, something caught my eye. Among the scrambling crowd I caught sight of Pamela. She was rail thin—she couldn't have weighed more than 95 pounds. Her eyes darted briefly across the brawl and then, just as quickly, she was looking down, rummaging distractedly through her purse. In an instant, my attention was pulled back to the judge as he pounded his gavel and gruffly called, "Order! Order!"

Robert stood next to his attorney, observing the melee, an arrogant smirk twisting his thin lips. He laughed as he watched his brother get dragged to his feet, spit at the closest deputy and yell "Fuck you!" at the judge as he was escorted out of the courtroom.

Earl was handcuffed too, but he seemed to sense his resistance would be futile; he let two more deputies remove him from the courtroom. At the exit, he made one last threat: "You haven't heard the last of me!" With that, he was shoved hard through the doorway.

The judge called for order again, and the onlookers settled back into their seats. Deputies were posted at each door, and as I scanned the room, I again fixated on Pamela. She seemed oblivious to the commotion, now dumping the entire contents of her purse into her lap, doggedly searching for something. I watched in fascination as she took her left shoe off, put it back on and took it off again.

From the bench, the judge firmly announced charges of contempt were being filed against Robert's brother and uncle for their outburst. Sentencing for Robert would take place later in the week, but the judge made it clear that these were significant charges. Robert faced up to 20 years in Stillwater prison. For a man facing the prospect of being locked away for a long time, he seemed to possess an eerie calm. Perhaps these were the characteristics that had drawn him and Pamela together—two devious minds that feared nothing.

"Sentencing of the defendant is this Friday, Oct. 20, 2000, at 9 a.m. Court is hereby adjourned." He pounded his gavel one final time, vacating his seat.

* * *

As expected, the courtroom brawl appeared on all the local newscasts. Robert's brother and uncle were both charged with contempt for their disruption and would be dealt with separately. In their stories filed from the courthouse, reporters alluded to both the Carter brothers having extensive criminal histories, as well as their uncle's own troubles on the Minneapolis police force and eventual dismissal for corruption.

On Oct. 20, Robert was sentenced, and we were again disappointed. Instead of the maximum 20 years or anywhere near that, he was sentenced to four years in prison. Including time already served and any additional time off for good behavior, he might easily get by with less than three years.

Pamela boasted that the sentence was a victory, noting in a phone call to Paul that Robert "got off easy and will be out of prison in no time." Worse than her bragging was news that he would be released from jail briefly in the interval before being transferred to Stillwater prison. Paul's ire at Pamela's having Kaitlin while Robert was out of jail led to another volatile confrontation. Appearing at our office unannounced, Pamela engaged Paul in a carefully choreographed public display.

"I do not want Kaitlin in the house with Robert," he told Pamela, his rising fury turning his face beet red.

"How dare you! This is entirely your fault. Robert was only protecting me. He gave me a sense of security after you destroyed our marriage, broke up our home and threatened to kill me. Don't tell me who can stay in my house!"

As Robert was being released for his brief interim of freedom, Pamela abruptly changed her mind and disposition, asking Paul to care for Kaitlin, which was a great relief.

During the six days Robert was free, a morbid curiosity drew me to his and Pamela's Bloomington home like an insect attracted to a bright light on a muggy summer's night. I devised every excuse to slowly drive by the house, diligently observing. I would pull off the busy thoroughfare of Portland Avenue and park across the street in a city park. There, undetected, I would document the number of cars, license plates and descriptions of the constant stream of people moving in and out. Surely, I would catch them in the throes of some sort of illegal activity. Once and for all, Paul would gain full custody of Kaitlin. Pamela would go to jail for a long time, and she would finally be out of our lives.

In the stillness of night, I thought of nothing else, my head alive and buzzing, eventually rising to drive to Pamela's. On the second night, Tim woke up and groggily inquired, "Kay, where are you going? It's 2 o'clock in the morning."

"Don't ask me any questions, all right? There's something I need to do, and I can't sleep."

Turning on the bedside lamp, Tim squinted against the light to see me dressed in black. "You're going to Pamela's, aren't you? What could you possibly discover that we don't already know?"

"I want to know what's going on over there. It could provide useful information."

Tim yawned and shook his head. "You're obsessed and you're doing this out of spite. There's no reason—"

"Stop," I said, holding the palm of my hand toward him. "You won't change my mind."

Tim sat up in bed, arms folded. "Suppose someone sees you? What will you say then? That you were just passing through?" Tim shook his head in frustration at my stubbornness. "Kay, spying on Pamela and Robert won't solve anything; it'll just be dangerous."

"They're so busy celebrating, the last thing they'd expect is someone watching them."

Realizing he would not be able to budge my resolve, he said with resignation, "I'm going with you. I won't sleep knowing you're over there."

"No," I said firmly. I saw the worry in his eyes and the guilt welled up inside me, but the fixation of witnessing the illicit activity of my ex-sister-in-law and her criminal boyfriend was stronger. "I'll take my cellphone, and if anything should get hairy, I'll call you. I'm not afraid of them. I have to know what we're up against."

Tim probably heard me leave every night, but if he did, he let it go.

From my perch among the long shadows of the park's trees, I observed the unremitting traffic of people. The lights were always on, music always playing and the door always open. Covertly, I snapped pictures of the people passing through. Robert's brother, freshly released from custody after the courtroom melee, appeared the first night, unloading cases of beer and liquor from a rust-pocked pickup truck, an ever-present cigarette dangling from thin lips. Big Earl, his massive belly hanging over his belt, showed up too, and I presumed the family viewed Robert's lenient sentence and fleeting freedom as a celebration of sorts.

I eyed them patiently, hoping to document Pamela involved in illegal or unsavory activities that could be used against her in court. My vigil, however, proved to be in vain, and at week's end I wondered if Tim's comment that I was consumed with vengeance might well be true.

chapter 28

Sometimes, perhaps more often than we'd like to think, we become so entangled in the dramas playing out in our own lives that we forget there are much larger events taking place outside the bubble. This was the case for my family and me in November 2000.

An election was taking place, this round a presidential choice with no incumbents. The race was tight from the outset, with the Democrats nominating former Vice President Al Gore and North Carolina Senator John Edwards. The Republicans countered with former Texas Governor George W. Bush and a stalwart face from his father's presidency, Dick Cheney.

Still, Minnesota politics were changing. The Wednesday after the election, the race remained too close to call. When it was over, after the protracted legal wrangling had gone all the way to the Supreme Court, the Bush ticket was declared the winner, although Gore had clinched the popular vote by more than 50,000—only the fourth such occurrence in our history. Al Gore carried Minnesota, but the percentages hinted at transitions in the state's political landscape. Having won the state with just under half the popular vote, Gore's small victory indicated that Minnesota, like much of the country, was leaning toward the conservative.

Normally, the Pierson family would have taken on our usual active roles within the DFL party, but the legal barrage from Pamela kept our attention focused elsewhere. Instead of thinking about the state of our country or the state, I found myself obsessing about how Pamela had monopolized our lives.

One evening, Tim sensed I needed a distraction. "I'll make popcorn and you pick a movie," he suggested.

Settled into the sofa, I selected one of my favorite black-and-white classics, "Casablanca." When the main character, Rick Blaine, made his sardonic observation that "the problems of three little people don't amount to a hill of beans in this crazy world," I felt like a lightbulb had exploded above my head. Pamela's ability to cause my family distress had been merciless, but did the problems of a small group of people really matter when played out against events of greater and far-reaching consequence? As challenging as our personal tribulations seemed, they were mere specks in the vast intrigue of life.

After the movie I told Tim, "There are much bigger problems to solve in the world." And I made a promise to myself to be a little less consumed with Pamela.

Shortly after Thanksgiving, on a late afternoon that was dissolving into dusk, I came into Past Treasures Antiques to find Mother busy at work signing Christmas greeting cards. The large pile captivated me, as the cards appeared to be family picture Christmas cards, but we hadn't had a family portrait taken since the disastrous evening when I noticed Pamela's wedding ring was missing. I picked up the card and realized, based on Kaitlin's appearance, the picture was two years old. "Why are you using an outdated picture for your Christmas card?" I asked.

Mother continued signing "The Piersons" on one card after another and said simply, "Look closer."

Scanning the back row, I saw Dad, Kaitlin, Tim, Jack and Paul. In front of Dad was Mother, followed by Michelle, Ruthie, Sam, me ... and Lisa. I looked intently at the photograph. It was clearly the one taken when Pamela was living in Rochester and still part of the family.

"Isn't it wonderful?" Mother said, setting aside her pen, the twinkle in her eyes one of sheer mischief. "I had Pamela digitally erased and replaced with Lisa. You can't even tell."

I laughed loudly, caught up in Mother's enthusiasm. "How much did it cost you to have this done?"

"Sixty-seven dollars for a hundred cards and let me tell you it was better than therapy," Mother said with a snap of her fingers. "Just like that, and Pamela was out of the picture. Now, if we could just get her out of our lives that easily."

"That would be wonderful," I agreed.

I admired Mother's ability to make light of what had been a heavy situation for far too long. Even more, I appreciated her unwavering ability to provide a sturdy foundation for our family. Through the highs and lows and everything in between, she had always been a grounding force. She'd taught me many important lessons throughout my life. I could still learn a thing or two from her about not letting Pamela get under my skin. I would continue to remind myself there were much bigger problems to solve in the world.

chapter 29

The flashing red-and-blue police lights had slowed traffic to a crawl as drivers stretched their necks for a look at what was going on. Far enough back from the scene, I couldn't tell whether it was a traffic stop or an accident, but as if this slowdown was not bad enough, heavy snowflakes began to fall at a brisk clip, eroding visibility.

What I thought would be a good time to avoid the Christmas shopping crunch was a miscalculated venture. Our offices in Edina were near Southdale Center, which had made its place in history as the first climate-controlled enclosed shopping mall in the country. I reasoned that with dozens of shops just a few blocks away and time running out, I could not delay my shopping any longer. Many others, unfortunately, used the same logic. Crowds packed the mall, clogging the parking lot and surrounding streets. My expedition a failure, I inched along the corridor of France Avenue, lined with gleaming office towers, stores and apartment complexes, toward the I-494 freeway. With the accumulating snow, the evening rush hour traffic was beginning to knot into a mass of cars, all trying to get somewhere and going nowhere.

Approaching the site of blazing police lights, I was anxious to get past this tightening bottleneck and onto the freeway. An SUV was the offending vehicle, pulled off into what was normally a right-turn lane, backing traffic up even further. The vehicle was blocked from any movement by a police car in front and one at the rear, and judging by the number of police, I assumed it was more than just a traffic stop. Slowly driving past, I noticed the dark blue Jeep Grand Cherokee was the same make and model as Paul's.

Braking in the middle of the road, I stared aghast at the scene. On the opposite side of the Jeep, Paul was spread out against the vehicle in the process of being frisked. In the back seat, Kaitlin was strapped into her car seat, clasping her favorite blanket, visibly frightened and crying.

A blaring horn from the truck behind startled me, and I drove my car around the second police cruiser, pulling into the crowded turn lane. Annoyed motorists honked their mounting irritation. Before I had turned the motor off, a police officer had made his way through the traffic and was at my window. "Can I help you, ma'am?" he said through the glass.

I brought down the glass halfway. "Yes," I answered, unbuckling the seat belt with my free hand. "That's my brother Paul Pierson you've stopped. May I ask what's going on?"

"Ma'am," the officer said curtly but politely, "we're acting on an anonymous tip regarding a police matter."

I was trying to open my driver's-side door, but the officer's bulky frame stood in the way. "What? Can I talk to him?"

"I need you to stay here, ma'am."

"I can prove who I am," I said, delving into my purse for my wallet and identification. "If you won't let me talk to him, at least let me comfort my niece." I handed the officer my driver's license through the window. "The little girl crying in the back seat is my niece Kaitlin, and it's pretty obvious she's scared. Ask Paul who I am."

"Just a moment. Wait here, please," he said, returning to the parked patrol cars. I closed the window and slowly got out, avoiding the vehicles maneuvering around us. I wanted Paul to know that someone familiar was here.

From my position, I could see that the police, now numbering three cruisers and four officers, were taking everything out of the Jeep. The removable seats, floor mats and spare tire were propped alongside the vehicle, quickly becoming covered with the falling snow. An officer in the front seat was in the process of removing the contents of the glove compartment. They were searching for something; instinct told me it was drugs or alcohol.

There was a sinking feeling in my stomach like I'd just descended a 300-foot drop on a rollercoaster; my insides were in a free fall. I looked down the length of the turn lane, where Paul stood speaking with an officer. If this was a DUI stop, there would be tests he would be required to perform, and so far they seemed more interested in the contents of the Jeep. I ached to talk with him myself, to see he was indeed sober and to find out what exactly had precipitated this.

I walked up onto the curb pacing back and forth on the sidewalk, retracing the same patterned footprints repeatedly in the snowy cold, gloved hands jammed into my coat pockets. On the street, the traffic was chaotic and nearly stopped. Then suddenly I spotted her, over the snarled lines of cars and trucks, at the furthest edge of the Dayton's Home Store parking lot. Her blonde hair flailing in the wind, Pamela's form stood out against the vacant recesses of the lot. She was holding a video camera.

I peered hard for a moment to be certain. Her white Camaro was parked nearby. "Hey!" I yelled and started jogging toward Paul and the group of police officers, motioning frantically with my arms.

The officer I'd spoken to turned around. "Ma'am, please return—"

"There's something you need to see. All of you. Right now," I said, cutting him off.

Briskly I led two of the officers to the spot where I'd been standing when I first spotted her. I didn't run or point, so as not to attract Pamela's attention. "Look across the street into the Dayton's Home

Store parking lot, at the edge by the trees. See that blonde woman in the red coat?"

The two officers who followed me craned for a glimpse over the traffic, and as they did, Pamela lowered the video camera. "Yeah, I see her," the younger of the two said.

"That's Paul's ex-wife, Pamela Pierson, and she's been videotaping this whole episode. So will you please tell me what the hell is going on?"

"You're sure that's her?"

Across the street, Pamela was moving toward the white Camaro. "Yes, I'm positive it's her. The white Camaro she'll get into is most definitely her car. You said something about an anonymous tip?"

"That's correct. A tip that Mr. Pierson was in possession of narcotics," the older of the two police officers explained.

"Goddamn her!" I shouted, hitting my clenched fist against the hood of my car. "And of course, you found nothing!"

The surprised younger officer waited a split second before he spoke. "Yes, ma'am."

"For good reason! That wasn't an anonymous tip; it was a setup. Pamela set up my brother, and I can assure you, we'll be contacting our attorney immediately!" I was so angry I could hardly breathe.

"Ma'am, we need you to calm down, please," the older and larger officer said. "Wait here, I'll be right back." Jogging to his squad car, he slid into the front seat and got on the radio. The younger officer stayed beside me.

"I can't believe this," I muttered angrily. "I just cannot believe this."

"We will find out what's going on," the officer assured me.

I did not say anything more; I knocked the snow off my shoes, staring toward the parking lot. In dismay I watched Pamela's car exit the home store lot, heading out the back toward York Avenue, where she disappeared among the traffic. Paul and the officer accompanying him were at the Jeep's door, Paul getting inside to comfort Kaitlin.

In a few minutes, the other officer rejoined us, my wallet and driver's license clutched in his muscular grip. "I've made arrangements for your niece to be turned over to you. There are some questions we'd like to ask your brother, which he's agreed to. But I want you to know that any suspicions you have that the tip was false will be investigated," he explained, handing me my license. "We don't take these things lightly."

"Good," I said. "Our family will most definitely want to know the specifics."

Both officers returned to the Jeep, helping Paul carefully wrap Kaitlin in a blanket. The younger of the two carried her over to me with the diaper bag slung over his shoulder, speaking softly as they approached.

"Here's your Aunt Kay," he said. "She'll take good care of you."

Kaitlin came to me, big blue eyes filled with tears. "Daddy come?"

"Auntie Kay's here. Daddy will come soon. Let's go see Grandma."

"Daddy come?" she asked again.

"Soon, sweetheart. Soon."

The officer surveyed the scene, speaking to me again. "We won't keep him long."

"Please tell him I'm taking Kaitlin to our parents."

"I apologize for any inconvenience, ma'am, but we'll get to the bottom of this."

I secured my niece into the car seat and found a favorite stuffed toy tucked in the diaper bag to keep her company. I climbed into the front seat, starting the engine. As I cautiously merged back into traffic, I saw in my rearview mirror that each of the four officers had their arms filled with Paul's possessions, and they were returning everything they had removed.

* * *

The Edina police stopped Paul on the suspicion that he was in possession of illegal drugs. Bob Rolfson was issuing a subpoena for the tape of the anonymous call made to Crime Stoppers, which, even if successful, might take several weeks. All we knew for sure was that the caller had been a woman.

Paul provided key details, helping both the police and our family understand how Pamela had so conveniently managed to be present with a video camera as he was stopped.

"Several times over the past week, I'd noticed a white car in the vicinity of my neighborhood, Kaitlin's day care or the office," he explained. "But I thought I was just being paranoid."

Pamela presumably had been stalking Paul, patiently following him until the police acted on her bogus tip. I wasn't surprised, though I had a couple of questions: What was her motive? And how was she able to follow him all day when she was supposed to be working? Was she calling in sick? If she was calling in sick, I thought Pamela's employers had the right to know just how she was abusing her company time. I made the call to Twin Cities Bio-Medical the next morning.

"May I speak with Pamela Pierson's immediate supervisor, please?" The receptionist who answered the switchboard paused indefinitely. "Hello?"

"I'm sorry, Pamela Pierson no longer works here."

"What?" I replied, more taken aback than I expected. "Could I speak with human resources then?" The operator transferred me. "Human resources. How may I help you?"

I knew there were only certain questions that would get answered, and I started with her dates of employment. "Yes, I'm calling to confirm Pamela Pierson's dates of employment with Twin Cities Bio-Medical."

There was a pause, and then the voice on the other end said, "Just a moment," placing me on hold. She returned to the line and quickly rattled off Pamela's start date, which I paid little attention to. It was her dismissal date I was after. "Pamela Pierson worked here until Nov. 22," she said crisply.

"May I have the name and title of her direct supervisor, please?"

"That would be Walter Rixmann; he's the owner of the company."

I scribbled some notes on a pad before asking the question I already knew would not get answered. Yet it was worth a try. "Was there any specific reason for Ms. Pierson's dismissal?"

"I'm sorry, but I can't give out any further information."

I hung up the phone, absentmindedly tapping my pen against my ceramic coffee mug, which made a pinging sound. Pamela was released from Twin Cities Bio-Medical the Wednesday before Thanksgiving, not the most convenient time to lose one's job. It certainly provided a motive for her to launch what was beginning to look like an extortion scheme.

If legal action was pursued, we would need proof that Pamela devised an elaborate ploy to have Paul stopped and searched by the police. It hardly mattered that no contraband had been found; the videotape could still do enormous damage if it was shown to uninformed parties.

I walked the hallway between Jack's and my offices, wanting to discuss this. At the open doorway, he had turned his chair, the high back facing the entrance and shielding his words. As I drew near his large mahogany desk, he spoke bluntly into the phone, "That videotape proves absolutely nothing."

My fear had already been realized. He swiveled the chair around to face me, motioning to shut the door. I sat in front of Jack, listening intently.

"There's no way in hell we'd ever allow Pamela to gain full custody of Kaitlin without a fight," he answered forcibly. "Take my advice, Annette, before you start believing some video and spreading rumors that are patently false, you need to take a good, hard look at your own family." He waited and stared at me, his clear blue eyes smoldering into steel gray. "You go right ahead and call your lawyer, Annette, because I can guarantee we're calling ours." With that, he slammed the receiver into the cradle.

My body flattened, as if I had been punched in the stomach. "This is never going to end, is it? She just keeps hammering and hammering and hammering."

Jack whistled softly. "Pamela thinks she can wear us down. And right now, she might be succeeding. She's already shown Annette the videotape, who of course thinks it proves that Paul is a dope fiend."

"I knew it!" I spat. "It doesn't matter who sees it; without context Paul is screwed."

Jack clasped his hands behind his head and tilted back in the leather chair. "It gets better—or worse, depending on your point of view."

"Let's hear it," I said, bracing myself.

"Pamela has filed to reopen the divorce settlement."

I sat up ramrod straight, suddenly remembering what I had come to tell Jack in the first place. "This is starting to make sense, believe it or not. I wondered how Pamela could spend days tailing Paul and not lose her job. Well, she was let go right before Thanksgiving."

"She's out of work less than three weeks, and already she needs the money."

I scooted to the chair's edge. "Probably, but what we need to find out is why Pamela lost her job. Doesn't Sandy Baker have a friend working at Twin Cities Bio-Medical?"

The leather upholstery made a squeaking sound as Jack came forward. "She did. I can't think of her name offhand. Let me give Sandy a call."

I stood, feeling the pull of my stiff muscles. The anxiety and stress were closing in, and I felt the drain in my bones. "We need to make a plan to fight back," I said. I leaned over Jack's massive desk, my open palms spread out and supporting my weight. "And we need to do it now."

* * *

Sandy's friend at Twin Cities Bio-Medical was Juanita Chavez. She had known Pamela and agreed to meet to relay her own story. We met at Tim's and my home, gathered around the square of our dining room table, Jack and I on one side, Juanita directly across. Very pretty, with ink-black hair and warm olive skin, Juanita was about Pamela's age and had been employed at Twin Cities Bio-Medical since she had graduated from college. She was wearing a coral suit.

"Let me begin by saying this: Pamela is the devil, and she destroys every life she touches," she said in a soft voice.

Jack said, "Can't argue with that. Was she fired?"

Juanita folded slender hands on the table. "Not outright. Pamela's work record was lousy. She'd call in sick two or three times a month." She looked squarely at Jack and me. "For a long time, the gossip around the lab was that she had something over Walter, and that's why he didn't fire her."

"Walter Rixmann, the owner?" Jack asked.

"Yes." She had the slightest trace of a Spanish accent. "We assumed she was blackmailing him."

I shook my head in dismay.

"The rumor was that they were having—or had—an affair, and Pamela had threatened to tell Mrs. Rixmann. That terrified Walter, because his wife is a devout Christian, and we always thought he couldn't stand the humiliation. But no one ever actually caught them."

"That sounds like Pamela," Jack said emphatically. "Something must have changed for Mr. Rixmann if she lost her job."

"Yes, but he had to be convinced," Juanita replied. "Not only was

Pamela absent a lot, but she also made many enemies. She lied to cover up her mistakes in the lab and told Walter stories about co-workers that weren't true. After a while, we got smart and started documenting her errors, her coming in late or not at all, and other suspicions."

"What other things made you suspicious?" I asked.

"Pamela was always going at 90 miles an hour. It seemed like she was on something—we thought cocaine. Finally, enough of us started confronting Walter about her behavior and he couldn't ignore us anymore. But it took him a long time to get to that point, because he was scared to death of her," Juanita said, clicking her manicured nails on the table. "In November, Walter demanded that Pamela take a drug test, but she refused."

"And she was fired," Jack said, but Juanita was shaking her head.

"It's more complicated than that. After Pamela refused a drug test, Walter confronted her with all her mistakes and absences. They argued and Walter told her to clean out her desk, saying she was fired. That was the Wednesday before Thanksgiving, and Walter closed the office early, sending everyone home at noon. Pamela had caused so many problems that he didn't want anyone around that she could manipulate. He thought that having the security guard watch her would be enough, but it wasn't."

I felt the horrible sensation of my stomach falling, bracing myself for the worst. Jack asked quietly, "What happened?"

"The Monday after Thanksgiving, Pamela filed a sexual assault and harassment suit against Twin Cities Bio-Medical."

I asked, "Against Walter Rixmann?"

"No. Pamela had been socializing with a male co-worker. He was young. This was his first job after college. Pamela claims he not only sexually harassed her, but on the day that she was asked to leave, no one else but the security guard was supposed to be there. She is accusing this person, whom I won't name, of coming to the office while she was packing up and raping her." Juanita paused, taking a long, ragged breath. "Pamela has destroyed his life and nearly bankrupted the company. Walter is choosing to settle."

The color rose in Jack's face. "Twin Cities Bio-Medical isn't going to fight her? What about the security guard? Where was he?"

"The security guard said he was at the front desk taking a call from Walter, who wanted to know if Pamela was gone yet," Juanita responded warily. "They settled quickly to get rid of her, to act as if she never existed."

"But that's exactly what she wants them to do," I said, the sickening feeling pushing into my throat.

Jack asked Juanita, "What happened to this kid?"

"He was fired. Even though Walter, I think, knew that he was innocent, it all boiled down to removing her." She stopped again, as if the conversation was starting to overwhelm her. She stretched out her hand—the coral polish on her nails was the same shade as her suit—and took another breath. "Pamela knew the company was about to take its stock public, and rather than risk dragging out a nasty court case, Walter and his investors paid her off."

"Do you know how much?" I asked.

"Rumors were $200,000, but we don't really know," Juanita replied. She looked at us, her lovely features twisted in despair. "Honestly, Pamela terrorizes everyone she touches. I hope she burns in hell."

This was all too familiar. How many lives would suffer the blight of Pamela before someone dared to stop her? Juanita Chavez shared her story with us, but fear engulfed her. She would not testify against Pamela, and she doubted Walter Rixmann would either.

After she left, Jack and I remained at the dining room table, immobilized by defeat. This was the story we desperately needed to tell but could not.

Slumped in his chair, Jack mused, "Juanita is certain that Walter and his investors would never admit there had been a sexual assault and harassment suit, much less a settlement."

"People could be subpoenaed, but hostile witnesses will do us no good," I replied wearily.

Jack concurred. "Pamela has enough dirty laundry of Walter's to seriously damage investor confidence in Twin Cities Bio-Medical and put him in divorce court."

"You were right," I said. "You once said manipulating the truth is Pamela's vicious gift. And it's true."

"I forgot about that," he replied dryly, unexpectedly sitting up. "But here's what really scares me. Pamela's badgering is so calculated and relentless, it probably won't stop until she's dead. And even then, I'm not sure it will end."

chapter 30

The dream was always the same, and in the weeks before Christmas, it occurred nearly every night: On board the family sailboat in the middle of Lake Minnetonka, we are caught in a raging storm. Tossed about over the rising waves, the sailboat begins to break apart amid the crashing walls of water. One by one, my family is thrown into the howling depths to perish. Worst of all is the sound—the shrieking, maniacal laughter. Pamela.

So vivid was the nightmare that I would wake with a violent start, flailing and sweating. Sometimes my frantic, heaving gasps would awaken Tim. But his consoling words and tender embraces could not stem the terror. Many nights, I didn't fall back asleep. I had never smoked this much before, sometimes a half-dozen cigarettes a night. Anything to vanquish the darkness.

The mounting squall was tearing my family apart. Pamela had devised a multipronged attack, and fighting it became akin to plugging a hole in a leaking dike. As soon as one leak was blocked another sprouted, and soon we had more holes than chewing gum.

Pamela said the Crime Stoppers incident and videotape grew from her fears that Paul was using again. She had followed him and taped the police stop only to bolster her story. Masterfully playing the martyr and terrified mother, she claimed her sole interest lay in protecting her child.

Bob Rolfson started the arduous process of compiling a list of witnesses to testify on Paul's behalf in the divorce and child custody hearings, but there was resistance. Heather Carlson, who had once served as Kaitlin's nanny, initially agreed to testify. Days later she not only recanted but signed an affidavit stating she had witnessed Paul's drug use firsthand.

"Pamela's the fucking master of blackmail," Jack railed. "She's got something on everybody."

"I would love to know what it is that made Heather do an about-face," I said angrily. "I'm convinced Pamela could dig up dirt on God himself."

Pamela's ex-husband Doug agreed to testify but warned that she would portray him as an abusive spouse. "I'm not afraid of her," he told us. "In fact, I'd relish the chance to set the record straight in court. But going against her will be ugly."

Pamela's attorney marshaled an extensive list of witnesses, including her parents, Donovan and Annette. Both signed affidavits claiming to have witnessed incidents that proved Paul to be an unfit parent. Pamela also culled from her list of ex-boyfriends Charles Dayton, the Minnetonka police officer who signed an affidavit stating that she feared for her safety.

All the legal wrangling was exhausting and expensive. Dad hired another private investigator, who accessed Pamela's credit records and determined that she was heavily in debt, having borrowed against the loan on her house. It explained her next tack of suing Pierson Properties over an apartment complex she claimed she had ownership rights in. Paul and Pamela briefly owned the property early in their marriage, but that agreement had long since been terminated. She was claiming those rights were dissolved against her will, and while the chances were slim of Pamela gaining a financial settlement, it meant more time, more lawyers and more money.

The stress was eating away at all of us, but especially Paul. In mid-December, I witnessed behavior from him that I had not seen for a long time. He declined to discuss what was happening, as if he believed that by refusing to acknowledge the truth it would simply vanish. Sullen and easily distracted, he began withdrawing from us, just as he had after Rachel died. We could not afford to lose him a second time. Under the guise of taking Paul to lunch, Jack and I confronted him.

We drove to Uptown, a trendy area in south Minneapolis teeming with art-house theaters, galleries, shops and restaurants of every ethnicity. Far enough from the office, it would afford us privacy and a change of venue.

"You look pretty rough. All this stuff with Pamela getting to you?" Jack said as soon as we'd ordered.

I was sure Paul would try to blow us off and pretend everything was normal, arguing we were just overreacting. Instead, he nodded his head, his dark eyes shifting between the two of us across the table. "I was never very good at concealing my emotions," he said in a relieved tone. "She's pushing me to the brink."

"This isn't easy for any of us," I said. "Pamela is attacking this entire family."

Paul emitted a long, tired sigh, staring through the water in a glass on the table. "I know. But the reality is that I married her and fathered a child with her. Without Kaitlin, no connection would exist between us, no reason for Pamela to constantly harass me and the rest of you."

"What exactly are you getting at, Paul?" Jack asked.

He inhaled deeply, adjusting his glasses in the absentminded way he had when he was nervous. I noticed the dark circles under his eyes; his olive complexion looked dull. Folding his large hands in front of him, he said quietly, "I'm thinking about relinquishing my parental rights to Kaitlin. That way, Pamela can no longer use her as a bargaining chip. I'd pay child support, but unless Kaitlin wanted to see me, I would not be a part of her life."

I felt as if someone had kicked me in the gut with a steel-toed boot. I was speechless, swiftly overwhelmed by the chatter of the other patrons, the scraping of silverware and the clattering of dishes. Jerking me back to reality was Jack, brutal and to the point. "Give up your parental rights? Are you out of your fucking mind?"

Paul clearly had not anticipated this kind of reaction, stammering over his words. "That's not what I ... I mean, she'll never ... she'll never quit."

I realized our middle brother could not see beyond this crisis to the future. I took in a deep breath and rested my left hand on Jack's tense forearm. "She won't stop then either, Paul," I spoke forcefully. "Terminating your parental rights won't solve this. This is about money, like it's always been, and there simply isn't enough in the world for her." I clasped Paul's trembling hand on the opposite side of the table. "Please don't give up hope or, worse, your own child. Kaitlin's just a meal ticket to Pamela. If you do this, it will only be your little girl who gets hurt."

Somewhat less abrasively, Jack added, "Kay's right, Paul, and Pamela's hitting us with everything she's got. But to me, that says she's desperate."

Paul sat in silence, his nervous fingers tinkling against the water glass. "You're both right," he replied, a bit self-conscious. "I've gotten better at handling her, and Lisa's been great." He paused, searching for the words. "I just want Pamela to leave us all alone."

Jack's eyes softened, a smile forming at the corners of his mouth. "Maybe what we should do is help Pamela find husband number three, so she channels her energy elsewhere."

A ghost of a smile turned up Paul's lips.

"But giving her custody of Kaitlin is out of the question. It's Kaitlin, it's our family legacy, that we've been fighting for all along. Like Kay said, don't give up. We need you to be strong, Paul, maybe stronger than you've ever been in your life. Is any of this easy? Hell no! But there's no room for self-pity."

We succeeded in pulling Paul back from the edge of the abyss that day. A week before Christmas, having completed the diversion program that would keep him from prison, Paul cleared his record, giving us cause for the tiniest bit of rejoicing.

chapter 31

Christmas was usually my favorite time of year. This year the decorations and twinkling lights I always looked forward to on homes and streets looked chintzy and misplaced, as though it were the wrong season. The usual holiday festivities struck me as hollow and frivolous, and I found my concentration easily tapped. All of my and the family's energies were focused on Paul's never-ending battle with Pamela, and I wondered if we could pull everything together to at least give the children a special holiday.

I forced myself to leave the office early and finish Christmas shopping. This foray had been more successful. At least I would have gifts to put under the tree. As I pulled into the driveway, waiting for the automatic garage door to rise, I noticed a large brown cardboard box propped against the front door. Not having done any mail-order shopping, I hoped I was not ruining a surprise Tim might have in store.

Bringing the package inside, I noted its heaviness and a typed address label, but nothing to indicate who the sender was. Ripping into the package, I found stacks of papers, bound together with a thick rubber band. On top of the stack was a typed letter, addressed "To Whom It May Concern."

It began: "The enclosed information regards my ex-husband, Paul C. Pierson, whom I divorced in 1999. As you are aware, I am requesting that both the divorce and child custody agreements be re-evaluated, as

Paul Pierson has sorely neglected his financial obligations. In addition, he has made repeated threats toward me, and I am gravely concerned for the well-being of both me and our daughter, Kaitlin."

I felt punch-drunk as I moved into the dining room. I brought a chair to the table, slowly sorting through the sheaf of papers. There were copies of the original divorce decree and custody settlements; statements from a physician, whose name I didn't recognize, detailing Pamela's illness relating to the "poisoning incident," implying someone had, in fact, tried to kill her; correspondence from Phillip Mattson on his concern for her welfare; and rationale for the various suits she had filed. Any articles regarding Paul that had appeared in the papers were included.

I returned to reading the cover letter. A paragraph near the bottom of the first page jumped out at me: "It is also a known fact that Paul Pierson is both a drug dealer and abuser, having at least one failed attempt in drug rehab in the summer of 1999. During our marriage, he dealt drugs out of our home, and these two things cause me to again fear not just for my own safety but for the safety of our daughter." I had the sickening feeling I had been closer to the truth than I ever wanted to be. I flipped through the pages, finding documentation detailing Paul's treatment in the outpatient program, highly confidential information.

"Holy shit," I said aloud. The squeaking of the garage door opening caught my attention, and I suddenly realized the casserole I planned for dinner was still sitting in the refrigerator.

Tim had discarded his shoes in the laundry room, standing behind me in his overcoat and stocking feet, planting a kiss on the crown of my head. "Hi," he said, looking over my shoulder. "Is this today's mail?"

I looked at my husband's handsome, bearded face as the color was draining from my own. "No. I haven't even checked the mail," I said, trying to control my quivering anger. "This is material sent to us courtesy of Pamela."

Tim perused the cover letter briskly. He whistled softly. "She just doesn't quit," he said.

I shook my head. "That's not even the worst of it."

The phone rang. "Hello?" I answered.

"Did you get a package from Pamela?" I could almost feel Jack's seething breath against my skin.

"Yeah, we did. You, too?"

"Mom and Dad, Paul's attorneys, both newspapers, TV stations, the police and several of our employees. Those are just the people we know about."

My head was throbbing. "She sent ours to the house."

"Same here," he confirmed. "Michelle called as soon as she found it. Have you gotten to the part about our mafia connections?"

I laughed aloud as Tim stood next to me, quizzically searching my face for an explanation.

"Go to page three, the fourth paragraph." I turned over the pages, and Tim followed over my shoulder, as Jack read Pamela's assertion: "I know for a fact that Paul Pierson and his family are part of a powerful mafia syndicate, who will stop at nothing to destroy me. I beg of you to protect me and my child from this evil and cunning family."

It was absurd and chilling at once. The allegations were ridiculous, but I had no doubt that Pamela had made a believer out of Phillip Mattson. He would demand they be investigated, which would give them credence. That none of this was true would get pushed aside as an afterthought.

"If we were lucky enough to actually have mafia connections," Jack said ironically, "there would be no Pamela problem."

I was trying to think through the madness and be reasonable. "The first thing we have to do is keep Paul from confronting her, which will just end in a shouting match."

"Which Pamela would, of course, tape-record, then twist to her advantage," he replied.

"Exactly. We've got to know who else received this."

"The good news is, Paul and I have already talked, and he won't have any contact with her except through our lawyers. What we need to do now is stop the flow of false information. Our attorneys are putting together materials proving she's lying. Dad's contacting the police, and I'm handling the television stations. Can you contact the newspapers?"

"Of course. One question: How did Pamela find out about Paul's being in a drug treatment program?"

"We've got the private investigator checking into how the patient confidentiality was breached."

"That's a crime. When will we get the rebuttals?"

"Delivery by special courier this evening. We'll probably be up most of the night, but we won't let her get by with libel and slander."

* * *

I was meeting with Margot Paliulionis at the Minneapolis Star Tribune on Thursday afternoon, Dec. 21. I read and read again the documents from our lawyers, making certain I was familiar with every aspect. In front of the bathroom mirror applying makeup, the woman in front of me looked far older than the one who'd never before been intimidated by the approach of 40. The lines around my eyes and mouth were deep, and for the first time, I genuinely felt old.

I arrived at the sprawling four-story Star Tribune complex downtown before 2 p.m., and the security guard let Margot know I was in the lobby. The building was decorated in the traditional trimmings, which made me feel a bit of holiday cheer. I recognized Margot as she exited the elevator, although I had to admit she had changed over the years. A tall and slender brunette, she bore no resemblance to the gawky adolescent with braces who had often floated through her mother's piano lessons.

We made the preliminary small talk riding the elevator. Margot guided us through an intricate network of cubicles, humming computers and the steady drone of voices as reporters and staff researched their current stories.

"I graduated from high school with one of your brothers," Margot was saying as she offered me a chair in the glassed-in cubicle that was her workspace. "Jack, the one with those blue, blue eyes." She laughed at an apparent recollection. "I always had a bit of a crush on him. He was so cute and quite the athlete. But a little wild, too, organizing every kegger our class had."

"He was always popular with the ladies," I acknowledged. "It was never dull."

Margot tittered nervously. From a corner of her desk, she moved a large stack of papers to the center. From the top page I recognized the materials we had all received. "The most pressing question is how did you know I got this?"

"Nothing more than a hunch," I said. "Everyone in our family, our attorneys, co-workers, the police and numerous media outlets were sent this. Since you had reported on the wiretapping case involving Paul, I figured you'd be her natural contact."

"'Her' being Pamela Pierson?" Margot interrupted.

"Yes, that's correct. In any event, I'm here to warn you that the information you've been given is not only false but also defamatory. Confidentiality was also breached to obtain some of the material, another element we're investigating."

Margot fanned through the stack of pages. "There are some pretty incredible accusations here, from what I've read. I've talked with my editors, however, and the consensus is there's the concern of malicious intent on Pamela's part, for the reasons you've mentioned. We'll have the documents destroyed."

I jumped in. "If you don't mind, I'd like to take them with me."

"That shouldn't be a problem," Margot responded, pushing the stack toward me.

Our meeting was proceeding much better than I'd anticipated, but there was one point I still wanted to address.

"If you have the time, I'd like to revisit the wiretapping hearing and the subsequent coverage," I said.

The ballpoint pen poised in Margot's right hand twitched, and a defensive tone crept into her voice. "I know the story didn't portray your brother in a particularly positive light, but those were the facts as I knew them to be."

I smiled, wanting to present my argument diplomatically. "There was one factual error, which drastically changed how those events actually happened in the overall story."

The pen still twitched in Margot's hand, and shades of dismay registered in her eyes. "Which facts do you believe were incorrect?"

I kept positive, being certain my body language didn't send a confrontational message. "In the story recounting the hearing, you wrote that Paul was tapping the phone of his 'estranged wife,' and it was presented as though they were living in separate residences and he was stalking Pamela. In fact, Paul had tapped the phone in his own home, because he discovered that his wife was having an affair, and he believed that person posed a threat to his infant daughter."

Margot sat there momentarily, carefully reviewing the hearing and subsequent article in her head. "Wait a minute," Margot said. "Pamela referred to Paul as her estranged husband on the witness stand. And he needed a judge's approval to tap the phone."

"True enough," I conceded, recalling the hearing and the fact that Paul's attorney hadn't corrected Pamela's statement. It occurred to me that Pamela had wagered no one would confront her on this point, and she'd been correct. "I think I owe you an apology."

Margot's pen tapped against the desk. "An apology isn't necessary. I can see how reporting that they were estranged rather than still married and living under the same roof greatly alters the story's slant. But there are other facts you need to know," she said. "I interviewed Pamela after the hearing, and she emphasized they were separated. If it wasn't true, why didn't your family demand a correction?"

My chest heaved a deep and tired sigh. "It shouldn't surprise me that Pamela made sure you got only the information that made her look like a victim, while we blew an opportunity to at least give the true facts, however flawed they might have been."

"You know, I did try to interview your brother after the hearing as well, but neither he nor his attorney were offering any comment." Another chance lost, and it had come at a price. Margot and I regarded each other in pained silence for a moment, the activity of the newsroom whirring around us. "Do you want the paper to run a correction? My editor can approve it for tomorrow."

I signaled a negative response with a wave of my hand. "The hearing was in July, five months ago. No one will remember or care. That's why we chose not to pursue a correction then, because honestly, who reads those anyway?" I paused, realizing that Margot had, in fact, done her job. "Anyway, I came here today to stop the dissemination of false information, and you'd already figured out the information you received was about a personal vendetta and not a news story."

"If she's defaming your family, you should fight her."

"We are," I said, trying hard not to sound overwhelmed. "But frankly, waging a battle in the media while Pamela continues to play the victim hurts us far more than it would help us."

Margot and I ended our meeting on cordial terms. There was no newspaper story to worry about, but I now knew why she had written the wiretapping story from a point of view favoring Pamela.

On Dec. 22 I had an appointment on the other side of the Mississippi River at the St. Paul Pioneer Press, where Pamela's news attracted less attention. Pamela's allegations fell on indifferent ears there, and the Pioneer Press gladly handed over the materials.

In contacting the television news stations, Jack discovered all believed there was no story. "If we broadcast every nasty letter somebody wrote about someone they knew, we'd be out of business in a heartbeat," one producer told him. The news organizations were more than happy to relieve themselves of such calumnious material, as were our employees who had found themselves receiving Pamela's missive.

There was the additional worry of how many cities she had contacted, particularly the reaction from law enforcement. Fiercely determined to protect our family, Dad marshaled several of his friends in law enforcement to verify the agencies in question. As it turned out, the Bloomington and Minnetonka police were the sole recipients. Again, the consensus stood that they were baseless charges not meriting investigation.

There was one group Pamela delivered the materials to, however, that we had neglected to consider. Dad was alerted by the Minnesota Bar Association that several attorneys our family had relationships with had all been recipients. They willingly gave him the unopened documents.

We had collected the mounds of paper from across the Twin Cities. I suggested the best way of destroying the documents and their malicious intent was to simply burn them. The chosen site was the fire pit in the backyard at Goldenwoods. It was cold but not bitterly so. A full moon cast a shimmering halo off the thin ice covering Lake Minnetonka.

Jack's fury was ferocious. "Every new incident with Pamela is a goddamned game of endurance," he said, building a teepee of wood at the center of the pit. "Too bad Robert wasn't smart enough to get rid of her for good."

I removed my cigarette lighter from my pocket and, with a sharp flick, lit the fire. As I added the reams of paper, the blaze sparked and crackled against the chill. The amount of paper continually increased the flames licking upward into a spectacular orange bonfire. Pamela's pages of lies evaporated in front of us, becoming a plume of towering smoke that billowed into the moonlit sky.

chapter 32

Christmas Eve arrived and somehow lights twinkled, decorations were in place, presents were tucked under the towering gold-trimmed fir tree, and the cupboards were stocked for the holiday feast. How we had managed to do it all, I could not fathom. As we gathered at Goldenwoods in preparation for church, I looked forward to the message of hope more than ever.

Letting myself in through the back door, I came face to face with Ruthie in a green velvet Christmas frock, her golden curls trimmed with a matching bow. "Ruthie, you look so pretty. Merry Christmas," I said, hugging my niece.

Released from my embrace, Ruthie crinkled her nose. "Mommy always wants me to wear a dress for special occasions," she said, all of 10 going on 20. "I'd rather wear jeans."

"I know, sweetie. But you still look nice."

"Thank you," Ruthie said. Michelle called her from the front bathroom, and she scampered out of the room.

The door opened behind me. Paul entered carrying a brown sack of groceries. "Merry Christmas, Sis," he said.

"You too. What's this—some last-minute shopping?"

He gave my shoulder a hearty squeeze and shook his head. "Mom forgot the rolls for tomorrow, so I ran over to Byerly's and picked them up."

Outfitted in a cream-colored Christmas sweater embroidered in green and gold, Mother elegantly strolled into the kitchen. She deftly balanced Kaitlin, who was all ready for the holiday in a burgundy satin dress and black patent leather shoes. "I thought I heard you, Kay. We're just about ready."

"We've got time. It's not even 7:30, and church doesn't start until 8 o'clock. Hi, cutie," I said, facing the two of them. "Mom, you look great, and that's a darling dress for Kaitlin."

"What do you say?" Mother asked gently, and Kaitlin smiled shyly.

"T'ank you" came her sweet reply.

"Mom, where do you want these rolls?" Paul asked.

"In the breadbox."

"Will Lisa be joining us?" I said, turning to address him.

"Her family is celebrating Christmas at her sister's in Duluth. We'll have our own holiday later in the week."

Clustered in the kitchen, everyone talking and laughing, we had not heard the front doorbell chime. I heard Dad yell from the master bedroom, "Is somebody getting the door?"

"I'll get it," Michelle said.

Mother was giving Kaitlin a sip of milk as Paul and I stacked the rolls. "How many rolls did you order?" I asked, taking one box after another out of the bag.

"Six dozen," Mother replied and wiped Kaitlin's mouth with a damp cloth.

"Mom doesn't want anybody to go hungry," Paul smiled. "Like anyone has ever gone hungry in this family."

"I just want to be prepared," she said. "Yes, Grandma just wants everybody to get enough to eat," she said, planting a kiss on Kaitlin's forehead.

"Paul, there's someone here to see you." Michelle stood in the archway; her dress matched Ruthie's, and her auburn hair fell to her shoulders. The warm colors stood out against the paleness of her cheeks.

Mother asked, "Michelle, who is it?"

She looked at each of us, one by one, her green eyes full of fear. Her voice was small and shallow. "It's the police."

"The police?" Mother handed Kaitlin to me and cut a brisk path through the dining room toward the foyer. Dad had beaten her to the front door, and we heard a cacophony of voices.

I looked to Paul for an explanation, and he shook his head in confusion. "I have no idea what's going on." The two of us followed. Mother and Dad stood under the entryway chandelier speaking with a uniformed police officer.

Dad said curtly but politely, "I think there's been a misunderstanding." Turning toward us, he continued, "Paul, this officer is investigating a complaint of a scuffle at the grocery store involving you."

Paul stared in silent amazement. "I don't know what you're talking about. I was in Byerly's for less than five minutes to pick up some rolls in the bakery. They gave me the order; I paid for it and left."

Dad's concern was evident. "What was the complaint again, Officer?"

"We got a call there was some shoving and name-calling in the parking lot. The person who was allegedly pushed is making the complaint."

I moved to the front of our group toward the open door, holding Kaitlin. I stood behind Mother and Dad. The officer was in his early 40s, powerfully built, sporting a brown mustache.

Paul said, "I absolutely do not know what you are talking about. I got the rolls, paid for them and came home. I didn't encounter anyone in the parking lot."

"You acted on this 'complaint' quite quickly," Dad said, his tone questioning the officer. "Paul's only been back a short while."

"Not even five minutes," Mother added.

The officer smiled, pleasant but professional. "We like to check these things out and get the problem handled."

"Daddy, let's go!" came Kaitlin's tiny voice suddenly, and I said, "Just a minute, sweetheart." My eyes traveled over the officer's square-jawed face, across his jacket to the badge over the pocket. The name read "Dayton."

I pushed past Mother and Dad to within a foot of the officer, shifting my wiggling niece to my other hip. "Do you know Pamela Pierson?" I asked tersely.

Facing Officer Dayton I couldn't see Dad's expression, but I sensed the annoyance in his voice, as though I had uttered an obscenity under inappropriate circumstances. He said, "Kay—" but I interrupted, asking the officer a second time, "Do you know Pamela Pierson?"

His posture stiffened and chest puffed out, assuming an authority-figure stance as he answered. "Yes, I know Pamela Pierson. But I don't believe it has any bearing on this situation."

I felt caught between what I knew to be the truth and possibly putting my family in a difficult position. I wanted to say, "I think it has plenty to do with this," but instead I said, "As my father mentioned, there appears to have been an unfortunate misunderstanding. Unless you have additional information on who made this complaint, we're due in church at 8 o'clock."

"Yes, we do need to be going," Mother said. I saw from the corner of my eye that she realized something was amiss.

Dad noted the officer's name badge too and was pressing for more details. "Officer Dayton, who did you say made the complaint?"

Jack came down the stairs at a fast clip chasing Sam, unaware of the situation in play. "Hey, guys, we need to get going if we want a place to sit."

Sam abruptly stopped upon seeing the officer. He asked with both fascination and concern, "Are you a policeman?" as Jack halted one step behind.

"Yes, that's right," Officer Dayton replied, smiling at my young nephew, the arrogance gone.

Not quite satisfied, Sam furrowed his brow and asked gravely, "Is somebody in trouble?"

Jack whispered, "That's enough, OK, bud?"

"Nobody's in trouble," Dayton offered, perhaps sensing the distress he was causing. He faced Dad. "In answer to your question, sir, it was another patron, but it appears there's been a mistake. Sorry for the inconvenience."

Dad said, "It appears someone has overreacted."

"Yes," Officer Dayton said. "You folks have a merry Christmas."

We watched him walk to the cruiser parked in the driveway, Dad pushing the massive oak door shut. "I'm sure the neighbors wonder what's going on," Mother said, plainly irritated. She turned to me. "Kay, how did you know that policeman knew Pamela?"

"Yeah, how did you know that?" Paul asked. "You don't think she has something to do with this?"

"It's a long story; I'll tell you on the way to church." We were slipping into coats and deciding who was driving with whom. I was explaining Officer Dayton's involvement in the raid on Dan Kinney's private investigating office and Pamela's relationship with him when the front bell chimed again.

"We'll be lucky to make church by Easter," Dad said, exasperated. He threw open the door, all of us twisting to find Pamela standing on the porch in her red wool coat, blonde hair shimmering under the porch lights. Her arrival had occurred less than five minutes after Officer Dayton's departure.

For a few seconds, the only sound was the ticking of the grandfather clock in the hall; we were all holding our collective breath. Dad was the first to speak, cool but polite. "What can I do for you, Pamela? We're in a bit of a hurry."

"Oh, I'm sorry. I didn't know. I just wanted to wish Kaitlin a merry Christmas, since I won't see her until tomorrow."

"Oh man," Paul muttered, exiting the darkened house.

The pieces were falling together, but I needed to confirm my hunch. "Look, sweetie, it's Mommy," I said merrily, carrying Kaitlin to the doorway.

"Merry Christmas, sweetheart," Pamela said. She pulled a gorgeous gift-wrapped box crowned with a gold bow from behind her back, handing it to Kaitlin. "Santa will come to Mommy's house tomorrow, too, but you have to have something on Christmas Eve."

Mother was calling from the garage, and Dad excused himself. "Should she open it now?" I asked, steadying Kaitlin and the square box in my arms.

"No, I need to be going. I just wanted to drop it off."

My smile plastered in place. "You drove clear across town to give her a gift and you don't want to see her open it—that's silly."

Jack was behind me motioning to Sam, "Hey, Sammy, let's help Kaitlin open her present." He pried off the gold bow, handing it to me while the children tore into the box. In seconds, shredded paper covered the floor of the foyer.

Shyly, Kaitlin smiled and said, "Oh boy," as Sam held the Elmo game for her. "El-mo!"

"What do you say?" I prompted gently.

"T'ank you."

"Let's walk your Mommy out to her car," I said sweetly.

Pamela protested, "Oh, no, that's not necessary."

"Yes, we'll walk you out," Jack chimed in.

Pamela's eyes narrowed as we thrust through the door, the four of us gaily following her out to the white Camaro, the license plate of which, I noted, read "Single." Pamela opened the driver's side, activating the dome light and illuminating the interior. Leaning on the door, she wedged her body at an angle in the space of the open door, making it difficult to see inside the car. I said to Kaitlin, "Can you give your mommy a kiss?" Pamela looked agitated.

As my niece kissed her mother's cheek, my gaze traveled to the front passenger's seat. And there it was—her video camera. Jack and I exchanged glances, and I nodded toward the passenger's door. He walked around the vehicle and saw exactly what I'd wanted him to. "Merry Christmas, Pamela," he said as he and Sam made their way to his vehicle.

The garage door opened behind us, the taillights of Dad's Mercedes illuminating. "What time will you pick Kaitlin up?" I said.

"Paul said 9 a.m. I'll pick her up at his house," she said briskly, any traces of her contrived enthusiasm having vanished. Pamela slammed the door shut and started the engine.

"I'll be sure Paul has the correct time. Let's wave bye-bye," I said, but Pamela was not paying attention as she threw the car into reverse, tires screeching out of the driveway.

Jack grabbed onto Sam's coat sleeve and walked toward me. He leaned in to whisper, "Now she travels with a video camera? This was all a setup?"

"Yep," I replied, as Dad brought the Mercedes to a halt. "We'll talk later" was all I said.

By now, it was almost 8 a.m., and we would be hard pressed to make church on time. The first hymn was being sung as we entered and found seats at the back. I sensed Tim's growing alarm as his gaze traveled over the congregation in search of us. When our eyes finally connected, relief flooded his face.

Thoughts of what had happened crowded my head, and I admonished myself to enjoy the service. *It's Christmas Eve; don't let Pamela spoil this too*, I thought wearily. There would be plenty of time to explain.

* * *

"Officer Dayton was here with bogus charges that would hopefully get Paul riled and angry," I clarified, at ease on a sofa in the great room. Following the service, we had returned to Goldenwoods for hot chocolate and a chance to discuss the strange events that had transpired.

"And in case there was a confrontation, shouting or threats, Pamela just happened to be lurking around the corner, where she could conveniently videotape the incident," Jack said.

"Then present it in court as part of her ongoing campaign to destroy Paul's life," Mother said, her tired voice spiked with bitterness.

Michelle's head swayed back and forth, her normally bright green eyes clouded by fatigue. "My mom confirmed that Charles Dayton had an affair with Pamela. People actually witnessed them together."

Dad propped his face in one hand, carefully digesting these tangled events. "Being so public about an affair isn't very smart."

"She held that over Charles Dayton's head," I said. "And when she needed the use of his authority, called him on it."

Jack agreed. "Pamela is fucking relentless, and she won't ever stop." I expected to see Mother or Dad cast Jack a look of displeasure at his choice of words, but neither did so.

Paul removed his glasses and rubbed his tired eyes. "She's tried to get me disbarred, sent to jail, take my daughter away, sue for more money and harass my family. And it will only end if we give her what she wants."

"Maybe not even then," Tim said.

The grandfather clock in the hall sounded 11 chimes, and Jack nudged Michelle. "We better get the kids home. I still have toys to put together, and they'll be up early."

Listening to Paul's frustration, Michelle had started to cry. "Sorry," she sniffed. "But this is just so sad and just so—"

"Grueling?" Mother interrupted.

"Yes. I never thought I'd encounter someone so purely evil."

Jack tenderly rubbed Michelle's back. "We've taken the high road, done what's considered right and ethical, and gotten nowhere."

"I'm tired of it too," Dad acknowledged, "but we can't just magically make Pamela disappear. We've got a new legal team and a strong list of witnesses for the custody hearing. I'm not backing down from her threats. Put Pamela on the stand, and she'll get caught in an intricate mesh of lies and deceit. It'll unravel eventually."

Paul stared at the floor saying nothing, but his defeated body language told me he no longer believed we could win. Jack rose from the couch, surveying all of us. "It's Christmas Eve, and it's late, and we've all had enough of Pamela. If we do nothing else, we should make it our resolution for the new year to put an end to Pamela's madness once and for all."

Observing the fatigued faces of my family, I knew he was right. Pamela would stir up trouble at every opportunity, intent on wearing us down bit by bit, finally tiring us to death.

* * *

Our family managed to face Pamela again, but not without extraordinary efforts to remain gracious. On Christmas night, Pamela agreed to drop Kaitlin off at Goldenwoods sometime around 8 p.m., since it was closer for her than driving an extra half-hour out to Paul's new house. When she finally arrived, it was nearly 10 p.m.

The doorbell sounded its musical chimes, the talking ceasing in mid-sentence. We looked around at one another's tentative faces to see who should answer. Paul started to rise from the couch, looking as if it took all the willpower he possessed to bring himself upright. "I guess I'll go," he started to say, but Dad interceded.

"No, stay where you are," he said. He addressed Mother, "Bev, why don't you and I greet our granddaughter?"

Paul began mumbling in protest, but Mother shushed him. "It's better for you if your father and I talk to her."

Nobody moved, but we pulled forward in our seats, listening attentively as Dad said, "Hello, Pamela. We were starting to get worried."

"It's not my fault. My parents were late coming from Northfield. Then I have to drive all the way out here to Minnetonka to drop her off—"

Her tone was arrogant and peevish, and Dad cut her off. "Pamela, if this was inconvenient, we would have been happy to make other arrangements."

"That's not what Paul told me." Her irate tone startled Kaitlin, who had been asleep, and she began to cry.

"Come to Grandma, sweetheart," Mother comforted, immediately bringing her into the great room with the rest of our family. Rubbing her tired eyes in the warm light of the room, Kaitlin spotted Paul, who took her with open arms. "Hey, sweetie," he said.

In the foyer, Dad said, "What exactly did you understand Paul to say?"

"It doesn't matter now. I've already come. Here are her things."

Dad remained controlled, his voice steady. "Just so there is no further miscommunication, Pamela, when are you planning to have Kaitlin next?"

"That's an issue between me and Paul," she shot back.

Paul handed Mother the baby, who nestled deep into her shoulder. He joined Dad in the foyer. "Pamela," he said quietly, "it would help me a lot if I knew when you'd like to have her. That way I can be prepared."

"I don't know when," Pamela said briskly. "I'll call you in a day or two."

It seemed to me that Pamela was orchestrating a circular conversation in which she could say the Pierson family refused to cooperate with her. But I was too tired to care. I was relieved the entire Christmas affair had not turned into a round of incendiary accusations.

chapter 33

The week between Christmas and New Year's was peaceful, giving us time to re-energize. By Dec. 30, I could feel the aches and pains of a cold or flu coming on, but I had much to do. New Year's Eve fell on Sunday, and we closed the office at noon, giving co-workers an extra holiday. I was busy laying out newspaper ads for the coming week at my computer, deliberating the best placement.

I was surprised to hear the building's alarm being turned off and see Jack sailing into my office. Dressed in jeans and a brown leather jacket, he exuded casual confidence. "Hey," I said in greeting.

"We have a problem," he stated tersely, the set of his strong jaw so rigid I saw angry muscles bulging in his neck, the redness registering across his features. "I need your help."

"What's wrong?" I asked with trepidation.

"Paul's in trouble. Again." Jack peeled off his brown leather gloves, bunching them together in his right hand. "Pamela has had him arrested and charged with assault and battery."

I closed my eyes tight, tasting the rising bitterness of nausea in my mouth. Jack called my name, the words echoing in my head. "Kay, hey, Sis, you're gonna have to help."

My eyes blinked open, taking in his stern features. "Sorry, I'm just in shock," I replied, as if I were trying to wake myself from another nightmare. "What's happened?"

Jack slapped his gloves systematically against the open palm of his hand. "Here's what I know. Pamela claims she asked to have Kaitlin for the day on Dec. 29. Paul agreed and dropped her off. Later in the evening, when he went to pick her up, there was an argument, during which Pamela claims that Paul became violent. She went to Phillip Mattson with the alleged charges yesterday. The police showed up at Paul's with a warrant for his arrest this morning."

"Where's Paul now?"

"He's being held temporarily at the Bloomington Police Department. But if we can't raise bail money by 5 o'clock, they'll transfer him downtown to the county jail. Bond was set at $25,000. We need to come up with $2,500. Cash."

"It's Saturday afternoon. My bank is closed," I said, slowly giving myself the bad news to actually hear and absorb it. "They won't open again until Tuesday, Jan. 2." I glanced at my wristwatch. It read 3 p.m.

"Mine too. She's going after him on a holiday weekend when there's minimal access to money. The way the holiday falls, he could be in jail a good two days."

I came from behind the desk, grabbing my black wool coat from the coat tree. "Twenty-five thousand dollars is pretty high bail for an accusation with no proof," I said, wearily throwing my coat over my jeans and sweater. "Or has Pamela conveniently provided that?"

"Yesterday, when Pamela and Phillip Mattson went to the police, they presented photographs they claim were taken shortly after Paul attacked her, as well as exhibiting bruises present on her face and neck."

Halfway through buttoning my coat, I met Jack's tense stare. "If she has bruises, there's any number of explanations. Lisa wasn't with Paul when he picked up Kaitlin?"

"Of course Lisa wasn't with him. No witnesses. This way, Pamela gets the police involved, while playing the martyr and the victim," Jack said.

"What about petty cash?" I asked Jack.

"I just checked the safe. It's all gone. We used it to buy gift cards for the staff for Christmas. It won't be replenished until next week."

"Shit."

We exited, Jack pulling the main door shut and punching in the alarm security code. "It makes for a very happy new year," he added facetiously.

I did not reply, instead poking through my purse, fishing out my wallet from the bottom. "I only have a few dollars on me, but I can hit the ATM and stop home to see what Tim has."

"Michelle and I scrounged up $500, and Mom's looking to see what's in the safe at the shop."

Outside it was snowing, the cold making my bones throb. "Where's the best place to meet you?"

"Goldenwoods. Lisa's there with Kaitlin. After the cops showed up, she was pretty upset."

"Can you blame her?"

"Hell no. I'll meet you there. Once we've got the money, I'll take it to the police department. Dad's gone to the station, trying to get the story straight from the police."

"I'm going with you," I said, and surprisingly, Jack did not argue. I pulled my sleeve away from the face of my watch, which now read 3:15 p.m. "I'll bring as much money as we have."

Once home, Tim and I scraped together $500. By the time we departed from our house, it was 4 p.m. Speeding along the increasingly snowy freeway, no room existed for delays. "This is a new low, even for Pamela," Tim said. "A couple days in jail is too many."

At Mother and Dad's, Jack's and Lisa's cars were parked in the driveway. We entered through the garage. "Poor girl; she's probably a wreck," Tim said.

"Hello?" I called out, walking into the empty kitchen.

"We're in the great room" was Mother's composed reply.

"Where have you guys been?" Jack asked irritably. "We've got 40 minutes."

"We've got $500," I said, hugging Lisa. "We'll get him out." I turned toward Mother. "How'd you fare?"

"Between all of us, we've got what we need," Mother said. She handed me a stack of bills.

Jack motioned for me to follow. "Let's go."

"Have you talked to Dad recently?" I asked, rushing behind my brother.

"About 15 minutes ago. You know your father; he won't rest until he gets some answers. He's very suspicious, and the police have fortunately been accommodating. Getting immediate legal counsel may be tough, however. Bob Rolfson and most of his associates are spending the holidays in Aspen. Cellphones go directly to voicemail. No idea where they're staying."

Jack tugged hard at my sleeve. "We're running out of time."

"I'll stay here with Bev and Lisa," Tim said. He gravitated toward Lisa, who was crying.

"Sorry," she sniffled, having difficulty finding any tranquility. "This is so awful—coming up with bail money for something Paul didn't do. I never thought I could wish harm on anyone, but I hope Pamela gets what she truly deserves."

"There's a long line ahead of you," Mother replied.

The scenic snowy landscape blurred as we sped across town. I stopped looking at the speedometer when it passed 90 miles per hour. *Please God, don't let us crash or get a ticket!* We debated what Pamela thought she could gain by having Paul thrown in jail, on top of her other accusations. "If Pamela can publicly humiliate Paul, it stands to reason that would give her more leverage in all the lawsuits she's filed but especially in the custody fight," Tim said.

"But she doesn't even want Kaitlin," I said.

"You have to stop being logical about this, Kay. For the kind of money Pamela's after, she needs to paint Paul as an abusive, drug-addicted liar. Success at getting him arrested and jailed will just be more 'proof.'"

At exactly 5 p.m. we entered the Bloomington PD. There was immediate confusion and a tense discussion about whether Paul would, in fact, be released. Beyond impatient, Dad reminded the officer that we had met the deadline with the correct amount of bail money. "I want to speak with a supervisor—now," he demanded.

The shocked administrative officer vanished behind a locked door. Jack and I exchanged anxious glances, my stomach bouncing around like a rubber ball. If Paul were held over the long weekend, I was truly fearful of the effect on his fragile state of mind. Jail might be the definitive push.

Time seemed to loop backward as our wait dragged on, Dad providing additional details. "She's pulled out all the stops. Phillip Mattson is also claiming Paul has been threatening Pamela and provided phone conversations she's taped as evidence of a continual pattern," he explained angrily. "Your brother has had one helluva day, and I've had no luck reaching Bob Rolfson. I am not happy."

"What have the police said?" I asked.

Dad stood between the two of us, lowering his voice. "They're caught between a rock and a hard place, frankly. They have a domestic violence complaint, which they were bound to act on. Very much like the Crime Stoppers incident. Pamela gives information or files charges, and the police have no way of knowing they're false."

"What was her explanation for waiting a day?" I inquired, my own heated anger rising.

"Too frightened and upset" was Dad's curt reply. "Supposedly Annette convinced her to go to the police."

After 45 minutes, a sergeant buzzed open the door and approached us. He assured us Paul would be released shortly.

Another half-hour passed before a uniformed officer escorted Paul to the waiting area. Clad in a pair of faded University of Minnesota sweatpants and a Timberwolves T-shirt under a down jacket, he was rumpled and unshaven, as the police had arrived before he'd had time to shower. He looked drawn and tired yet clearly relieved.

"Hey, guys," he said quietly. "Thanks for getting me out of here."

"Are you kidding?" Jack said, giving Paul's shoulder a squeeze.

I hugged Paul close, feeling the tension in his tired muscles. "You know we'd never just leave you here. Were you treated all right?"

Paul shrugged weary shoulders. "As well as can be expected. Lots of questions, and they took a statement. But that doesn't make me feel any less like a criminal."

Back at the house, Dad hadn't parked the car before Lisa was out the door to meet us. As Paul climbed out, Lisa reached for him, her face streaked from continual crying. "I'm really dirty, and I smell pretty bad," he said, trying to inject a bit of humor.

"I don't care," she said, and they melded together in a tender embrace.

Mother stood at the door, holding Kaitlin, who waved her hands excitedly. "Daddy's home! Daddy's home!"

"Yes, sweetheart, your daddy's home," Mother replied.

"Hey, sweet pea," Paul addressed her. Jack and I joined them.

Dad said, "Your mother's got a ham in the oven if you're hungry."

Paul and Lisa held hands, as if they never wanted to let go of one another. "Are you hungry?"

"Not really," Lisa replied. "Your mom's kept me pretty well fed."

A half hearted attempt at a smile over his lips, Paul said softly, "If you don't mind, I'd just like to take Kaitlin and go home."

"The ham will keep," Mother said.

* * *

In the remaining days of 2000, Tim and I had taken to arguing, which, all things considered, seemed the most appropriate way to finish the year. I'd made clam chowder from scratch, a favorite meal we savored over the holidays. As we cleared away the dirty dishes and started to clean the kitchen, our conversation focused on the craziness of the past year and so much wariness for the future.

"We can only hope 2001 is better," Tim said matter-of-factly as he placed empty soup bowls on the granite counter.

I stood at the sink, scraping off dried food before I placed the rinsed dishes into the dishwasher. "I don't know if I can be that optimistic. Jack's right. Pamela is not only relentless, but pure manipulative evil, devoid of any human decency."

Tim poured the remaining chowder into a Tupperware container as he spoke. "This year has been tough on everybody, and Pamela is in a large part responsible. But there is still good in her, however deeply buried it might be. There's always the chance for redemption."

Tim's comments agitated me, and in that moment a ceramic serving bowl slipped from my wet grasp, careening to the hardwood floor, where it splintered.

"Shit," I angrily gathered up the pieces. "I know you truly believe that, but in this case, it just isn't true."

I tossed the broken dish into the garbage can, the noise of further shattering temporarily disrupting our conversation.

From across the island, Tim faced me. "Kay, we're all sinners, and while Pamela has done malicious and even evil things, she's not completely devoid of decency. There is the possibility she will eventually see the harm she's caused and make amends."

I stood opposite him and stared, my hands flailing like birds unable to take flight. "You always say that! Always look for the best in even the worst of circumstances! But Pamela is different, Tim. She's harassed

Paul endlessly, had him arrested under false pretenses, smeared our family name and now is engaging in blackmail. She's not interested in amends; she's interested in destruction—the complete destruction of our family for her own financial gain. Pamela is a monster."

"I'm not saying she hasn't caused us pain and suffering through sinful acts," Tim acknowledged. "I'm only saying you can't completely write her off."

"No," I shook my head in angry rebuttal. "This time you're wrong. Pamela is well past redemption. It's not possible for her to be good or decent, and if we can't recognize that, then we're all as good as dead." I was fuming, my breathing coming fast and shallow.

"I admit that some people make a conscious choice to forego goodness, but it's still present," Tim replied, his frustration mounting. "The best we can do is to continue to take the high road."

As Tim and I argued, and I felt myself on the losing end, I heard my voice pitch higher, my words tumbling out over one another. I tried in vain to make him see that his naiveté was clouding over the nasty truth. "Sure, we're taking the high road, but it isn't doing any good, is it? We've been twisted into the aggressor every time, while she plays the victim. We are dealing with someone who's not just manipulative and cunning but intrinsically evil."

Tim tossed a towel limply across the counter. "OK, so let's say you're right and Pamela is an irredeemable monster," he said, sighing in irritation. "That's between her and God when her time comes. But I would like to believe that Pamela will recognize what she's done and make amends, not necessarily tomorrow or the next day, but sometime in her life. If not for her, then at least for Kaitlin." With those words he walked out of the kitchen. Stomp, stomp, stomp as he climbed the stairs, his footsteps overhead in our bedroom.

We had had this argument many times over the last year. Generally, it ended in a truce, to not keep pressing the issue. But we stood on opposite sides of the chasm.

As the clock approached midnight, I crept upstairs to fetch a pack of cigarettes. I turned on the hall light and slipped into our darkened bedroom, the light from the hall casting a yellow crescent over the floor. At the side of our bed, I looked over Tim's still form and his serene face.

"Still mad?" he said into the darkness.

"I'm not angry," I said, my lips brushing a kiss across his forehead. "I just disagree with you."

"I shouldn't try to force my opinions on you."

"You're entitled to your beliefs. And I'm entitled to mine."

Tim emitted a long and mournful exhalation, knowing there was no sense in revisiting this. "Pamela has affected more lives than she'll ever know."

I stood briefly at the foot of our bed. "'Affecting lives' doesn't begin to cover what she's done."

He said nothing when I closed the door and padded down the stairs. Outside, it had started to snow again, so I pulled on a long coat. On the front porch, I lit a cigarette and watched intricate flakes cover the ground in snowy solitude.

Tim was resolute in his belief that regardless of what Pamela had done, there was still good in her, however obscured it might have become. I inhaled deeply and blew rings of smoke that captured a cluster of snowflakes before fading out against the night.

The image in my mind's eye was of Paul, exhausted and grimy as he was being led out of jail. I saw in his eyes not just defeat but shame. I had come to see Pamela as a person never exhibiting the slightest hint of remorse or conscience, only malice, cunning and brazen fearlessness. How could she continue to torment my brother, her daughter, our family? Only a psychopath exhibited such qualities.

chapter 34

In the ensuing days, Phillip Mattson argued vigorously that Paul was a danger to Pamela and contended he would prosecute him to the full extent of the law. Fingers were pointed back and forth, as Bob Rolfson demanded a copy of Pamela's police report, the Crime Stoppers videotape and other records. Then, out of nowhere, Phillip Mattson offered an out-of-court settlement. For $1,000,000, the charges would be dropped. Dad was outraged. He saw any type of settlement as an acknowledgment of guilt and accused Pamela's attorney of engaging in blackmail. He advised Paul to flatly refuse, but the stress left no one untouched.

The virus I had contracted during the holidays knocked me flat between shaking chills and a fever, leaving me worn to the bone and in need of rest. With one crisis on top of another, Tim and I postponed our holiday visit to his family in northern Wisconsin. On Jan. 3, I insisted he go alone.

"Go and have a good time," I reassured him. "I don't want to risk getting everyone else sick."

"You're sure? I can wait."

"No," I said emphatically. "Your family has postponed Christmas long enough. I'll get plenty of rest and minimal human contact. I'll be shipshape when you get home."

Tim did not like leaving me, but I persisted. "It's only six days."

The illness, however, evolved into what appeared to be stomach flu. I was alone and bedridden when Michelle came to my rescue three days after Tim left for Wisconsin, bearing bland foods and liquids to keep me hydrated.

* * *

Each year before Christmas, Malcolm McBride, the insurance agent who represented our business and personal interests, held a small appreciation luncheon. Between battling Pamela and my illness, the gathering was rescheduled for Jan. 9, 2001.

Malcolm's sprawling Minneapolis home was situated on an expansive, wooded lot one block from Lake of the Isles near the city's center. The house had been refurbished, with huge windows offering a panoramic view of the lake, dressed in snow and ice. As this was still a holiday party, the Christmas decorations remained, the colorful twinkling lights poking through the murky gray of early January.

Sipping refreshments in the warm glow of a crackling fire, our group of Mother, Dad, Jack and I shared conversation with Malcolm and his wife. The only person missing was Paul.

"Most of the decorations are heirlooms or antiques," Malcolm explained. "They were passed down through our families, or we discovered them in antique stores."

"But," his wife said with emphasis, "as soon as the luncheon's over, they're coming down."

"Nice of you to keep them up for us," I said with a smile.

Seated at Jack's elbow, I noticed him glancing at his watch, a frown darkening his face. Whispering at my ear, he said crossly, "Paul's always a little late, but this is bad even for him; he's 45 minutes behind."

"Let's tell Malcolm to begin serving lunch. You and I have an appointment at 3:30, and surely everyone here has commitments as well."

Mother overheard us talking. "I can't imagine why we haven't heard from Paul. He's usually so good about calling if he's running late."

The group moved into the dining room for the first course. As the main entrée was served, the bells at the front door chimed. We heard voices, and I could have sworn I recognized Kaitlin's happy chatter. Malcolm excused himself, and the voices moved in closer.

"We have an extra guest," he announced cheerfully. Frazzled and in disarray, Paul held Kaitlin in one arm, the bag he was carrying sliding off his shoulder.

"Sorry I'm so late," he apologized. He looked thoroughly annoyed. "Pamela was supposed to take Kaitlin today, but she never showed up. I've been waiting at her house for over an hour."

Seeing Mother, Kaitlin's sweet voice exclaimed, "Gamma!"

"Hi, sweetie," Mother said, taking her granddaughter into open arms.

Paul plopped onto a chair, clearly exasperated. "I didn't have a backup plan, so I hope bringing her was OK."

"Not a problem," Malcolm said, carrying an old metal and vinyl high chair into the room. "We used this with all of our kids and never got rid of it."

Mother fastened Kaitlin into the seat, and she inquisitively inspected her new surroundings, banging happily on the metal tray.

Malcolm's wife chuckled. "Every garage sale, we say we're going to sell it, but we can't part with it. Might as well save for grandkids!"

"Thanks, I appreciate it," Paul said.

Dad asked Paul, "What time were you dropping Kaitlin off at Pamela's?"

"At 11:15. I left two messages on her voicemail as reminders. I've been calling her cellphone, but it goes right to voicemail and she's never responded to my messages."

After a leisurely lunch, our family departed, gathering in the driveway for a quick chat. Paul tried phoning Pamela once more but again reached voicemail. Punching off his phone, he asked, "Where is she?"

"Paul," Mother said gently, "I'll take Kaitlin home with me. When you get ahold of Pamela, I'll bring Kaitlin to her. But she's not home, and there's nothing you can do."

His hands shoved in the pockets of a camel topcoat, Jack asked, "When was the last time you spoke to Pamela?"

"On the 4th, right after the holiday. She specifically asked to have Kaitlin today and overnight. Pamela made it clear she was giving me advance notice, as Dad had requested on Christmas Eve." Paul's shoulders sagged in dejection. "If I don't show up with Kaitlin, she'll accuse me of violating the custody agreement again."

Jack didn't hide his sarcasm. "That was a week ago. Pamela's a remarkably busy girl, and child care is not typically a priority for her."

Mother said, "Regardless, Pamela is still Kaitlin's mother and has the right to see her. And like it or not, we don't dare deny her right now."

"Your mother's right," Dad said. "Perhaps when you hear from Pamela, she'll have an explanation."

Paul agreed. "As soon as I reach her, I'll let you know. You're all witnesses I've held up my end of the arrangement, so she can't cast blame."

Throughout the day, he left several phone messages receiving no reply. Well past 10 p.m., he called Mother and Dad with curious news. For the first time in months, Annette phoned. "She was civil, wondering if I had heard from Pamela. The last time Annette talked to her was the same day I did, on the 4th of January."

chapter 35

On Thursday, Jan. 11, the Schaeffers filed a missing person report with the Bloomington Police Department. They communicated with various media outlets, but interest didn't start building until that third week in January. That Tuesday, Paul and I were sharing lunch in the office kitchen discussing the media coverage Pamela's strange disappearance was attracting.

"Annette told police the last time she talked to Pamela was on the afternoon of Jan. 4 on the phone," he said, swirling a finger absentmindedly in his drink. "That's almost two weeks ago. All the news stations are doing stories, and I believe Margot Paliulionis is doing an interview with Annette and Donovan."

"That's not surprising," I replied. "Jeanne called this morning with information too. You know all the contacts she has in the Twin Cities. Apparently, the Bloomington Police Department has interviewed Lula Faye Simmons and Phillip Mattson."

"They're talking to a lot of people, including me," Paul replied.

"Lula Faye isn't providing much of an alibi, including where she and Pamela were over the New Year's holiday. She's claiming she dropped off Pamela at her house Jan. 4," I said. "Do you remember what time Pamela called you?"

Paul stroked his jaw. "It was still morning, maybe 11 o'clock or so. She and Lula Faye could have been out of town."

"True. She might also be the last person to have seen Pamela."

Paul shook his head. "What about Phillip Mattson? I'm still waiting for him to implicate me in all of this."

I removed an entrée from the beeping microwave. "Jeanne is a gold mine of data," I said. "Apparently Phillip Mattson told police he spoke with Pamela on the 4th too. Apparently, he and Pamela had another meeting scheduled for Monday, the 8th, but she never showed."

"She needs to come back from wherever she's been," Paul replied. "Otherwise, everyone's suspicious of me."

I massaged my brother's shoulder. "You volunteered to take a polygraph test, and the police have said it isn't necessary. As the ex-husband, it's only natural the police would look to you first. But you're not the only one with motive. Plus, this is not her first disappearing act."

* * *

The media attention surrounding Pamela's disappearance became more intense. Margot Paliulionis called me requesting a comment from our family for the article she was writing. "I really have nothing to offer," I said. "It's a missing person case, being handled by the police, as it should be."

I could hear the impatient tapping of Margot's pen on the other end. "I got an anonymous tip that Pamela had quite the reputation for sleeping around, as well as for blackmail," she said. "That wouldn't have come from you, would it?"

The source had to be Doug Castleton letting the world know the image Annette and Donovan were presenting of Pamela was a fabrication. "It was not me. Beyond that, neither I nor anyone in the family has anything to add."

Margot's story ran in the Sunday edition of the Star Tribune on

Jan. 21. She included the fact that the Bloomington police searched her home for clues. Nothing had been disturbed or was found to be missing.

The following Tuesday, Michelle and I met for coffee. I mentioned the subject of Pamela's past disappearances. "Remember last year over the new year when Paul had been unable to contact Pamela for several days, too?"

"That's right," Michelle said, warming her hands against the ceramic mug of steaming liquid. "It's been a couple of years in a row." She drank deeply. "Here's what I think—Pamela's met someone, and she smells money, a commodity she's running short of. Maybe she's in Vegas again, and this time she got lucky."

That Friday, Jan. 26, I stopped home for lunch. A noontime phone call startled me. Dreading another telemarketer, I almost didn't answer but then realized it was Jack's number displayed on the caller ID.

"Pamela's made the news again," he said.

"Did they find her?"

"Not exactly," he replied, and I could make out the sound of the television in the background. "Channel 5 just reported Pamela's car was discovered at a secluded area of Beaver Creek Valley State Park near Caledonia at the Mississippi River. There's no sign of her, but I thought you'd want to know."

I switched on the television and caught the end of the story reporting Pamela's white Camaro had been discovered by cross-country skiers, off the road in a remote section of the park, hidden by the heavy brush and snow. No one was certain how long the Camaro had been in the park. One theory held that its white color had blended in with the snow, making detection more problematic. Authorities were examining the car for fingerprints, body fluids, hair and skin samples that might offer hints to Pamela's mysterious vanishing.

By dinnertime the local news was reporting that the results of tests run on Pamela's car would be known in a few days. At this early stage, the police were not venturing any guesses as to whether a crime had been committed.

"Are Michelle and I the only ones who think Pamela's probably in Vegas or LA with a new boyfriend?" Tim asked.

"I don't know. Mom and Dad think she's lying low, waiting until the divorce settlement and custody cases are about to be heard. Paul thinks Annette and Donovan are in on it, helping her stay in seclusion. He figures Pamela's story will be that she went into hiding as protection from him. Jack, of course, isn't saying what he thinks."

"I don't know that I buy Paul's theory that her parents know something. They certainly seem to be worried."

When tests on Pamela's car were completed, the Minnesota Bureau of Criminal Apprehension notified Annette and Donovan. They told Paul that of the fingerprints and hair samples found, law enforcement officials were only able to make two matches. Both were from males, and each was called into the BCA for in-depth interviews. The men relayed a familiar story: They had met Pamela in bars in Bloomington near the airport. Both were able to provide confirmable alibis.

As January 2001 ended, Pamela had been missing officially for three weeks, and no one seemed to have the slightest idea of where she might be.

* * *

By Monday, Feb. 12, there had been nothing notable concerning Pamela's whereabouts. Annette began hounding Paul, as if he could make her reappear. Dad enlisted the attorneys to intervene, citing her for harassment. They reasoned that the police would most likely contact her and Donovan with any pertinent information first.

I had been putting in a grueling number of hours preparing to launch a major marketing blitz on the new Lakeside subdivision. Early one morning, well before anyone else arrived, I was at my desk. I heard the office front door unlock, followed by the heavenly aroma of rich coffee. Jack appeared with a cardboard tray holding two large paper cups of Caribou coffee and a bag of baked goods, a rolled copy of the newspaper tucked under an arm.

"Had breakfast?" he asked casually, setting the tray on the corner of my desk.

"Just coffee," I said with an appreciative smile. "I'm definitely due for something a little more substantial."

He handed me one of the steaming cups. "Double latté with skim milk." Unrolling the top of the brown paper bag, he produced two large muffins. "One's cranberry nut and the other's banana. You pick."

I made my selection as Jack deposited his topcoat and leather gloves across an empty chair. "This is a nice surprise. And the paper, too? I'm impressed." I relished the first sip of good coffee.

"I figured you hadn't eaten breakfast or read the paper yet, and there's something I want to show you." Separating the sections of crisp newsprint, Jack stopped at the Metro/State section, which he laid in front of me. "Take a look at this."

The headline was gruesome enough: "Dog returns home with severed leg." I noted the byline was Margot Paliulionis and looked at my brother.

"Just read it," he said.

I started reciting the story aloud. "The owner of a German shepherd near Chisago City made a grisly discovery when the dog came home Tuesday with part of a woman's leg," the article began. I took a deep breath and continued, "The dog's find has prompted an intensive search in the heavily wooded area north of Chisago City, near the Wisconsin border.

"Although police are not certain they are dealing with a homicide, they are hoping a tattoo on the woman's leg may offer clues to her identity. The tattoo, found on the ankle, includes the drawing of a red rose with the inscription 'Foxy Lady.'"

The steam from the coffee hovered between us as I stopped reading and looked up at Jack.

"It's Pamela," he spoke frankly. "It's gotta be her."

I read the rest of the article in silence. Pathologists were still examining the leg as the police continued reviewing missing person reports from Chisago, Hennepin, Ramsey and surrounding counties. Information was vague until pathology tests could be completed. I folded the paper, passing it back across the desk. "You're assuming Pamela is the only woman with 'Foxy Lady' tattooed on her ankle."

"But this tattoo with the red rose is an exact match with hers. After you pointed it out in court, I made sure to look for it."

I sat back in my chair with my arms loosely folded over my chest. "OK, let's say, for argument's sake, that it is Pamela. Besides the tattoo, what else makes you so confident?"

Jack handed me a napkin and split his muffin into two pieces. "Pamela's got an expensive habit. Paul estimated she was doing $1,000 a week in cocaine when they were married. Add to that her large debts and the fact that every lawsuit she filed against us is also costing her money. She needs cash, but she has no job and no guarantee of winning a new settlement. In her desperation, she has definitely become less choosy about who she sleeps with in order to feed her habit."

I listened intently, and when he was finished, I asked one question. "Do you think someone deliberately planned to kill her?"

"Not necessarily," he said, sweeping muffin crumbs into his palm before depositing them into the wastebasket. "There are dozens of people, however, including any one of us, who would have had good reason to. I think she picked up some guy and either tried to blackmail him for money or maybe the sex got rough. Either way, she winds up dead, and there's a body that's got to be disposed of."

"That's really horrible, Jack."

"It doesn't matter how horrific it is," he replied. "The point is that Pamela is dead."

* * *

Eight days after the first grisly discovery, the German shepherd returned to its owner with a new find: a section of the woman's other leg. The evidence prompted another intense search of the Chisago City area, as dozens of sheriff's deputies, police dogs and a helicopter combed the densely wooded land.

Area newspapers reported that law enforcement officials determined the legs were not from any area hospitals, due to the absence of formaldehyde and the type of amputation. The sheriff's deputy interviewed was blunt in his assessment. "There is no doubt we are dealing with a homicide," Lieutenant Glenn Petersen of the Chisago County Sheriff's Department said. "We are dealing with someone who went to great lengths to conceal a murder and make it difficult to identify the victim." The Minnesota Bureau of Criminal Apprehension took over the investigation, coordinating the massive search.

Test results reported by pathologists indicated the victim was a white female between the ages of 18 and 40 who was killed several weeks before discovery. Decomposition had been minimal; the cold of winter slowed the decay. The tattooed markings had not proved helpful in determining an identity.

Pathologists were continuing to conduct tests. Blood type determined from tissue, muscle and bone marrow told investigators little. Comparing the characteristics available so far against missing person reports, police had whittled their list of potential victims. For the first time, Pamela's name was included as a possibility.

Articles in both the Minneapolis and St. Paul papers, as well as local newscasts, indicated this was the most frustrating yet challenging type of police investigation. One official was quoted as saying, "This is why we come to work in the morning—for cases like these."

The answer to one question surrounding the case arrived on a routine Wednesday in March, a day somewhere between the chill of winter and the thaw of spring: DNA evidence had tentatively identified the two severed legs as belonging to Pamela Pierson.

* * *

Tests positively identifying Pamela as the victim came within a few days, and Jack reminded me that his theory had been right all along. "It couldn't have been anyone else. Pamela essentially set her own demise in motion, making impaired choices and taking risks that could only end in tragedy," he said.

Interest in the case was high, and other stories on the crime appeared on the news and in the papers. Margot Paliulionis wrote that the owner of the property near Chisago City where the legs were found had been in the process of renting out the house situated on the acreage. Now he was having great difficulty landing a tenant due to all the publicity surrounding the shocking discoveries. The landowner arranged for a cadaver-search dog to scout the area.

His plan made perfect sense. He wanted to prove—and do so publicly—that no more body parts were entombed on the land waiting to be discovered by the next unsuspecting tenant. The strategy backfired; the golden retriever uncovered a human skull that the police believed was Pamela's. Within the week, a forensic odontologist used dental records to identify the skull as Pamela's.

Three days later, in the muck and snow, a severed right hand was found in southern Wisconsin. As they had done in Chisago City, authorities swarmed the area in the hope of finding additional body parts and perhaps cracking the mystery of who killed Pamela. The severed hand was also confirmed as Pamela's, but this only led police to the frustrating conclusion that they not only had no leads but that these discoveries simply meant whoever had killed her had gone to great lengths to scatter her remains.

* * *

No other body parts were discovered after that, and interest in the case of Pamela's murder faded. Fresher crimes would occupy the media and the police. Wanting to erase any doubt of his innocence, Paul requested and passed a polygraph test, and attention was turned elsewhere.

Annette and Donovan attempted to keep Pamela's unsolved murder a newsworthy story by regularly contacting various media outlets. They gave interviews in which they stated their belief that Pamela had been portrayed unfairly in the press. As the questions persisted about Pamela's drug abuse, numerous sexual encounters and enormous debt, they answered repeatedly, "She was a good mother and loving daughter."

For a few weeks afterward, rumors swirled that Robert Carter might have knowledge pertinent to Pamela's murder. The story persisted that he was furious at her for having already replaced him with a new lover and had her killed. Claiming the police were looking to frame an innocent man, he balked at taking a polygraph test, even on the chance it might prove he was telling the truth. The police investigated but found nothing to substantiate such accusations, and the gossip gradually disappeared.

Disbelief that Pamela was indeed dead reverberated within our family for months. It seemed too optimistic to think there would be no more hounding, no more lies, no more threats, no more fear. Even faced with the shock of the crime, the rage that had held our family hostage for so long was difficult to shed. In time, there was the realization that Paul would someday have to explain to Kaitlin what had happened to her mother. Everyone was torn between the revulsion of the brutal fate Pamela had suffered and the undeniable relief that we were, at last, free of her.

Everyone except for me.

I have come to understand that goodness and evil each present us with choices, and they are never as simple as they might appear. What one may view as the ultimate act of malice, another may see as the necessary destruction of evil.

I acknowledge this single fact: I alone made the cardinal choice to end the darkness casting deepening shadows across my family.

The thoughts had been creeping into my mind for months. Usually, I had been able to force the idea aside, understanding that what I was contemplating was morally repugnant. But as Pamela's actions became ever more threatening, taking an increasingly cruel toll on my family, the idea returned more frequently. Eventually, I realized I had devised a plan.

Luring Pamela to her death was easier than I predicted. A simple anonymous note, offering seductive promises of monetary gain and revenge, had enticed her to the seclusion of the park. I lay in wait for her, as all good hunters do, the dense night and brush providing cover. When she arrived that Friday night at the designated place and time, a predetermined signal of three bursts of light brought her within striking distance. As she approached, I flashed the light, blinding her. I fired a single gunshot at close range, piercing her heart. She clutched her chest, a sharp gasp emitting as she fell to the ground.

Retreating into the shelter of the woods, I watched the scene from a distance until I was certain she had come alone. Even as the crimson blood seeped out of her dying body, I felt no guilt at my actions, nor fear, only the surging release of pent-up fury. It would take only a few minutes for Pamela to exhale her last frantic gulp of air, and I was patient, wanting the assurance she was indeed dead.

Only then did I set about my task. The process of dissecting a human corpse is not much different than gutting a deer or dressing a duck carcass, processes with which I was intimately familiar. Just like all the times I assisted the hunters, I carefully dug out the bullet from her heart, placing it in a plastic bag. Forensic experts would face more difficulty proving cause of death without that evidence. I severed each limb and wrapped it in plastic, placing them in rubber containers for transport. Deep in the woods, impending snowfall and Mother Nature would restore the area to its natural state.

Pamela's remains were discarded across the black forests, steep valleys and thick terrain of Minnesota and Wisconsin, remote locations I'd been scouting as potential sites for weeks. The weapon, a 9-millimeter Glock handgun, had been pilfered from Mother and Dad's gun safe. I replaced the cleaned firearm in the safe undetected. The rest of the evidence—the crumpled anonymous note, clothes, gloves, shoes, tarps, saws, the telltale bullet and containers—were burned or hidden within isolated dumpsters heavy with refuse. Scattered across faceless towns, those remnants disappeared into the vast jaws of landfills.

I feigned my illness, the irony not lost on me in employing a tactic Pamela had used. I did not care. Allergic to peanuts, I wouldn't suffer anaphylactic shock, but consumption brought on vomiting and chills, which I passed off as a bad case of the stomach flu. I had the tiniest alibi in Michelle witnessing me in the throes of cramping nausea. Yet I knew the charade was risky.

My instincts of survival and the protection of those I loved aroused the desires of a primal hunter to attack and shield. I lied to my family and temporarily put Paul under suspicion. I regret nothing in my justification. Should the intrinsic evil brought upon us remain unvanquished, it was bound to swallow us whole.

Occasionally, one of Tim's favorite biblical passages, Psalm 51, drifts through my thoughts, and I am always caught by surprise: "Have mercy on me, O God, according to your steadfast love; according to your abundant mercy blot out my transgressions. Wash me thoroughly from my iniquity and cleanse me from my sin."

Beneath the mundane events of a conventional life thrust beyond its limits, I wonder if I should fear more than I do. Perhaps one day I will reach out toward the soothing touch of unconditional grace and forgiveness and admit my guilt. Today, however, the whispers go unheeded, my decision resolute to shield one truth into the deep hush of eternity.

an interview with the author

Where did the idea for "Darkness and Grace" come from?
"Darkness and Grace" was inspired by real-life events involving people I know in the early 1990s. Each time I would discuss the true occurrences, people would comment, "This is a great story. You need to write a book." After initial trepidation, I recognized this was not only a story worth telling, but it was one that comes to an author only once in a lifetime.

It was originally published in 2007 under a pseudonym with the title "Shades of Darkness, Shades of Grace." I worked with a new editing team to polish it and take it to the next level. "Darkness and Grace" is still a work of fiction, and the characters are entirely fictional.

Since the book is based on real-life events, what were some of the challenges you faced writing it? How were you able to overcome them?
Writing about people you know, even as fiction, can be tricky business, as they may see themselves and not like how they are portrayed. There are elements of truth to the characters that are inspired by real people, but that is all. As far as the events depicted, some are expanded upon. In the author's note, I acknowledge that the newspaper accounts are authentic. Names and physical characteristics of those depicted have been changed. Some incidents, however, were so outlandish I couldn't

make them up. I will also say this—the real story was even more convoluted. I had to tone some instances down for fear no one would believe they happened.

The genre for the book is domestic thriller—what makes it so? Are there other titles in that genre that have a similar vibe to "Darkness and Grace?"
Typically, a domestic thriller is defined as a subgenre of crime fiction that is best described as a psychological thriller that focuses on interpersonal relationships, often those between husbands and wives or parents and their children. What drives the story in a domestic thriller is the domestic disturbances, secrets and tensions that exist. The main feeling, in my estimation, is the underlying dread and suspense that all is not what it seems on the surface and the realization that true evil exists in the Piersons' world. Evil is a common denominator in other domestic thrillers such as "Turn of the Key" by Ruth Ware, "Behind Closed Doors" by B.A. Paris and "Gone Girl" by Gillian Flynn.

The setting for the story is the Twin Cities area of Minnesota—did the real-life events take place in Minnesota? What do you think Minnesotans will appreciate about it?
No, the real setting wasn't Minnesota, but the events did take place in the Midwest. To write the narrative, I employed aspects of historical fiction, using authentic news accounts and world events in the late 1990s and early 2000s, and settings and descriptions of Minnesota cities and landmarks. I have lived in Minnesota for a total of 28 years, for eight years in the 1980s and permanently since 2002. Much of what is written is from my perspective as a transplant. I think Minnesotans will appreciate that I think this is the best place in the world to live. I consider it God's country.

What was your process for researching the events of the period and the location?

The research was similar to the in-depth internet investigation I undertook for my crime novel, "Salvation Station." In a way this book was easier because I have stacks of files on the real events and the period from the mid-1990s to the year 2000. Some proceedings I remember very clearly. But I also am fortunate to have an editor who is a native Minnesotan. She corrected information when it was wrong, for which I am grateful.

Tell us more about the main character, Kay Pierson-Scott—what do you hope readers will think and feel about her?

Kay certainly has her flaws, but I want readers to empathize with her and perhaps see some of themselves in her. She is happily married but also very independent and in no way helpless. She is smart, loving and perfectly capable of holding her own. Like anyone, there are many dimensions to her.

Family is important to the Piersons—what do you hope readers will think and feel about the Pierson family and how they handle adversity?

My hope is that readers will recognize and appreciate that a strong, loving family is one of the most important gifts there is in life. Like the saying goes, you don't get to choose your family. I acknowledge there are plenty of dysfunctional, toxic families, but I'm extremely fortunate to have a family that will drop whatever they are doing to offer support and encouragement to any one of us. Do we still annoy each other? Of course!

In terms of adversity, the Piersons try to take the high road and not act in a malicious manner. Part of their frustration (and this was true in the real story as well) is that just because you are determined to take the high road does not mean doing so is going to pay off. Sometimes you attempt to do everything that is good and right and continually get knocked down.

What's the overall theme of the book?
There are two main themes. One, that when people are confronted by true evil, they are not prepared to handle it. No one ever thinks encountering evil will ever happen to them. The second theme is that anyone can be pushed by circumstances to take actions they would otherwise never consider. Both of these themes tie into the idea that no matter how close you are to someone, or how well you think you know them, close relationships can prove to be far more dangerous than the world at large. We want to believe people we are close to are decent human beings who respect and love us. Domestic violence or child abuse are prime examples of when those that are the most dangerous are right in front of us.

If the book were a movie, what actor would you see as Kay? Who would you see playing Kay's sister-in-law Pamela?
This is a very tough question, as the people I originally envisioned are too old now. When Sandra Bullock was in her 30s, I always saw her as Kay. As Pamela, I could imagine Margot Robbie. She's beautiful and smart, but she can play someone very calculating and dangerous.

acknowledgments

I am forever grateful to my friend and colleague Chris Olsen and the incredible team at Publish Her for their thoughtful suggestions, ongoing support and professionalism. Without them, this book would not be a reality.

about the author

Kathryn Schleich has been a writer for more than 30 years. Her crime novel, "Salvation Station," was published through She Writes Press in 2020. Kathryn has also published the short story "Reckless Acts," featured in "After Effects: A Zimbell House Anthology," and "Grand Slam," published in The Acentos Review. She is also the author of the academic book "Hollywood and Catholic Women: Virgins, Whores, Mothers and Other Images," which evolved from her master's thesis. Her guest posts have been featured on the Women On Writing blog, The Muffin, and she writes for the Amherst H. Wilder Foundation's volunteer newsletter. When she's not writing, Kathryn is volunteering in the education and arts communities in the Twin Cities, Minnesota, where she lives. Friends, family, good food, wine and traveling are important aspects of her life.

For more information about Kathryn, and to read her latest works, visit www.kathrynschleich.com.

Made in the USA
Monee, IL
15 May 2023